INNER PASSAGES

INNER PASSAGES

by

Carl Brookins

DEDICATION

This one is for Tom, absent friend and stout sailing companion.

He would have been pleased.

Acknowledgments

While writing is a solitary occupation, it isn't done in a vacuum. It can't be. That's particularly true of crime fiction in which we must look to society for our inspiration; else go to prison for murdering ourselves.

Like others who have gone before me, many people had a hand in the process and in sustaining me during the process. For encouragement, for thoughtful criticism, for editing, for believing in the project, and for teaching me so much, I particularly want to note these folks who deserve far more than the small token of my affection herein offered: my wife Jean, Julie Faschiana, Scott Haartman, Betty James, Michael Kac, Kent Krueger, Jean Paul, Betsey Rhame, Susan Runholt, Anne Webb, the Tarvers, and the staff at Top Publications.

Inner Passages

A Top Publications Paperback

First Edition
12221 Merit Drive, Suite 750
Dallas, Texas 75251

ISBN#:1-929976-01-1
Library of Congress # 00-131587

The characters and events in this novel are fictional and created out of the imagination of the author. Certain real locations and institutions are mentioned, but the characters and events depicted are entirely fictional.

Printed in the United States of America

Author's Notes

The principal setting of this book is the Inside Passage, that spectacular waterway between Puget Sound and the northern end of Vancouver Island along the western coast of British Columbia. A great many wonderful people live and work in that region. Some of them, and the places they live, are in this book. Some of them were removed by the magic hand of the novelist, just as a few geographic features were altered, for the sake of the story. This is, after all, a work of fiction. None of the events depicted happened, except in the mind of the author, and it is truly coincidental if any reader finds him or herself depicted in these pages.

1

They were all three up at dawn, inhaling the still, salt-laden air, gazing in delight at the pale sky overhead and listening to the scree of the gulls that circled 'round the masthead and swooped across the deck to land gracefully on the blue water. It was a perfect day to go to sea, even if, as in this case, it was not the Pacific Ocean, but only the Inside Passage. High over the dark green mountains behind them tendrils of golden-rose clouds hung suspended. Michael Tanner hummed a silent tune and bent his slender six foot frame over the bow of the Queen Anne. He hauled the dripping anchor out of the bottom of the sea and secured it to the rail. His bright yellow sea jacket rustled and sent nearby birds swirling up off the water. They quickly settled again, round dark eyes ever watchful. Tanner went back along the deck of the Queen Anne to the mast where he hauled the mainsail taut.

The little sloop slowly sailed away from Garden Bay on the British Columbia coast, her sail barely drawing in the almost non-existent breeze. Tanner dropped into the cockpit and grinned at the woman holding the tiller.

Alice George, graphic artist and Beth's long-time friend, grinned back. "Where away, O Captain, my Captain?"

"Just keep her pointed in that general direction." Tanner inhaled and the tang of fresh-brewed coffee mixed with the sea air teased his nose. He glanced down the hatch and met the warm gaze of his wife, Elizabeth. She rose, like Venus from the sea, only fully dressed and carrying a steaming mug of coffee in each hand. Tanner took the coffee from her.

With her own mug in hand, Elizabeth Tanner--Beth to her

close friends and family--settled on a cockpit cushion beside her husband. Then she leaned down and rubbed her ankle. It reminded Tanner of the day, years ago, when she'd injured that ankle. He'd been in Redmond, making a final presentation to a potential client when a call had come from the hospital in Seattle. Mrs. Tanner had fallen and an ambulance had brought her to the hospital. It was feared her ankle was broken. Tanner had abruptly terminated the meeting to rush to her side, leaving a board room full of open-mouthed executives.

That story, along with others of a similar nature over the twenty years of their marriage, still made the rounds of the advertising community in King County and enhanced the reputation of Tanner and Associates. Beth straightened and shook out her auburn curls.

"Well, well. It looks like a nice day. After breakfast, I'll bring the log up to date."

"Here," said Alice, "you know I hate steering. One of you take over and I'll go make breakfast."

Tanner smiled and shook his head, then reached for the tiller. Alice was game for any task on the little boat except steering. He waggled the tiller and glanced around. They were alone on the still water, Garden Bay still just off their stern.

"What's your course, Michael?" Beth called from her place at the table in the tiny main cabin of the Queen Anne, where she was writing in their trip log.

Tanner looked down at the top of her head and smiled. He always smiled when he looked at Beth. Tanner had two enduring loves in his life, his wife and his successful public relations agency. He looked at the compass fixed to the side of the cockpit in front of him. "Hey, Beth, we're only going over there." Tanner pointed west, over the bow. "No need to be so precise."

"C'mon, Michael, humor me. For the journal." Beth looked up through the hatch.

Tanner shrugged. "Well, Toots, the compass says due west, give or take a point."

"Two-seventy degrees, right?"

"You got it."

An hour later, the day's bright promise had faded. When they'd started across Malaspina Strait from Garden Bay, Texada Island was easily distinguishable. The distance wasn't great and they could even make out individual trees against the morning sky. But now the island was indistinct, a dark wavering mass. Tanner rubbed his head and ran his fingers through his hair. His eyes narrowed in a deep, uncharacteristic frown. Mists rose and fell, sometimes obscuring the outlines of the distant shore. Clouds had moved in, changing the sky from blue to gray and driving away the sun and its warmth. Tanner dropped the sail and switched on the engine. With the fog, the light breeze had died away to nothing but occasional puffs. Now the Queen Anne puttered along at a steady pace in a gradually shrinking gray world.

Alice George appeared from below and flopped down beside Tanner. "Things getting a little boring up here, Mikey?"

Tanner sighed. "Just a little fog, nothing to worry about. But I'd rather sail than motor."

"Oh, I'm not worried." She waved a negligent hand. "I have complete faith in the two of you to get us to--where are we headed?"

"Texada Island. We should be there in another three or four hours at this pace. Less if we get some wind."

"What happened to all the scenic beauty, the grand sweeping vistas you promised me on this trip?" She glanced around. "All I see here is fog."

"Sweeping vistas? We said that?" He laughed. "Hey, they're out there somewhere, you'll see." Tanner looked around. She was right. It was as if the fog--dank and cottony--had been waiting for their inattention. The hills and trees of Texada were entirely gone, as if wiped away by a giant hand. Now they were surrounded by unrelieved gray.

They were all natives of Seattle and fog in the city was

common enough. But out here on the water, this fog was different, alarming in some way they couldn't quite describe. They'd encountered other natural forces they hadn't bargained for, such as tides.

Ocean tides are well known to blue-water sailors and people on seacoasts anywhere. The daily newspaper routinely published tide tables but before this sailing jaunt, the Tanners had never dealt directly with the immense power of the ocean. It wasn't just the moon-influenced rising and falling of the water level. Tidal currents were often powerful, demanding forces; just how forceful they'd dicovered early in their trip. For hours, one day, they'd struggled against the falling tide outside Campbell River, but the engine wasn't big enough to get them back to port. There were warnings printed on their chart where small boats had been swamped when wind and tide opposed each other.

At home they'd never paid more than cursory attention to weather reports, but here on the sea, wind direction, temperature and the silent, stealthy, ocean currents became important factors in their daily lives.

They had planned to make an easy, short passage from Garden Bay to Lasqueti, a small island in the Strait of Georgia just west of Texada. According to their chart, there was a small deep harbor on the island's western side where they could anchor for the night. Since the beginning of their charter they'd been skirting the continental shore of the Inside Passage, skipping into the little bays and inlets, reveling in the scenery, and plucking fresh oysters off the tidal beaches. But Tanner wanted the experience of sailing on some big water. So they headed for Lasqueti.

He wasn't worried by the restricted visibility as yet, but he knew that if they missed the island, they'd face thirty miles of open water before they reached shelter on Vancouver Island. On a good day, with air pollution blown off-shore and the sea mists burned away by a hot sun, it would be a grand trip with the huge white-capped crown of Mount Rainier dominating the southern horizon. They'd had such days, of course, when the thirty-foot Cal sliced through the chop with exhilarating speed, leaving a creamy white wake behind them. But not today. Today thick fog surrounded and blinded them. They couldn't see other boats on the water, and they couldn't be seen.

"Maybe we should turn back," said Alice.

Beth peered up at the masthead which sometimes disappeared in the overhead fog. At times their horizon was limited to mere feet. Everywhere they looked, there was fog. Silently, inexorably, it had swept down and turned a bright day of promise into a gloomy, dripping cocoon.

"God, it's getting thicker," Tanner murmured, peering ahead. "I can hardly see the forestay shackle at the bow and it's only thirty feet away." He tried to focus his hearing as well. Few pleasure boats would be out today, but the commercial traffic never stopped. He knew their little yacht would hardly be noticed if they ran afoul of one of the big freighters that traveled the Inside Passage.

2

"Listen," whispered Beth. From somewhere far away came the sound of a heavy foghorn. Tanner had turned off the engine so they could listen for other boats. As the fog laid its damp grip on the strait, the gulls and terns had gone and quiet descended.

"So, tell me again about this piece of water we're heading onto," said Alice. She brought Tanner a refill of coffee and with her own mug sat down beside him. Beth went down to the cabin and picked up the log book. She smiled. "Watch it, Alice. You know how he likes to expound on things."

He laughed. "Okay. I'll keep it short. This water is called the Inside Passage. It's an important commercial route between Washington and Alaska. It's also where a lot of the seafood you love to eat comes from.

"Southbound traffic enters Georgia Strait north of Vancouver Island through Johnston Strait, then comes down the east side of the island to another strait called San Juan de Fuca. That's the way ships get into the Pacific Ocean. Ships heading north are supposed to stay on the east side of the strait. It's something like a highway."

"A lotta straits, none of which run in a straight line," quipped Alice. "Why don't they just use one name? Be a lot simpler."

Tanner had no ready answer. He started the engine and adjusted the throttle on the little diesel. Then he settled back again, one hand resting easily on the tiller.

"Up north the passage is only a few hundred yards wide, see this?" He pointed to a spot on the chart Alice was holding. "Down here, about where we are between Nanaimo and Vancouver, it's about 35 miles wide."

A fog horn sounded again, somewhere west of them.

"Is that close?" Alice's voice was sharp.

"I don't think so. It sounded like a freighter. They don't generally come this near the eastern side of the strait."

"Is there a lot of traffic out here?"

"Sure. Ship traffic of all kinds, from those huge container barges you see along the waterfront in Seattle to small coastal freighters. Just about everywhere you look are the salmon fishers. There are ore boats that service the mines and plants all along the shores. Then you've got all the pleasure boats, like us, and log booms."

"Log booms?"

Tanner nodded. "You know about the logging up north in the mountains? The mills are all down here, along the water. After they cut the trees, the loggers wire the logs into big loose rafts and a tugboat pulls them down the water to the mills. I guess the rafts are huge things."

"So to sum up your lecture, thank you very much, it's pretty busy out there."

"You got it."

"If we hit something in this soup, bad news."

"Right. But there'll be a lot fewer ships out there because of the fog. And we're real careful."

"What are the mountains called?" Alice had a habit of abruptly switching topics without warning.

"The Coastal Range."

"What's the Sun Coast?"

"The resort area along the water just north of Vancouver-- the city, not the island."

"Misnamed, seems to me. At least this week."

Tanner nodded and looked around him again. Alice subsided into contemplative silence.

The air got damp and colder. Tanner's sandy-blond hair curled tighter. He shrugged his shoulders to loosen the knot of tension he could feel on his shoulder. He was forty-one and at the top of his game, a respected public relations executive heading a successful public relations agency. He leaned toward the hatchway, gazed all around the boat at the grayness, and then at his watch, noting the time in his mental calendar. "Ahoy below," he called.

"Yo, Michael?" responded Beth.

"Come up, we need a conference."

"Hang on. I haven't quite finished bringing the log up to date."

"It can wait."

"No, my liege, it cannot. In spite of your fabulous memory, I think we have to keep up with the log. Since you won't, I'm going to do the job."

Beth's long-time college friend, Alice George, stirred on the cushion beside him. Alice was a little unconventional from Tanner's conservative view of life. She lived a blunt in-your-face style. Sure of herself; a tall, and talented artist, she was sometimes employed by Tanner's agency for special projects they undertook for arts organizations in Seattle. This was her first overnight trip on a sailboat, and her first sailing experience with the Tanners.

Tanner glanced at her. "I've been getting this uneasy feeling you really don't approve of sailing."

"You mean as a way to travel?"

"Something like that."

Alice said, "I sailed to South America on an ocean liner, you know, but I've never been on anything as small as this. I like being with you guys, and I thought it'd be fun. But this fog sucks, and this boat is just too little. I fart and you hear it." She shrugged and went back inside herself, hunching over and tucking her chin into the collar of her rain jacket.

Tanner looked back at the bow. He'd attended the University of Washington, where he studied journalism and advertising and where he met Beth in a Humanities class. After graduation, he and Beth married. That same summer they formed the agency, Tanner and Associates, with two other partners.

"Sounds like early days at the agency, Michael." Beth smiled at her husband, swiping back a hank of hair from her forehead as she clambered up to the cockpit. "Calling a conference."

"Yeah. Remember when we moved to the Baxter Building? We finally had a place big enough for a conference table." He grinned at the recollection.

"Even before there was anybody to confer with. Long time ago. And we still have the table," she said to Alice. "You know, we spent hundreds of hours, cooped up in those offices in the early years."

"I can remember getting to the office before dawn sometimes and not getting out until after dark," Tanner said.

"Guys," chimed in Alice, "before you get all weepy on this nostalgia trip, remember that I was there a lot of the time. Besides, don't we have something to decide?"

Beth nodded and frowned out over the stern at the dinghy, out of sight in the fog.

"Don't you think we ought to turn back?" she said, always the more cautious of the two.

"Well, I like it. It's kinda fun. A little spooky, though," Alice responded.

"You surprise me, Alice. I thought you didn't like this sailing stuff," said Tanner.

Alice shrugged. "If we keep going, we'll get to land sooner, right? And as I just said, I kinda like this, even without the vistas."

"I didn't get a good position fix before the fog came," Tanner said, "so this heading is only more or less okay."

"Currents, leeway, something like that?"

"Right. If we miss Texada and Lasqueti, we'll go right out into Georgia Strait. Then it's a long way to the next stopping place."

"And slow going in this soup. Which is another point. Can we even get back?" Alice wondered. "How much time would we lose?"

"If we go back to Garden Bay and spend the night, we'll be out here again tomorrow," said Tanner. "But we've still got a week before the boat has to be in Anacortes so there's plenty of time."

"Been to Garden Bay. I want new vistas. I vote we keep going," Alice said.

"The advantage of turning back to Garden Bay is that we know where it is and what our heading should be," said Beth. "On the other hand, this fog should blow away before long. Isn't that right, Michael?"

Tanner nodded. He wanted to go on, confident of his ability to find his way to their next anchorage. He was sure the fog would lift before nightfall. It almost always did.

"I know, Michael, but blindly motoring through this fog is a little scary." After a minute of silence, Beth sighed and nodded her agreement. "It's only a couple of hours more, and it's farther to go back. We're all a little tired and the island is closer." Tanner looked at his wife. She looks tired, he mused, tired of being on the boat. Alice was starting to get on their nerves, with her sidelong looks and perpetually raised eyebrow. Last night, when he'd started to make love to Beth, she'd pushed him away, whispering that Alice was right on the other side of that thin partition, listening.

So they agreed. Tanner started the engine and the Queen Anne puttered on into the fog. Half an hour later, Tanner reached to shut off the engine, but it died before his fingers touched the switch. They looked at each other. If the engine refused to run, they would really be in trouble.

3

"Damn thing," Tanner muttered in a soft voice.

Tanner didn't have any mechanical training. Everything he knew about engines he'd picked up dealing with his automobiles. He'd read the manual for the Queen Anne's diesel, but he assumed that engines just ran, as long as you gave them reasonable maintenance. He'd not been sailing long enough to know that on the water, things often went wrong at the worst possible moment. When that happened, limited space made repairs difficult, assuming you could figure out what the problem was. He knew the boat carried a few spare parts, but he doubted he could diagnose an engine problem. Fixing it was out of the question.

While they drifted he looked at the engine dials. They didn't tell him anything new. So they sat and listened. Except for the faint bleating of a distant foghorn and the sea lapping softly against the hull there were no sounds. The sailboat rode easily on the water making no wake. The line to the dinghy that trailed behind them sagged back into the fog, dipping into the water from time to time. Tanner knew the sea was pushing the yacht a little faster than the dinghy because the yacht had a bigger hull. He remembered that the tide was still ebbing, flowing toward the Pacific through the Strait of San Juan de Fuca many miles to the south, and it was carrying them with it. But that wasn't the direction they wanted to go. When he turned the starter key, the engine responded immediately.

After another period of slow motoring, he shut the engine down again and listened for nearby boats. Alice napped in her bunk in the tiny forward cabin while Beth kept Tanner company in the cockpit. Noon came and Alice prepared bowls of fragrant hot soup. It wasn't cold, but the damp from the fog penetrated everything. Small droplets of water formed on the horizontal surfaces of the boat. Other beads of water collected on the lifelines and then dripped off to the deck below. They were constantly wiping off the cockpit cushions.

"It's like we're all alone in the whole ocean, maybe the whole world," Beth said quietly, staring up the bare mainmast to the spreaders where the mast disappeared into the fog. "I kinda like it, isolated in the fog like this." She smiled at her husband and put a hand on his leg.

"Yeah. It's quite a change from life in the city. What do you think now about buying a boat?"

"I think this is the wrong time to decide."

Tanner laughed and jiggled the tiller. "Maybe we ought to buy a motor launch instead of a sailboat."

Like other successful couples, the Tanners were acquiring more grown up toys for their rare play times. Sailing was a recent interest. They'd planned this charter to help them decide whether or not they wanted to buy a sailboat.

Beth looked up at her husband, standing at the stern, the tiller in one hand while he peered ahead. His bright yellow slicker rustled as he twisted to look back over his shoulder. He jiggled the tiller again.

"Listen, hotshot," she said fondly, "I agree that something like sailing would be a good way to unwind, especially since we live so close to the marina at Shilsole Bay."

Tanner was something of a workaholic, often working through the weekends. Beth had understood the long hours when they were getting started, but recently she'd been suggesting that she wanted them to be able to enjoy their success. She told her husband that since he seemed to enjoy sailing on friends' sailboats, she'd thought a two-week charter would help them decide if there was a sailboat in their future.

"Sure, with the boat docked at Shilsole, we could have a quick evening sail whenever we wanted to," he'd said.

"Or a weekend if you would. You could use something like sailing that puts you in a position where you have to be patient. Do you some good."

Now she smiled and tapped him on the knee. "The sea and the wind can't be swayed by your glib tongue and your good looks. You just have to be patient and wait it out."

Tanner laughed and looked around at the gray curtain. "Do you hear something?"

The fog eddied and broke. A large white-hulled motor vessel was revealed as if it had just been placed there, fifty yards ahead, motionless on the water. It was a big yacht. Tanner estimated it at more than ninety feet in length. He stared at it, open-mouthed. He could see several decks, each outlined by dark smoked windows that somehow gave the ship a remote, dangerous look.

Tanner and Beth saw three figures standing on the open wing of the bridge, looking toward them. One was holding a cane or a stick. When Beth raised one hand in a tentative wave, none of the people on the yacht responded. The yacht's engines suddenly rumbled into action with a muffled roar. White water bubbled up at the stern. The vessel turned away into the fog bank. Beth and Tanner watched the yacht until it was quickly swallowed up, leaving behind only the disturbance in the water and the fading sound of its engines to mark its presence. They were only able to read part of the ship's name, the letters GOL-- on the stern.

"What is that? Golden Hind? Gold Finger?"

"Goldilocks," said Beth, smiling. "Well, they're gone and we still have to make it to Lasqueti."

The Queen Anne puttered on across the sea. Again Tanner shut off their engine. "I think I hear a different boat," Beth said. "Listen." In the distance the metallic sound of another marine engine grew steadily fainter until it was gone. Tanner wondered about it. It had sounded as if the other boat was running at high speed, which was dangerous in heavy fog. Maybe the air was clear where the other boat was. He had learned that fog can sometimes alter perceptions of sound and distance. He'd read of sailors even misjudging directions in thick fog. Because fog is denser than dry air, sound carries farther and can appear to change direction. Tanner wondered how extensive the fog bank was. He reached down and twisted the starter key.

"Is the fog lifting?" Beth asked from where she was curled up on the cockpit bench. "It seems a little lighter now."

"It is, it is," Tanner replied. "Every so often I get a feeling it's going to clear off altogether. Then back it comes, thicker than ever. I'm getting tired of it, aren't you?" He shivered.

Beth nodded. Minutes later the fog receded a hundred yards to reveal again the same white motor yacht. This time it was not just resting on the water. This time it was driving straight at them. Tanner put the tiller full over and turned away from the big ship. He nudged the throttle forward. The sudden hard turn brought Alice to her feet in the cabin below where she'd been napping. She cried out sharply. Beth called down the hatch, reassuring her that they were all right. Queen Anne rocked as the big yacht slid by. Tanner swung the tiller again, bringing them back to their course. The two boats again slid into the fog, blind to each other.

"That was close," Beth said. "Do you think they didn't see us?"

"I don't know how they could have missed us. Maybe they're just screwing around, or not paying attention. But a ship that large must have a professional crew that knows what they're doing."

"Well, if we see them again, I'm going to get the name of that boat and register a complaint of some sort."

The distinctive sound of the other vessel's engines was quickly smothered by the fog and the sound of their own motor.

Alice, now fully awake, climbed the ladder from the cabin and joined Beth and Tanner in the cockpit.

Shaken by the sudden reappearance of the big yacht, all three sat quietly, immersed in their own thoughts. Queen Anne's engine coughed twice, then continued its duties.

Finally Beth roused herself. "I'm going to make fresh coffee," she said and disappeared below.

Alice looked at Tanner, hunched over the tiller in the stern. "What do you suppose they're doing out here in all this fog?"

"I guess they're waiting for it to lift so they can continue up the strait."

"They could have hailed or sounded a horn and we would have missed them. Beth told me she thought we would have missed each other anyway. Do we have a fog horn," Alice asked?

"Such as it is." Tanner lifted the small horn screwed to a can of compressed air and pressed the trigger. The beep was small in the unrelieved grayness. The fog swallowed it quickly.

The tension they all felt took its toll, bleeding away their energy. The water was still quiet, almost mirror-like. Except for their wake, they seemed to be suspended in this gray world, their sedate forward movement an illusion. Tanner began to wonder if they'd missed the southern end of Texada altogether and were already into the Georgia Strait. For the third time in an hour, Beth looked at the chart and consulted her watch.

He expected some sign if they were in the strait proper, a change in temperature, a different rhythm in the water, something. There was nothing, nothing but unending fog drifting over the silent water. The fog seemed more and more to become a palpable force. It was as if some unnamed malevolence waited there, out of sight over the side of the little boat, ready to swallow them up, should they make the smallest error.

Alice had been standing in the bow for a long time, one hand holding the steel forestay, staring out over the water. Now she returned to the cockpit "Listen!" she said, cocking her head.

Faintly at first, then more loudly, they all heard the

burbling sounds of exhaust and throbbing diesel engines.

"I think it's the same boat," said Beth quietly, looking south over the port side. "That boat had a very distinctive sound."

"But why would they come back?" Tanner stretched his arms overhead, holding the tiller with one knee while he eased his cramped muscles.

"It's the same ship. I'm sure of it. It sounds like they're coming right at us!" Beth's voice rose.

Tanner sounded the little fog horn. He was suddenly uncertain what to do.

"I hear another boat," cried Alice, pointing ahead over the right side.

Again Tanner sounded the fog horn, but there was no response. He began to feel as if they were caught in a massive pincer between two boats, each unaware of Queen Anne's location. He tried to remember the rules of the road in such a situation. Did they matter? Being legally right wouldn't mean much in a collision. Especially a collision with that big motor yacht.

"Coming about," he said quietly and put the tiller all the way over. The little sloop responded smartly, heeling as they reversed course.

Beth lost her balance at the sudden maneuver and dropped her coffee mug, which broke, splashing warm coffee on all three of them. They glanced down at the mess. When Tanner raised his gaze to the bow, the fog had parted. The white motor yacht was there, broadside this time, running at right angles to the Queen Anne. They watched in sudden horror as the big vessel swung around to present her high, knife-edged, steel bow to them.

Alice raised one arm and spread her fingers apart as if her gesture would turn the yacht aside. Beth stood transfixed in the cockpit, clutching the coaming and stared across the water. They heard the rising thunder of her engines as the big white ship gathered speed and rushed directly toward them. "Michael!" Beth cried.

Tanner kicked the throttle lever against the stop and the engine responded immediately. He slammed the tiller across, changing direction. His quick action caught the other boat by surprise and the two slid side by side for a moment. The wake of the larger ship shoved the little Queen Anne rudely aside. Tanner glanced up at the deck above him and saw a man standing jammed against the rail. Their eyes met briefly, then flame blossomed from the stick the man was holding.

The shotgun boomed twice as the two boats rushed apart.

Tanner stared, shocked, at the ragged hole in the Queen Anne's cabin roof where heavy shot had penetrated. With little conscious thought, he shoved the tiller to starboard and turned at right angles. It was a desperate bid to disappear into the fog. He might have stopped his engine, once the fog covered them, but he'd recognized the radar housing mounted just above the bridge of the other ship. He knew the crew of the big motor yacht could find them, even in thick fog, unless they could reach the obscuring shelter of land. But where was the nearest land?

Alice dissolved in semi-hysterical sobbing. She crouched down in the companionway and covered her eyes. Beth stood in the cockpit, rigid, staring at Tanner.

"My God, Michael!" she cried. "He shot at us! Why?"

"Don't know," he gritted, looking wildly about.

Again the motor yacht roared toward them out of the fog. This time there was no escape. The bow of the sleek white motor yacht sliced into the Queen Anne forward of the mast. Her hull was crushed as if it had been made of balsa wood. The forestay parted with a sound like a rifle shot and the ragged end of the stainless steel cable slashed down, ripping at the deck. The loss of tension caused the mast to bend back and down to the deck. As it fell, the mast cried out in that strange, screeching, unnatural sound of tearing aluminum.

The mast crashed down across the cockpit, bringing with it the boom and a confused tangle of writhing wire rigging. Queen Anne's engine still shoved the little sailboat through the sea. The forward thrust of the sailboat's propeller increased the flow of water into her ruptured hull. Her watertight integrity shattered, the Queen Anne died in seconds. Her lead ballast and engine dragged her to the bottom, smothering her death cries and those of her human cargo.

4

Tanner's first certain impression as he swam upward through the murk of semi-consciousness was the salt smell of the sea air. The faint impressions that wavered though his mind were unclear. Was he dying? Was this what the last moments of life were like? When he achieved real sensation he discovered he was blind. When he tried to open his eyes, the lids were stuck shut. His right arm was numb and didn't respond. He used the fingers on his other hand to smear away the blood on his face and pry open his eyelids. The world was blurred and when he moved his headache was excruciating. He had no idea how long he'd been unconscious. Tanner tried to raise his head and passed out from the pain.

The second time Tanner regained consciousness, he was still sprawled across the middle thwart of the little dinghy. His head rested face up on the gunwale. It was very cold. The dinghy hung motionless in the water. He heard nothing, not even gulls. Slippery, greasy blood clogged his ears, blood still running down from the split in his forehead. He peered at his fingers, holding them close in front of his face, wiggling them in drunken fashion. His head throbbed. An image of the mast falling toward him swam in his brain and he flinched, then rolled his head to one side. The pain grew so intense that white flashes flared behind his eyeballs, but this time he didn't pass out. His sea boots were gone and his foul weather jacket was ripped and bloody He shivered, beginning to feel the cold touch of the raw air. Again he tried to sit up and the dinghy rocked dangerously. His stomach heaved from the sharp pain in his head. Blood still oozed from his forehead and ran into his eyes.

"Oh, God," he moaned aloud. "Beth, Beth, where are you?" Only silence responded. He looked down and realized there was a lot of water in the bottom of the dinghy and he was drenched.

With small, slow motions, Tanner raised himself enough to discover he was not alone. Alice's sodden form was draped across the stern thwart. Gone was her vibrancy, her sharp tongue, the golden glow that she carried with her. When Tanner reached for her limp hand, it took him two tries. He curled toward her, leaning over his feet, reaching out. When he finally was able to grasp her fingers, they were so cold if felt as though he was holding the hand of a doll. Tanner slid his fingers up to Alice's wrist but he couldn't find a pulse. He sat up straighter. His headache slammed about in his skull again. He gasped in pain. He rolled over and crawled toward the stern. The bow raised alarmingly, but no water came over the sides. Tanner bent over Alice like a lover and reached for her head. His fingers slid into her hair, hair that was soggy, matted, and dark with blood and seawater. When his trembling fingers probed deeper, her skull beneath the hair felt soft and pulpy.

"Oh, God, Alice, what happened?" he mumbled. "Where's Beth?" A slow worm of blood seeped in a wandering path down the shoulder of Alice's tattered jacket. Tanner braced himself awkwardly against the gunwale and gently turned her head so he could see her face. Her half-shut eyes were glazed, the pupils clouded. He sighed and laid her head back on the thwart. He knew she was dead.

The pain in Tanner's head reasserted itself until his eyes wouldn't focus any longer. The only coherent thought he could manage was for Beth. Over and over again the question ran through his brain. Beth. Where is Beth?

He fell back on his heels onto the floor of the dinghy. When he twisted around toward the bow the dinghy rocked heavily. His movements unbalanced Alice's body and she slid over the stern. There was a gentle splash and he turned in time to see her slip into the water. Her body floated away, rolling slowly until only the back of her bloody head and her arms floated on the surface. The dinghy's oars were gone. When Tanner tried to paddle toward her with his hands, his efforts brought more excruciating pain and he couldn't continue. He lay half across the gunwale and watched while the sea gently took Alice away.

Tanner never knew how long he lay in the dinghy, staring at the water where he'd last seen Alice. His head still throbbed and he drifted in and out of consciousness. There were times when he thought he heard engines nearby and he became afraid that men from the motor yacht were circling through the remains of the fog, still searching for him. Trembling harder, he crouched in the bottom of the dinghy. Fear rode his shoulders, pressing him down. The little dinghy drifted aimlessly through the fog at the whims of the tide and an occasional breeze.

Once he awoke with a start and came upright in the dinghy, calling "Beth!" in an agonized screech he didn't recognize. Tears ran into his open mouth. He spiraled down once more into insensibility.

The dinghy, carrying the unconscious Tanner, grounded hours later on the southern tip of Lasqueti Island. The bodies of Alice and Beth were never found.

5

In the elevator descending to the garage from his apartment, Tanner scratched his bristly chin. He frowned, realizing he'd forgotten to shave that morning. Since the murders of Beth and Alice three months earlier, he'd had occasional lapses like this but forgetting to shave before heading out to his office was a first. Fortunately, he thought, his beard was light so it would be hard to see and he had no client appointments that day. The staff would put up with it. Most wouldn't even notice.

When he arrived at Tanner and Associates, the place was humming with its usual level of activity. Tanner failed to notice the surreptitious glances from some of his employees. He'd barely settled at his desk when his phone trilled. "Mr. Tanner, the project files you requested are up from filing."

"Thanks, Marie, bring 'em in, please."

Marie Clark smiled her way into Tanner's big office and placed a foot-high stack of folders on the corner of his desk that was informally designated "incoming." Tanner reached for the first file and bent his head over it. Marie's smile faded, replaced by a look of concern. She noticed the sun glinting off her boss's light stubble of beard. She was aware of the considerable speculation inside Tanner and Associates, and elsewhere around the city, about the future of Tanner and Associates. Competitors were beginning to wonder about his ability to recover from Elizabeth Tanner's death. Some whispered that he'd lost his touch. Others muttered that Beth had been the real creative force in Tanner's agency. Now she was gone, they said, the agency would decline. The professional vultures circled closer, waiting to see the high-flying Tanner agency crash and burn. They wanted to be first in line to snatch up the contracts, lure talented staffers, tear at the carrion. In the constantly shifting world of public relations, where inside knowledge and the latest speculations were eagerly sought, even a vague hint that Tanner's agency was in trouble could generate its own movement of nervous clients to seek other agencies. No one wanted to be associated with a loser.

Inside the agency the mood was more upbeat. Tanner's employees knew just how good he was, even if he wasn't currently working up to his usual standards. He was respected and even idolized by some within the agency. But Tanner's conduct since the death of his wife had become worrisome. That he had changed, there was little doubt. The question being debated was whether the changes were permanent. Formerly outgoing and nearly always of sunny temperament, he had, in the past, rarely demonstrated anger or frustration. Now he was more often moody, turning sullen and morose for days on end. When conversation drifted close to the subject of his wife's death he turned and became uncommunicative. And he was drinking more.

Stories circulated that he'd been seen staggering drunk or on the edge of drunkenness in clubs and bars around Seattle. There were other whispers that he'd begun to frequent some of the more unsavory bars in the city. Most of the staff discounted the rumors and stories, buoyed by the other partners' assurances that the rumors had been started by competitors trying to take advantage of the circumstances.

However, many of the stories were true.

Tanner looked at Marie's departing back and reached for the topmost file. It was a report on an old campaign they'd completed for the agency's most important client. For years, Orienta Corporation had been privately held, a benevolent giant among major corporations in the Northwest. Orienta traced its roots to the earliest frontier days of Seattle's youth. Well established by the end of the twentieth century, Orienta's fortunes continued to expand exponentially. The corporation, personally prodded by Tanner, was beginning to return to the community some of the benefits it had reaped through the years, by making a series of sizable grants to Seattle's museums and colleges.

Tanner and Associates had handled advertising and public relations for the company for many years. Winning the account from an older, more established firm had been the coup that finally elevated Tanner's group to prominence in the business community. The relationship had grown more solid over the years and now Orienta and Tanner and Associates were considered to be almost permanently linked.

Eighteen months earlier the giant corporation was sold by the founding family. Orienta then went public with a large stock offering, but there had been no significant change in the relationship with its public relations agency after new management was installed. At the time of Beth's murder, Tanner and his partners were in the midst of developing a new advertising campaign for the corporation. The most recent response to a progress report and interim proposal from Tanner had been enthusiastic and complimentary.

The telephone rang and Tanner picked up. He was unprepared for the summons.

"Just come," said the voice of Art Meadows in his ear. Meadows was vice president for corporate relations and Tanner's key contact inside Orienta management. "The chairman wants to see you as soon as possible."

When Tanner arrived at corporate headquarters twenty minutes later he was immediately ushered into the big corner office where upper management of the corporation had obviously been gathered for several hours. There were dirty coffee cups on a side table and the four men present were in their shirt sleeves with loosened ties. Papers in untidy piles littered the tables. Tanner, uncomfortable with the abrupt summons, was suddenly conscious of his unshaven face. He glanced at an unhappy looking Art Meadows. But the chairman claimed his attention.

"Mr. Tanner," said the chairman as soon as the door closed on a departing secretary.

Why the formality, Tanner wondered?

The older man frowned at Tanner's unshaven face. "I am sorry to tell you this, but I'm sure you'll understand our position."

Tanner opened his mouth to demur that he didn't understand what he didn't know. The chairman swiveled back and forth in his big padded chair and went on without a pause. Tanner closed his mouth.

"Orienta derives a substantial share of its income from various ocean-linked enterprises. Our cargo fleet has an admirable record of safety on the sea. I think it's fair to say our safety record is envied by our competitors, and that record is good for business."

Tanner stood looking at the chairman, but his mind drifted back to the time right after his last meeting with a King County prosecutor.

Police in British Columbia had looked into the sinking of the Queen Anne, and so had the Canadian Coast Guard. They had taken no action. "Tragedy on the Inside Passage," local papers in Vancouver and Seattle headlined the sad tale. Tanner had presented his story to the prosecutor with an impassioned plea for help in locating the operators of the big motor yacht.

"They murdered us," he told the official bluntly. "Tried twice to run us down, and they hit us the third time, just ahead of the mast. A man on deck was shooting at us, for God's sake. With a shotgun."

Unfortunately, he had no physical evidence of his charges. The water was deep where Queen Anne went down and the sea refused to give up the bodies of the dead women. Since Tanner couldn't identify the killer yacht, the prosecutor and other authorities in both Canada and the U. S. reached the same conclusions.

In a futile attempt to get some satisfaction for Beth and Alice, Tanner used his contacts to be admitted to the Coast Guard base in Vancouver. He wanted to talk to the tall Coast Guard lieutenant, the captain of the Canadian cutter that rescued him from that Lasqueti beach. Now he watched the officer stride down the wharf toward him.

"Mr. Tanner," he nodded. Tanner rose from the big iron bollard where he'd been sitting and looked up at the tall dark officer. "I've already told you, sir, my superiors reviewed your statements and reached a final decision. The case has been officially closed. There's nothing I can do to help you." The lieutenant had agreed in his report that Tanner's version of the incident could have happened just as he said. He'd also stated that the Coast Guard had found no physical evidence to support the story.

"I understand. I read the reports," Tanner said flatly. "What I don't understand is why nobody believes me. Why nobody listens. It's not like I'm some irresponsible boat jockey with no experience or a bad record. Hell, I couldn't have chartered the Queen Anne if I weren't reasonably qualified."

"As I said before, Mr. Tanner, you came close to facing criminal charges." The man looked at Tanner from deep-set brown eyes. Tanner stared back. Was there something there? Some smidgen of sympathy? The feeling went away.

Tanner sighed. Frustration boiled up again like a bad taste in his mouth. He'd always been able to rely on his wit and his verbal ability. But nothing seemed to sway these people; they were unmovable, like the wind and the sea.

"Your record in Seattle as a responsible businessman is the only thing that saved you. It's highly unusual for something like the collision you described to occur and leave no evidence!"

Tanner heard the impatience in the man's voice. Heedless, he pressed on. "But I gave you a descript--"

"Tanner, look." The officer cut him off. "You know damn well your description fits dozens, maybe hundreds of vessels in these waters. You can't even give us the boat's full name! Or it's port of registry! Even if we identified a ship that matched the poor description you gave us, and even if that vessel was in the general area at the proper time, what then? Eh?

You've got no proof. It was a terrible tragedy but, man, you've got to put it behind you. That's the only thing you can do now. Believe me." The man looked hard at Tanner, then walked around him. Tanner turned and watched the lieutenant stride rapidly away and climb the gangway to his ship.

Deep inside he admitted the man was probably right. Tanner had been barely alive when he was rescued and his recollections were sketchy and not entirely lucid. The passage of time had done little to improve his recollection of that terrible day.

Tanner's shoulders slumped and he turned away. Michael Tanner was not in the habit of challenging established authority, in spite of his creative bent. Like most North Americans, he paid his taxes on time and he followed the rules. But the void in his existence left by Beth's death and his inability to get anyone to even look for the big white yacht threatened to overwhelm him.

He returned to the present with a start.

"Mr. Tanner? Are you with us?"

"Yes. Of course."

"It must be apparent," the chairman of Orienta went on, "that we cannot continue an association with a firm headed by an individual so intimately involved in an accident at sea, an accident that resulted in two deaths."

Tanner noted that the chairman carefully avoided directly accusing him of irresponsibility.

"We are therefore terminating your contract immediately. "Mr. . . . ah . . . Meadows," he glanced at a sheet of paper on the desk before him. "Yes. Mr. Meadows will discuss with you any charges which may be pending."

Tanner knew the loss of the lucrative Orienta contract, largest in their portfolio, would create difficulties in his agency. His mind raced. He said, "I'll resign from the agency if you leave the contract with my associates for the rest of the term."

The chairman waved him off. "No, no. The matter has been decided. Now I must ask you to excuse us." He turned away in dismissal.

Tanner realized there was nothing more to be said. "I'll contact Mr. Meadows shortly to arrange delivery of the work we've completed and to confirm any unbilled charges." He turned on his heel and stalked out of the room.

Alone in the elevator on the long ride to the street, Tanner's stomach fell in concert with the cage he rode in. He leaned his forehead against the cool burnished steel control panel. His mind went back again to the Coast Guard base in Vancouver. After leaving the lieutenant, he'd returned to his car in the public parking lot. As he hurried along, eyes on the ground, tears came to his eyes. A burly, dark-complexioned man with a thin black beard stood in the middle of the walk watching Tanner. As Tanner approached, he turned away and Tanner, in full stride, cannoned into the stranger, bouncing off his solid bulk.

"Hey, mate, watch where yer goin'!" The growling voice was harsh. Tanner regained his balance and looked at the man. He was wearing dark wool trousers and a heavily ribbed black sweater with a high neck. Over the sweater, the man wore an unbuttoned dark coat that looked like a Navy-issue peacoat. His hands were still in his coat pockets, but his whole image bespoke truculence and aggression.

"Sorry, sorry. Wasn't paying attention. Sorry." Tanner raised both hands, palms out, stepped off the walkway and hurried on, still concentrating on his own inner sorrow and pain. On the drive back to Seattle from Vancouver, he nearly sideswiped a car when he recklessly changed lanes. He tailgated relentlessly, and coming off the freeway into Seattle at the wrong exit, ran a red light. Then he went looking for a bar. He wanted a drink.

The next morning, while word of the Orienta loss circulated through the agency, Tanner talked to Marie. "We have to stop the fallout. The rumors will start a rush of business out the door. Move the Western Finance contract onto the front burner and call them right away for an appointment."

"We've just finished the prelims."

I know, but let's do an in-progress just to keep 'em in the

fold and reassure them the loss of Orienta isn't going to signal a disaster. We'll demonstrate we aren't losing our touch."

Tanner called his bank and arranged a transfer of personal funds to the agency to cover the Orienta shortfall so no one at the agency would be laid off.

Increasingly, Tanner's life was changing. Some former friends and several of Beth's relatives blamed him personally for her death. They refused to see or even talk to him. Only a few recognized that Tanner's judgment of himself was far harsher than that of others. Time became his enemy. Tanner strove to fill every moment to avoid thinking about those last awful moments. More and more, Tanner turned to drink to blunt his memories. He retained the apartment he and Beth had purchased a few months before her death, but the rooms carried unsettling memories and he frequently considered moving. Even the thought of finding a new place, and then the effort to actually move, was too much. He stayed where he was.

Again and again he replayed in his mind the last hours of their voyage. What, he asked himself, could I, should I, have done differently? Who was on that mysterious motor yacht? Why had they run down the Queen Anne?

The only answer that floated through his consciousness was that he should have turned back before the encounter. They would have avoided the mystery yacht, the killer yacht, altogether, had they retreated from the fog.

Tanner couldn't get his mind around any motives for the murders, try as he could. He even hired a local private detective in an expensive attempt to learn whether any of his competitors might have tried to have him killed. After a week of digging the detective met Tanner one evening at his apartment.

"Look, Mr. Tanner. You asked me to check out whether any of your business competitors might have tried to have you killed, right?" He watched Tanner take a long pull from the glass of whiskey in his hand. Tanner nodded and gestured for him to continue.

"I like your money just fine but I have to be frank."

"That's your name, right?"

"Sorry?"

"Frank," said Tanner, waving the glass and slopping liquid on his pants. "That's your name."

"Oh, right. Well, sure, you have plenty of business rivals, many who are jealous of your success, but I can't find anybody I'd classify as an out-and-out enemy, someone who'd turn to murder to destroy you. So it's tough to legitimately spend any more time on this--"

"So you're saying you can't do it?" Tanner interrupted.

"Sure, I can do it, but I won't. It'll cost a small fortune and I won't learn anything useful. You just don't have the kind of enemies who would do that."

Tanner sighed. "You wanna drink?"

"No, thanks."

"'S okay. I 'preciate your being candid." The man left and Tanner poured himself another glass of whiskey.

The weeks passed and although he seemed to be working harder than ever, things weren't going well. The quality and inventiveness of his work, so long a cornerstone of his pride, suffered. His partners diverted some of his unfinished projects to others in the agency when his productivity fell. He found himself thinking more and more about the big motor yacht, remembering small details, unable to concentrate on the task at hand. More than once he woke in the night, sweating, straining to see through that swirling fog the rest of the name on the receding transom.

GOL--.

It never worked. Tanner lost weight, quit his health club, ate erratically and drank heavily and more frequently. Many days he arrived at work late or hung over and some days he didn't put in an appearance at all. He began to miss appointments with potential clients. Late one night he realized he was in an unfamiliar section of Seattle.

"Hey, buddy."

"Hmmm?"

"Hey, buddy. C'mon. You can't sleep here. Cops'll

throw you in the tank."

Tanner felt someone shaking his shoulder. He pried his eyes open but he didn't recognize the figure looming over him. The streetlight behind the man's head cast his face in deep shadow. Blearily he peered around. God, he was half-lying on the curb on a seedy Seattle street, outside a bar. For a minute, Tanner stared at the stuttering neon sign above the bar's entrance, but he couldn't make out the name.

"Where'm I?"

The man leaned closer, his beery breath washing over Tanner, making his stomach lurch. "Hey buddy, lemme help you over to the park."

Hours later, when Tanner awoke to a thick tongue and throbbing head, shivering with cold, just as dawn was reaching into the city canyons, he found a twenty-dollar bill wadded into his shoe. He waved it in a passing cab driver's face and secured a ride to his apartment.

One night he woke sweating, reaching out, calling Beth's name. A heavy ache grew in his heart that weighed him down, made it difficult to breathe.

Tanner sat up and switched on the light. It was one a.m. I need a drink, he thought. In the refrigerator he found a pitcher of orange juice. "A little vitamin C will do me a world of good," he muttered. He added a generous slug of vodka to the glass and took a long swig, downing nearly half the glass. The leaden feeling didn't go away. He poured more juice and carried the vodka bottle into the bedroom.

It was noon the next time he wakened. He woke kneeling beside the bed. The empty glass lay beside him on the floor and the now empty vodka bottle lay on the bed in the middle of a wet spot. He staggered into the bathroom and vomited.

Days later, sitting at his desk, Tanner stuck out a hand and inspected his grimy nails. His fingers trembled.

"Well," he murmured aloud, "where did you go, steady Eddy? Have you abandoned me too?"

"I beg your pardon? Did you say something, Michael?"

His secretary was just bringing in some papers to be signed.

""No, sorry, Marie, I was just talking to myself."

He failed to notice the look of concern and sympathy that passed across her face.

One Saturday almost without knowing how it happened, he drove to the Seattle docks and bought a ticket on the ferry that crossed Puget Sound to the Olympic Peninsula. During the trip he paced the open deck, absorbing the sounds and sights of the blue, whitecapped water, and the green islands they passed. It was a brilliant, crisp, late January day. Tanner leaned on the rail and watched a white-sailed sloop effortlessly come about to avoid the huge ferry. Several people around him waved and Tanner saw the happy smiles of the crew on the sloop when they waved back. For the first time since the deaths of Elizabeth and Alice, he remembered what it was like to be aboard a sailboat. He could almost hear the wind in the rigging and feel the pulsing rhythm of the deck under his feet. For the first time in days, a smile came to his face.

He sometimes recalled in shame and discomfort a scene after the memorial service for Beth when her brother Tom stepped in front of Tanner on the lawn of the small, neat chapel in suburban Tacoma. The two of them had been close, Tanner remembered, and Tom was taking his sister's death especially hard.

"You son of a bitch!" he cried, blocking Tanner's path to the limousine. "I knew there'd be an accident! You must have been drunk or out of your mind to be sailing in that fog."

Tanner stared, then tried to step around the man.

Tom grabbed his arm. "Look at me, you bastard." His voice rose and people turned to watch. Tanner raised his red-rimmed eyes and stared at Beth's brother. He even looked like her.

"Tom, I swear to you, it wasn't like that. You know what I told the family, what I told the authorities. I wasn't lying."

"Everybody knows you take risks. You like it! You were

over your head out there or drunk. And Beth paid for it!" He sobbed and lunged forward, starting to swing at Tanner. Others stepped between them and hustled Tom away. Tanner entered the waiting limo and reached for a glass and the whiskey bottle.

6

"We have a problem, Michael," began Jeremiah Christian, "a growing problem." The least venturesome of the partners, Christian's responsibility was to the business routine of the agency. He managed the office and kept the books. His tall, spare body housed a solid precise mind for figures. His financial acumen had protected the partnership through the years.

"Only one?" asked Tanner. He sounded tired and he looked bad, slumped on the end of his spine in his chair at the rounded end of the walnut conference table in his office. It was the same table he and Beth had chosen years ago in the early years of the agency. His chin rested on his chest and he peered at Christian and Perry Barstowe, the third partner, out of swollen, half-closed eyes. Again the previous night he'd had little sleep

After her death, Beth's family made half-hearted attempts to continue their contacts with Tanner, but after the first uncomfortable dinners, dinners from which Beth's brother Tom was conspicuously absent, Tanner began to decline the invitations and soon they stopped coming. Last night his phone had rung and the answering machine hadn't kicked in. Tanner, finally roused from sleep at three in the morning, picked up and heard Beth's brother Tom blubbering into the phone.

"Yes, Tom," Tanner had agreed softly. "I admit it. It wasn't my fault that other ship hit us, but I was negligent." He dropped the receiver back in its cradle and slumped back on the bed, tears running down his face. He had no more sleep after that.

Now Tanner struggled to follow Christian's theme.

"The problem is this. Ever since we started this agency, we've been pretty frank with each other, right? And things have gone from pretty good to excellent. Even when you jumped into something without consulting us, we've gone along. It's been easy since you almost never made a wrong move. So, now we have to have some plain talk. Michael, to be blunt, the last six months have been a disaster."

"Since Beth's murder," Tanner interjected.

"That's right. Your attention wanders. You've lost your meticulous eye for detail. There have been a couple of embarrassing situations." With a quick glance at Perry Barstowe, Christian leaned forward and continued, staring into Tanner's blood-shot eyes. "You know we've recently lost several bids to other agencies."

Tanner waved it off. "Sure, Jeremiah, but that always happens. You know this business. We don't get every contract we bid on. Who does?"

"I know that, Michael, but we're taking some serious hits. We're making mistakes we never made before. What concerns me is that things seem to be getting worse, not better.

"You recall I maintain productivity files on everyone in the agency. Something we set up years ago."

Tanner nodded, wondering where Christian was going. He hadn't realized his troubles were so obvious to others.

"Even allowing for your ... loss, your productivity rating is running somewhere between zero and a minus twenty. We, Perry and I," Christian swallowed and gestured vaguely across the table. "We think something has to be done."

Perry Barstowe nodded. He and Jeremiah hadn't discussed Tanner's deteriorating condition in detail, just that they had to meet, something the partners had always done on a casual basis. He scratched his balding head and chimed in. "It's not just you, buddy. If it was only your personal projects we wouldn't be so concerned. But you've always been our leader, practically the heart and soul of this agency." He waved at the busy office on the other side of the glass wall. "All these people count on you. Now, however, your leadership has just gone missing. And what really concerns me is that things aren't getting better. Things seem to be sliding downhill." Barstowe shifted in his seat. Neither of the partners wanted to bring up Tanner's drinking, and he'd just come perilously close to the subject.

Tanner glanced up to see Marie hovering outside the office, a look of concern on her face. He nodded slowly, remembering. More than once in past years, his agency had won important contracts when it appeared there was no hope, because Tanner had driven himself and the staff to higher levels of productivity. Tanner and Associates had won and then maintained contracts against larger and more experienced competition through meticulous preparation and a demonstrated willingness to go that extra mile. But since the murders, almost seven months ago he'd been unable to find his way back to his old self. He'd sloughed off key responsibilities at times, and he'd missed some important personal deadlines with clients. He was also vaguely aware that alcohol was getting the best of him.

"Yeah, okay. I get the point. You guys want to buy me out? Is that it?" He felt as though the temperature in the room had dropped suddenly.

"No!" The response from both partners across the table was immediate. Barstowe leaned across the table toward his friend. "It really hurts us to see you like this, and that's distracting too. But the main thing here is to help you find your way through this. We think you need a rest, a change. I think you need to get away from Seattle for a while and heal. I think it will be easier if you don't have to worry about the daily grind here."

Tanner looked back at his partners through misty eyes. It had never occurred to them to buy him out and cut him adrift. "I am tremendously grateful to you guys," he said in a husky voice. "What do you want me to do?"

"I have a suggestion." Jeremiah cleared his throat. He almost never made suggestions at partner meetings unless they dealt with the balance sheet.

Surprised, Barstowe stared at Christian.

"Why don't you take a leave of absence?" Jeremiah continued. "Go lie on a beach somewhere for several weeks. A whole month, even. Maybe Mexico? You can certainly afford it, and so can the agency. Then when you get back, I think you should spend some time in research. Use the agency. After all, we've got the best research department in the state."

"For what?" Tanner couldn't see where the conversation was going. His bleary red eyes wavered over Jeremiah's animated features.

"Michael, I never doubted for a minute your version of what happened out there in the Inner Passage, and neither did Perry."

Suddenly Barstowe was grinning. "Damn, Jeremiah. You want us to help Mike find that yacht. Is that it?" He sat up straighter.

Tanner's eyes opened wider. Good Christ, I should have thought of that, he mused.

Christian nodded, still looking at Tanner. "Do you see, Michael? I haven't a clue whether you'll be successful, but at least you will have tried."

"Yeah," chimed in Barstowe, "which is more than the authorities ever did."

"I dunno," murmured Tanner. "Mexico I'll buy, but trying to find that yacht on my own? Seems like a pretty tall order. And what if I do find it? What do I do then?"

"Let's take this in easy stages. First, you get well. We'll deal with that yacht later. Both partners remarked after they left Tanner's office that he had been sitting straighter and scribbling notes to himself when they went out.

7

In mid-March, after a week in Mazitlan, Tanner moved farther down the coast to a quiet Mexican fishing village, infrequently visited by "gringo touristas." He found a small cottage, just a step above a shack, that was right on the beach. Most of the time he slept, wandered the village and listened to the sea. Two days before he'd planned to return to Seattle, he wired the agency that he would stay in Mexico at least three more weeks.

Tanner cut down on his drinking, and began to exercise. Every morning, just as the sun sent its first soft rays over the mountains in the east to paint the Pacific Ocean with its golden colors, he jogged along the beach. Soon he was running over the hard wet sand. One mile, two. Then five miles, sweat pouring off his body. Every day. He did push-ups and sit-ups and he sprawled on the warm sand and listened to the sea.

Tanner had watched the local Mexican fishermen set out each morning and return late in the afternoon with their catch. Frequently he bought a small grouper or yellowtail for his supper. Toward the end of his second week in the village, he went to sea on a small boat for the first time since the Queen Anne had sunk. One morning he appeared at the tiny anchorage before dawn. He was wearing faded ragged cutoffs, scuffed deck shoes, and a torn sweatshirt.

"I would like to fish with you," he said to the old, grizzled Mexican. The man was working with a young boy, getting their nets ready. "I will be your crew." Tanner spoke almost no Spanish and neither of the Mexicans spoke English. But with many gestures and finger-pointing, he was able to spend a day at sea with the old man and his grandson, setting and hauling nets. He discovered that his return to the water helped his healing. Bone tired, weary in every muscle, he fell into bed when they returned and spent a dreamless, peaceful night. It was the first of many such nights. He stayed another week and went fishing again with the Mexican and his grandson. His tortured, restless nights, and his nightmares, began to fade.

Back in Seattle Tanner reactivated his health club membership. He began to familiarize himself with the search capabilities of the Internet and spent hours in consultation with the agency's head of research. He also resumed some of his duties, reconnecting with contacts and appearing at business meetings in the city.

"I say, old chap. You are looking very fit." The small man next to him at the cocktail party spoke with a distinct British accent.

Tanner looked around, winked and smiled. "Tom Wallace. I haven't seen you in months." Tanner stuck out his hand. Wallace was one of Tanner's fiercest business competitors. Over the years their respective agencies had gone head to head several times in competition for new clients. Their respect for each other's business acumen was strong. "You're looking pretty healthy yourself."

"Susie and I are just back from a trip to Hawaii." Wallace's white teeth gleamed from his smooth tanned face. "We had a grand time. Big seas, fine winds." Wallace owned a 55-foot Gulfstar and was an experienced blue-water sailor. Realizing he was intruding into a painful area for Tanner, he smoothly changed the subject. "We've missed you in the ad wars. Business pretty good over on Pike Street?"

Tanner shrugged. "No complaints. I took some personal time and went to Mexico for a while. I'm also trying to be less of a workaholic. Barstowe was called away at the last minute or he'd be here today instead of me." He looked at Wallace a moment and made a swift decision.

He took the other man's arm and steered him away from the noisy crowd to a quieter corner. "Tom, you've sailed the Inside Passage. Maybe you can help me."

"So long as you don't want any trade secrets."

"I'll tell you one of mine, if you'll promise to keep it to yourself."

Wallace's eyebrows went up. "I'm all ears, so to speak." Tom Wallace's ears were large and stuck out from his skull in an obtrusive way. "Ears" Wallace was the unkind sobriquet jealous rivals had pinned on him behind his back. Tanner hadn't known Wallace was aware of the jibe.

"I need a job. No, Tom," he responded to the surprise on the other man's face, "I'm not quitting the agency. But I think there's a strong client potential among recreational boating service operators. The people who run marinas and repair boats. To make the right kind of pitch, I need to know a lot more about the business."

"Research? Why you? Just assign one of your people to it. Personally I think you're wrong. Those people are all very independent operators. They make up their own advertising. You can tell just by looking at some of the magazine ads. I know. I deal with a lot of them."

"I'm aware of that, Tom. Which is why I'm talking to you about this. You know my style. I have to see it for myself. Talk to the people on the job. Get inside the business. What I'm asking for is a reference, a personal reference. I want to spend a season working as a helper in one of the small marinas along the Inside Passage."

"Well, I think your idea is a non-starter, but now I have the secret of your success." He smiled. "Let me think a minute." Wallace took another sip of his highball and stared at the wall. "How about something just north of Puget Sound? Maybe in the San Juans?"

Tanner's pulse surged. "Good. There's a lot of traffic

between Seattle and the Sun Coast. It sounds perfect."

"We take our boat, Maid Merry, to Desolation Sound almost every year and we always stop at a particular island. I know the owner of the marina where we often refuel. What say I give him a call?"

"Thanks, Tom. I'll return the favor sometime."

"That you will, me boy, that you will. Now, how about another drink?"

"Thanks, Tom," Tanner said. "I'll take a rain check. I was just about to leave when we ran into each other." The two men shook hands and Tanner put his mineral water on a nearby table and left the room.

Across the bar, a small colorless man in a gray suit watched Tanner go. He turned to the woman next to him. "Excuse me. Who's the gentleman over there in the dark green jacket? The one with--"

"The big ears?" she finished. "That's Tom Wallace. He owns the largest public relations firm in Seattle."

"Thank you very much." The gray man turned away and walked toward the buffet table. From his inside pocket he took a small notebook and wrote in it. Tanner--Tom Wallace--chk, the note said.

8

"Phew!" Tanner jerked his head back as thick, evil-smelling liquid spilled over his fingers and ran down the sloping deck of the head. His nose stung and his eyes started to water. The heavy odor of waste threatened to overwhelm him. He was crouched in an uncomfortable squatting position in the tiny forward head of a sailboat named Last Chance. Tanner threw a wad of grimy wipes into a bucket and sighed. The chartering party had long since departed for home, singing praises for their just-completed week of sailing in the San Juan Islands. As they'd left, one of them had casually mentioned that the forward head might be plugged up. Tanner's summer job required him to clean it out before the next charter party arrived.

Tom Wallace had made good on his promise. A week after the gathering at the Seattle Hilton, Tanner received a call from John Martin, owner and operator of Martin's Marina on big San Juan Island. They met at a small restaurant near the Pike Street Market.

Tanner was not a prime candidate for the marina job and Martin was initially reluctant. But Tanner persuaded him that even though he said he wanted the job to continue advertising research, he'd give full value. Martin finally agreed after they met a second time. But he insisted that Tanner would be paid a regular salary. Tanner didn't tell Martin that his real reason for wanting the job was to continue his search for the motor yacht. The killer yacht.

Except for his Mexican sojourn, Tanner's physical activities in recent years had been directed toward maintaining a reasonably healthy body in a largely sedentary life, not one of physical labor.

He remarked ruefully to John Martin after his first day on the job, "I thought I was in better shape. I'd forgotten I even have some of these muscles."

"Well, Tanner, you'll get used to it. You'd better, or it's gonna be a very long summer." John Martin was a retired seaman. Although he now led a less active life, long years at sea had given him a steely inner core masked by a round body and persistently smiling face.

Tanner was amazed to discover what he didn't know about the world of boating.

"Take a careful look at what we offer here. When I took you on as a general helper, I also got me a salesman. You have to know what we can do for the boater who shows up here and you have to tell him about it. He may need some service or piece of gear we can provide, but he's not gonna buy it here unless we suggest it. Another thing. I probably don't have to say it, knowing your background, but the customer is king. You'll discover you have to put up with some real bozos in this business."

The days slid smoothly by. Tanner, always a fast learner, began to appreciate the complexities of the support structure that keeps recreational boat owners afloat and operating. Boats used both gas and diesel fuel that had to be transported into the islands and stored in huge underground tanks. Fresh, sweet water was always in demand, water that had to be pumped from deep wells or brought from the mainland. One of Tanner's jobs was to inventory and replenish the marina's stock of lubricants, small parts, rope and line and other merchandise displayed in the ship's chandlery.

Vessels that docked overnight were assessed dockage fees. Many required electrical hookups and other services . The marina facilities had to be kept in good repair. Tanner's job included being sure the floating mooring buoys strung across part of the harbor were in good repair.

He used the marina's Boston Whaler runabout for the purpose. One bright day he was idling across the harbor, checking buoys and mooring chains. He turned his head and looked across the little bay.

The harbor was a deep bowl-shaped indentation in the island that opened to the east. It was surrounded by moss and lichen-covered boulders. Visitors entering between the rocky arms saw a long wooden wharf running parallel to the shoreline with a large cluster of fingers jutting out into the harbor on the right. These were transient docks and were joined to a smaller cluster of permanent berths on the left that were reserved for island residents. Still farther to the left was another, smaller dock, with five slips for boats of guests at the resort hotel that shared the bay.

Midway down the main wharf was the harbormaster's shack and behind it the gas dock. The marina itself consisted of several white-painted cinderblock buildings of one and two stories. They looked, with their black-framed windows, like a handful of dice cubes randomly dropped on the shore by a giant hand. The cubes housed offices, showers, a laundry and several small stores.

The separately owned resort and Martin's marina shared a gardener who kept the lawns mowed and flowers blooming around every building and along the paths. Flags mounted at each corner of the buildings snapped in the breeze. Against the blue sky, populated with bright white clouds, the little harbor was a very pleasant place to work and play and, for Tanner, to watch and learn.

Tanner was responsible for cleaning and maintaining the small fleet of charter boats Martin ran from the marina during the summer. "Dammit, John! I've seen some dirty boats since I started here, but this last one was a real mess. Nearly as bad as the plugged head on Last Chance."

Martin chuckled and shook his head. "That's one job I wondered about your doing, being a big executive and all."

Tanner laughed. "To tell you the truth, if I'd known

everything I know now about what pigs people can be, I might have changed my mind about taking this job. Why d'you suppose they leave things so dirty?"

"Not their boats," grunted Martin. "Do we charge part of their deposit?"

Tanner thought a minute. "Twenty bucks, I guess. At least I didn't have to disassemble the head and nothing's broken on this one."

"You'd never make it in this business," chuckled Martin, "you're too easygoing."

A few days later, he looked up at Tanner from the paperwork scattered across his desk. He was reviewing a recent statement from his accountant, frowning over the small growth in revenues. "I dunno, Tanner," he said. This business is getting tougher every day. More competition."

"I have a couple of ideas for you. I think a new brochure might be a good move." Tanner knew Martin did his own design and wrote the brochure.

"I'm glad to look at new ideas, any time. Never did claim to be a P.R. type."

"Okay. And let me call the agency art department for a little help."

Martin reluctantly agreed. "I always pay my own way. I don't hold with taking big favors."

"Don't worry, I'll make sure you have the chance to pay me back, one way or another."

"Anything else?" Martin could see Tanner had something on his mind.

"Yes. I wasn't completely honest with you about why I wanted this job." He looked intently at the man opposite him. "Do you know who I am?"

"D'you mean do I know about the Queen Anne? Yes, I know about it. Your friend Tom Wallace didn't mention it, but I thought I recognized your name, so I dug out some old newspapers." He waited.

"My city friends hope this job will help me forget about

trying to find the killer yacht," Tanner went on. "But finding that yacht is the main reason I'm here. I hope I'll see her, or learn something that will help me find her."

"And if you do identify the ship, what then?"

"I'm convinced it wasn't an accident. John, they fired a shotgun at us! I think they didn't want to be seen. I think we interrupted something. Something illegal."

"Shot at you! Good God. Why are you telling me this now?"

"Because I want to be straight with you. Plus, I'm sure you won't talk out of turn about what I'm doing here."

Martin nodded and said, "I was beginning to suspect you had another reason for comin' here. You've been pretty eager to talk with the passing traffic. I'm glad you told me the whole story. I may be able to help. If you want a few days off to wander around up north, we can arrange it. But you're gonna need a plan. It's a big piece of water and there's lots of places up there where a boat could hide."

Tanner agreed. How was he going to find one motor yacht on those trackless waters and miles of twisting inlets and coves?

Over the next week Tanner and Martin talked several times. As gently as he knew how, Martin repeatedly encouraged Tanner to go back to Lasqueti Island where he'd been rescued, to the place where Beth and Alice had died. Tanner didn't want to think about that. He wasn't ready.

He put together some ideas and mapped out a modest, advertising campaign for the rest of the season. They ordered the new brochure Tanner designed with help from his agency's art department, and as the summer wore on, increased traffic was the result.

Martin began to encourage Tanner to return to his marina job the following year. "Unless you get lucky, you may have to spend another summer up here. What better place to base your search?"

"I don't know. I think I'm going to have to spend a lot of

time searching for them."

"I'll make sure you have the time available," Martin responded. "Have you thought any more about how you're going to do this search? As a start, maybe you ought to take a run up to Desolation Sound. Kind of scope things out." Martin was convinced that Tanner had to revisit the place where the Queen Anne went down, where his wife and Alice had died. For his inner healing.

"I'll think about it." Tanner changed the subject. "I've developed a plan of sorts. The research staff at the agency is compiling lists from Canadian and U. S. ship registries based on my less than precise description of that motor yacht and we're starting to trace them."

"Big job."

"I'll say. I have no idea how many similar ships are in these waters There are hundreds that have GOL in their names and might or might not look like the one that hit us.

"Yeah, well, lists and planning on paper are one thing. Being out there eyeball to eyeball with the Passage is gonna be necessary sooner or later."

Traffic on the Inside Passage that summer was brisk. There were the usual confrontations between commercial ship operators and unwary pleasure boaters, confrontations that kept authorities busy on both sides of the international border.

Tanner explored other ways of finding the ship he sought. In midsummer a big party of divers, headed for the underwater exploration of a late nineteenth-century wreck, stopped at the marina. He talked to the leaders of the expedition. They were initially interested.

"Well, Mr. Tanner, we'd certainly like to help you locate your boat. Where did she go down?"

Tanner described the approximate location.

"Not very precise. I don't suppose you have her log or recall your exact position when she went down? No GPS?"

Tanner shook his head and admitted he only had a general idea of their position at the time of the sinking.

"Let me spell it out for you," the dive leader informed him. "To have any chance of finding the wreckage, you'd have to hire a submersible, or maybe a drag boat. Problem is, it's deep, it's cold, and it's murky." He ticked off the problems on his fingers. "The tidal currents are another factor. I'm afraid you could spend a whole lot of time and an awful lot of money and not even come close, unless you can give us the latitude and longitude. Even if you could, tides and the depth make the odds very long for success."

Tanner was lonely that summer. He missed his wife badly. Female companionship was available, and one or two women at the resort even made it clear they were strongly attracted to him. But in spite of his loneliness, Tanner did not respond to their messages.

9

"Excuse me. Tanner, isn't it?" The man had a flat voice with no accent. Gray, Tanner labeled the voice, like the man's coloring. He was slight of build and gray-haired. His clothes were ordinary, like his image. The nylon fabric of his tan windbreaker rustled as he strolled closer. He was a man you'd forget ten minutes after he walked away.

"Yes?" When Tanner was busy he didn't encourage small talk. He'd discovered that hotel guests who were weary of the slow simple pace could waste hours of his time in idle chat if he allowed it. Still, being polite to the paying guests was important. Tanner didn't recall seeing the little man around the marina but he didn't see all the hotel's guests.

"I'm curious," the man said. "Have you been here long?"

"All summer." Tanner hosed the deck in front of him and set to work with a mop.

"You don't seem the type, somehow."

Tanner looked a question at the man who hadn't introduced himself.

He waved a casual hand. "I mean, most people I see working at jobs like this aren't as well educated as you appear to be." The stranger switched direction suddenly. "I'm interested in the recreational boat traffic up and down the passage. You service a lot of boats in this marina and I've seen you watching others going by. Maybe you can help me. I'm doing a bit of research, you understand. Have you seen any boats that seem to come by frequently? Vessels that appear to be making a lot of trips back and forth? Any boats you've recognized?"

Tanner shrugged. "Sorry. I've too much to do to keep track of such things. Ask John Martin. He might have records that would help. Or start keeping track of the traffic yourself." Tanner smiled to take the sting out of the words and went back to swabbing the deck with more vigor, splashing water about. The man stepped back quickly to avoid the spray. When Tanner looked up again the man was gone. Odd, he thought. Who was that? He was sure he'd never seen the man before.

Tanner grew restless. He wasn't getting anywhere in his search. One day he went to the rescue of a drifting ketch that lost her propeller during passage through the islands. It was one of those long, windless weekends when the weather was hot and sultry, the narrow strip of sand in front of the hotel was crowded and there was scarcely a ripple to mar the glassy sea all the way to the heat-blurred horizon. Overhead the sun rode unchallenged by a single cloud through a sky so brilliant it made his teeth ache to look at it.

The disabled ketch, Patience, had been enroute from her home port of Seattle to Desolation Sound. Just south of the Strait of San Juan de Fuca she'd hit some submerged debris. The collision bent the propeller causing serious vibration of the drive shaft. With no prospect for wind before nightfall, and the temperature rapidly rising in the cabins, Patient's captain called for assistance. Tanner was sent to her aid in the marina's Boston Whaler. Propelled by a big Chevrolet inboard engine, he was alongside Patience in less than an hour. Most of the guests sat about under a large white tarpaulin that had been raised over the main deck for protection from the hot sun. Without her engine, the ship's refrigeration system was shut down and all the ice aboard had long since melted, adding to the general discomfort. There was a languid cheer when Tanner drew alongside. He had come prepared and handed up a large pail filled with ice that soon disappeared into the glasses of guests and crew.

Negotiations over service and fees concluded, Tanner and

a crew member rigged a bridle from an unused anchor line and prepared Patience for the long tow to safety. Tanner resisted pressure to hurry preparations, knowing the strain from improper towing could damage the disabled yacht.

"If you want someone aboard to keep an eye on Patience while you drive, I'll volunteer." The tall slender woman hopped aboard without waiting for an answer. "Hi. I'm Mary Whitney. From Seattle." She put out her hand and gave Tanner a firm handshake.

"Whitney? THE Seattle Whitneys?"

She smiled slightly. "That's right, THE shipping Whitneys."

Tanner looked at her while she made herself comfortable beside him in the cockpit. He ticked through his mental file cabinet to recall what he could. Mary Whitney was in her mid-to-late thirties. He remembered that she was in the news frequently, usually on the society pages. He assumed she was like many other wealthy women he'd met. She'd be used to getting her way, perhaps a little spoiled, a woman who was frequently asked to sit on a company or organization board, more for the board's prestige than anything else. She would also, he supposed, spend a good deal of time supporting one or more favorite charities in King County and Seattle. He'd encountered several like her while making proposals to boards of directors. He would learn that his assumptions about Mary Whitney were off the mark. He told her his name.

"Tanner?" she frowned. "I know that name." She stood beside him, braced against the windscreen, facing the stern. "Have we met?"

"I don't think so," he said. "I would have remembered. Tanner and Associates is my company. We do public relations and advertising." Tanner turned his attention to the heavy line that now drooped into the water from the bow of the disabled Patience and rose again to heavy cleats on the stern of the powerboat. With a smooth touch on the throttle, he maneuvered the whaler to take up the slack smoothly in a straight line. That would minimize strain on the line and on the chocks and cleats on both vessels as they began the slow task of towing Patience to the marina.

"Oh, yes of course. You did a public relations campaign for one of my aunt's favorite charities," she said, closely watching him position the Boston Whaler.

Tanner listened to her low-pitched, slightly husky tone, thinking she had a nice voice.

A faint cheer went up from those aboard Patience when they felt her bow coming around in the wake of the powerboat. Tiny breezes crept along the hot decks.

Mary Whitney gazed at Tanner thoughtfully, swaying easily to keep her balance in the cockpit beside him.

"I don't understand. What's one of the city's top P.R. execs doing out here in jeans and a raggedy polo shirt being a boat jockey for some marina?" She looked at him thoughtfully. Elegantly turned out in expensive, white, light-weight slacks, a thin white short-sleeved blouse, and a white headband, she appeared to be from a different world.

Tanner glanced at her and then looked back at the towline. He nudged the throttle forward and the line between the two vessels came taut. Smoothly he increased their speed and the burbling engine sound changed to a rumble.

"Are you always so direct?" Tanner had to raise his voice slightly to be heard over the engine.

"Yes," she said. "I was raised in a seafaring family. We were taught to be direct." Mary Whitney was watching the towline and Patience so Tanner couldn't see her eyes when he glanced at her. The wind through the cabin's side windows ruffled her curly auburn hair, which she wore short so it just touched the collar of her blouse in back. "You haven't answered my question." Her lips bowed upward in a smile and little laugh lines appeared beside her right eye. Her lashes were very dark, he noted.

Tanner nodded and said. "Relaxation. Rest. Research. Business at the agency is pretty good right now and my partners told me they could get along this summer without my presence."

"I see." She turned her head and looked at him. Her eyes were dark like her eyebrows. Her long patrician nose had a slight bend and a dent halfway to the end. She saw him looking and smiled. "Broke it when I was seventeen. Granddad and I were sailing on the Sound in his old dinghy. The boom came over and whacked me in the face. Does your partners' dismissal bother you any?"

"No. Why should it? We get along. We have each other's confidence and trust. They'll call if they need me. Besides, it's not a dismissal."

Mary recalled the death of Tanner's wife last year and wondered if his partners thought he'd become a problem at the agency.

For the rest of the trip their conversation dealt with the immediate concerns of the tow as swells from a Pacific storm, far to the west, complicated the job. Two hours later, with infinite care, Tanner brought the disabled yacht into the marina entrance.

Patience, safely docked, would wait while her Captain arranged to have the propeller replaced and the rest of the powertrain checked. Most of her party booked ferry transportation back to the mainland, their sailing holiday terminated. Tanner handed Mary Whitney to the dock and said good-bye.

She looked down at him and said, "I've taken a room at the hotel. Would you have dinner with me tomorrow night? I have to go back to Seattle the day after that."

Tanner's self-imposed shell of resistance to women on the island suddenly developed a large crack. "Yes," he said. "I'd like that." She went away and his eyes followed her slim-hipped graceful way down the long dock.

"Good looking woman," commented the kid in the harbor-master's shack.

"Mmmm," responded Tanner with a sharp glance at the boy.

Wednesday evening Tanner dressed in his casual best, white duck shoes and white Dockers, pressed for the occasion, and a dark blue silk shirt. Mary Whitney wore a flowered dress with spaghetti straps and a short flared skirt that emphasized her slender form.

During their first cocktail Mary took the lead, filling in the conversational gaps. "I went to Vassar. Granddad and his brothers were heavily into timber. But Whitney shipping was established even earlier. Granddad's father started the company and they made scads of money."

"You're not married?" Tanner had noticed the absence of a wedding ring, although that wasn't a perfect clue.

"Divorced. I was supposed to come home after college and make a good marriage that would combine Whitney Industries with who knows what other corporation. I went to New York instead and met a stockbroker." She shook her head in sad amusement. "Classic case, I guess. Whirlwind romance, East meets West. My family was not pleased, although they liked Edwin well enough."

"Edwin?"

She nodded. "Edwin Tobias Baker, the third." Harvard, Harvard Law and then an MBA from Columbia. He's from a very Eastern, very clubby and socially upscale family."

"You didn't fit in, I suppose?" Tanner sipped his scotch, admiring the way the soft candlelight limned her cheekbones.

"Sure, I fit in. What d'you take me for?" She straightened up and raised her chin. She placed her hand over her bosom, fingers just touching her breastbone, elbow theatrically extended and said, "Entirely too well, in fact. I guess I got tired of the social shallowness. Mother says that fundamentally I'm just like granddad, all elbows and sharp corners."

Tanner smiled. He'd met the old man years ago. "Sure, strong-willed, opinionated, ambitious."

"Don't forget smart!" Her laughter was strong, satisfying.

"Oh no, I won't forget smart." Tanner was relaxed, enjoying social intercourse with a woman for the first time in months. He found this attractive woman easy to talk with.

"So, Michael Tanner. What do we know about him?" Mary held up one finger. "Successful P.R. type, big firm in Seattle. Local boy?"

"Tacoma."

"Udub?"

"Yep, Journalism and Advertising."

Mary's voice dropped. "Widowed last year."

"So you know."

"No, Michael Tanner, I only know the public persona. I only know what I read in the papers." She waited, watching him.

"That's about it, though. Right now I'm just hanging out, doing some physical labor for a while, combined with a little research." The conversation lagged. Dinner came and went. It must have been good, but afterward Tanner couldn't remember what they ate.

"I saw you looking at my finger." She held up her left hand and wiggled her fingers. It's been almost six years since the divorce. Afterward I felt lousy. Do you want to know what I did?"

"If you want to tell me."

"I went to sea." She nodded at his surprised look. "I took a sailboat and sailed to Baja, down the coast."

"By yourself?"

"No, with my uncle. But I was captain. It was very settling. It helped me ground myself." She glanced at her watch. "Oh, it's later than I realized." Mary stood and leaned over the table, one hand pressing on Tanner's shoulder, looking into his face. "I do that when things are rough. I go to sea. You should try it." She straightened and Tanner rose from the table. "Don't come out with me. I'm just going to my room. I have to leave tomorrow early, and I haven't packed. Thank you for a pleasant evening." She smiled, turned and started into the space between nearby tables. Then she stopped and looked back at him. "Go back to Lasqueti. I think you need to do that."

A few nights after his dinner with Mary Whitney, Tanner

discovered how difficult it was to remember Martin's axiom that the paying customer was king. Complaints had come to the office several nights running, about noise from a particular yacht disturbing the peace of the little harbor.

"Ahoy, Mistress II." Tanner's voice was hoarse from having just been roused out of a sound sleep by the night manager at the hotel. He was not happy.

"Yuh? Whaddayuh want?" The response was slurred and aggressive sounding, and Tanner knew he was in for trouble.

"Excuse me, buddy, can I talk to you a minute?" He didn't feel like a buddy. His voice didn't sound buddylike either. Moving closer, Tanner thought wryly that he was adding to the bedlam. On this warm night, portholes on the yacht were open and recorded music with a pronounced bass beat thumped loudly into the night.

"Sure, mac, c'm on aboard. Wanna drink?"

Tanner climbed the short ladder and dropped onto the promenade deck just behind the cabin. "You the owner?" he asked, ignoring the offer of a drink, and raising his voice over the music. It was after one in the morning and Tanner wondered where these people thought they were.

"Naw, m'brother owns her. Over there," accompanied by a vague wave.

There were ten or twelve couples aboard, Tanner estimated, most in semiformal dress, a few in casual clothes. He walked to the port side of the deck and addressed the man leaning against the rail talking with two others.

"Excuse me, sir. It's really late and we're getting complaints about the noise."

"Yeah? Well, don't worry about it. We'll be gone in the morning."

"That's fine. How about shutting it down now so the rest of the harbor can sleep?"

The man swung around violently and gave Tanner a hard stare. "Hey. Don't I know you?"

"No, sir," replied Tanner, a prickling of his scalp sending

out warning signals.

"Yeah, I do. You're the joker who got drunk on a boat and killed his wife, couple years ago, wa'n't it? Shit! I don' have to lissen to you. Get off my boat!"

A coldness settled in Tanner's chest. He was conscious that others on the deck were moving toward them, sensing a confrontation. Our primitive instinct for blood is still close to the surface, he thought, backing a step away from the finger pointing at him.

"I'm not the issue here," he said evenly.

"Yeah?" Increased belligerence from the other man blew over Tanner like a bad-smelling wind. "Get off my boat. You ain't no man."

The fellow leaned forward and again jabbed at Tanner's chest. Anger boiled up in Tanner. Here was this drunken fool, who probably didn't know port from starboard, calling him names. A year ago he might have backed off, but his lingering irritation with the maritime authorities, a season of physical labor at the marina and increased frustration at his lack of progress finding the killer yacht had toughened him. He had less tolerance for cruel insults. He swung one arm up and knocked away the other man's thrust. His other hand came up and he grabbed a fistful of shirt.

"I don't have to take this shit," he husked. "You weren't there. I was. Now close it up or I'll do it for you."

The man straightened and tried to pull away, arms flailing. But Tanner didn't let go. He yanked the man in close, tearing his shirt. The man in his grasp had no room to swing and his arms bounced harmlessly off Tanner's shoulders. For a moment they struggled against the rail. Tanner cocked his fist when John Martin, shirttail flying, climbed over the side of the yacht and stepped between them.

"Here you two! Knock that off!" Martin's voice was low and sharp with disapproval.

Instantly Tanner relaxed, belatedly realizing he had probably cost Martin a good customer.

He let go of the man's shirt and stepped back. The yacht owner stared at Tanner contemptuously for a moment, then turned and spat over the side.

Martin took the man by the shoulder and turned away, talking softly all the time. Tanner shrugged and left the yacht, aware of the stares that followed him.

As he walked back along the long wooden dock, past the harbor-master's shack, the din from the offending stereo suddenly stopped. He looked around and saw Martin climb over the side of Mistress II and head up the dock.

In the morning when he tried to apologize for losing his temper with the drunken owner of Mistress II, Martin waved him off.

"Ahh. You understand why we're careful so the marina doesn't get the wrong reputation. We have to walk a fine line between the guests who wanna party all night and those who want it real quiet. Party drunks are one of the trials of this business, but that one's a real pain in the ass. If we never see him again, it'll be too soon."

10

Not long after Tanner's confrontation with the owner of Mistress II, John Martin sauntered down to the dock to where Michael was sitting in the sun, repairing spare mooring buoys.

"Been thinking 'bout the other night."

Tanner looked up at him. Gulls screed in the silence, and a distant runabout purred across the harbor mouth. Behind them, a flag popped in the high breeze. Martin stretched elaborately and looked slowly around, surveying his domain.

"Also been noticing you seem to be gettin' a leetle tense, as the weeks go by." Martin grunted and scratched himself, signs he was uncomfortable or uncertain how to proceed.

Tanner decided to make it easier on him. "You want me to leave."

Martin nodded once. "Yep, but not the way you mean." Tanner's forehead crinkled. "I think you need to go back to Lasqueti." There was another pause.

Tanner looked down at the water lapping against the piling beside him. Breathed in. Tried to take a chest full of air. His throat closed. "You mean, back to the place where Beth and Alice died." The bitter memories welled up once more. "Mary Whitney told me the same thing," he muttered.

"Smart gal. I know I been bringin' this up a lot," Martin resumed, "but you ain't gettin' far enough tryin' to trace that other boat from here. Anyway things are slow right now." Martin raised a big hand and adjusted the cap lower over his eyes. "My sister Ethel, she and her kid are comin' down for a couple weeks. He's a big kid and they can both help out. They like it here. Take the Whaler. Fact is, you nose around up there," he waved toward the north, "you might find out somethin'." Martin turned away, then swung back, squinting in the glare off the sea. "Yeah, an' be sure you go to Lasqueti."

Tanner nodded. He knew Martin was right. He had to do it sometime. He had to go back there. Somehow it was tied to his search for the yacht that had almost destroyed his life. That was the past, but Lasqueti was also the future. He had to return to that rocky beach, to that section of the Georgia Strait. He had to see it again, this time without the sticky screen of blood in his eyes.

Tanner breathed in the clean, moist air, felt the sun on his back. A small creature scuttled across a plank and disappeared over the piling. Tanner sighed, appreciating the peaceful scene but not at peace with himself.

He rented a small motor cruiser from Martin, a Boston Whaler like the marina workboat. It had an enclosed foredeck, a tiny gas stove, a plastic cooler for an icebox, and a narrow bench that would serve as a bunk. Tanner collected the few personal necessities he would need, filled his water jug and shopped for basic provisions.

When he stopped in the marina office to say good-bye, he found Martin at his desk, writing a letter.

"Here, Michael. Here's a note to folks I know in the lower islands up there. I didn't say anything specific, just that you're a friend and to help out if they've a mind to."

"Thanks, John, I appreciate this." Tanner took the letter and slipped it into a large plastic envelope with his credit cards and navigation charts. "I'll look around the Gulf Islands for a while, see what I can learn, then head farther north. Maybe I'll get all the way into Desolation Sound. I'll call you if anything develops."

"People up there are friendly but not what you'd call forthcoming. You'll have to figure out a way to ask without seeming nosy."

"You mean be indirect."

"Right. Besides, if the people you're chasing get wind of the fact you haven't given up, they could come lookin' for you."

The next morning, a bright August day, the sun was high, the weather and the sea were calm. A gentle breeze barely rippled the blue water as the Boston Whaler threaded its course among the scattered sun warmed San Juan islands. It was a good day to search for a killer yacht.

Tanner went first into the Gulf Islands which lie along the eastern side of Vancouver Island, north of the American San Juans. They are a thirty-mile-long group of islands reaching from Nanaimo to Sydney. Sydney is the small community that serves as the ferry boat port for the larger city of Victoria, which lies at the very tip of Vancouver Island. Tanner peeked into Sydney's harbor and then continued north.

The Gulf Islands are home to many people from the United States who settled there during the turbulent sixties. Tanner discovered that a lot of those old hippies and drop-outs seemed to be generally suspicious and intensely private. They lived close to the earth and minded their own business. Tanner briefly visited North Pender Island, then went on to Fulford harbor on Salt Spring. His letter from John Martin gave him easier access to the taciturn harbor and marina operators, but they weren't particularly helpful. Either the ship he sketchily described was unknown to them or they recalled so many that Tanner couldn't keep track. None of the suggestions touched his memory. He began to wonder if he was looking for an apparition.

On Galiano, a long sausage-shaped island, he stayed several days at Roche Point, anchoring alone in a small bay just over the low tip of the island from the main strait. The weather remained stable. On the morning of the third day, a long, low motor launch appeared. Tanner recognized the storekeeper from the harbor on Thetis Island, but the other two men on the launch were strangers. He waved, but none of them responded.

During the next couple of hours Tanner had his own cold

lunch and watched passing traffic in the strait with his binoculars. He was half-lying on the sun-washed foredeck of the Boston Whaler, leaning against the windscreen, when he noticed that the launch had drifted closer as the men prepared to leave. One of them stood up at the wheel and shouted at Tanner across the narrow strip of water that separated the two boats.

"A word of advice, Mister Tanner." The man spoke with a strong Scottish burr. His gray hair shone in the sunlight that streamed down. "What is it with you, man, whining after a phantom boat? Best you accept what the authorities say and get on with your life."

Tanner was stunned. He stared at the man a moment and replied, "I'm sorry, I don't understand what you're referring to. I'm just wandering about up here. Sort of a vacation." He was about to explain that he was intent on finding the mysterious yacht and didn't intend to give up the search. But he thought better of it. He had no idea who these men were or where their loyalties lay.

The engine in the big launch coughed, turned over and with a puff of blue-gray smoke, they swung away, the three men again ignoring Tanner.

Well, thought Tanner, watching them go. If everybody feels like those three, I'll have a devil of a time learning anything.

For several more days he poked about the islands and the southern reaches of the strait, mostly examining passing traffic close up or through his binoculars. From time to time when Tanner talked with men he encountered, his questions always the same. The answers were nearly always the same, a shrug and no information.

Tanner's meandering journey, with its self-enforced isolation, the constant necessary attention to weather and tides continued the healing process. At times, he allowed the natural rhythms of the water and the spectacular vistas of mountains and sea to lull him into lassitude and inactivity. Sometimes his loneliness and isolation reminded him more strongly of his loss. He knew he was delaying Martin's admonitions to return to that beach at Lasqueti. But the subject was always there, like a scab to be picked at. An itch to be scratched. One Friday morning he awoke and looked out at a gray overcast sky that hung quietly over the silent sea. A pale yellow sun struggled to cut through the high clouds. Tanner drank the last of his orange juice. The ice in his cooler was gone and he realized he needed other supplies as well.

His spirits were low but he headed northeast across the strait toward Lasqueti Island where the Canadian Coast Guard had found him almost eleven months earlier. He'd been lying half dead in the beached dinghy. The Coast Guard had saved his life. By then it had been more than thirty hours since the Queen Anne had gone to the bottom. He still had no recollection of how he'd gotten to the island.

Lasqueti rose out of the sea and Tanner sighed a great sigh as he motored slowly to the point where the Coast Guard had found him. His stomach knotted. The sea was calm and he had no trouble running the little boat up on the beach. He stepped off into water that barely wet his ankles. His tall bright-yellow sea boots made a stark contrast to the dark gray shore in front of the gray-green pines that lay thickly over the land. The tide was in. He stood there breathing deeply, feeling the emotions surging through him. He realized with something like relief that he would never know exactly where the Queen Anne's dinghy had grounded.

Tanner walked slowly along the beach. He stumbled occasionally on the rough terrain. This was no sandy beach attractive to sun-worshippers. This was a beach of gray and black, smoothly polished stones and a few scattered, sea-rounded boulders. Tanner stood at the water's edge, staring east, toward the mainland, across several miles of unbroken sea. Somewhere there beneath the gray heaving sea, beyond his vision, his beloved Beth, her friend Alice and the broken remains of the little sloop Queen Anne lay buried. Tears came then, hot stinging tears that flowed freely while he stood there at the edge of the land.

"Oh, God, Beth. I miss you so much," he cried aloud.

Only the high screeching gulls gave response.

Tanner returned to the motor launch and turned south, toward the San Juan Islands and home. Depression picked at the edges of his consciousness. He wondered yet again whether his was a fruitless quest. Perhaps, he thought, it was time to put it all to rest. To get on with life. To simply forget.

"Yeah, right. As if I could ever forget. Damn," he muttered aloud. He couldn't decide what to do next. It was an unusual feeling for Tanner.

Routinely he checked the barometer and tuned in weather radio. They both indicated an approaching storm of considerable size. Great, he thought. First, I need a harbor. This tub isn't worth much in rough water. He altered course and hurried west across the Inside Passage toward the tiny port of French Creek on the eastern coast of Vancouver Island.

The storm moved faster than predicted. The wind rose swiftly and the chop became a surge. Whitecaps appeared. Dark gray clouds rolled across the overcast. Tanner's light boat, with its small keel, became increasingly difficult to control. Waves smashed more frequently over the bow, sending long streamers of foam into the air. Michael realized that he was tearing across the water, slamming repeatedly into larger and larger waves, but making slow progress toward the harbor and safety. He began to doubt his ability to cope with the sea and the storm. Darkness was falling by the time he had the shore line in sight.

"Let's see." Tanner was talking out loud to keep himself company. "I've never been to French Creek before. Where's the damn chart?" Standing with feet wide spaced and braced against the lurching, rolling deck, he scrabbled in the big plastic envelope until he found the right chart. In one corner was a detail of the harbor entrance. It was tricky, reading the chart in the uncertain light and keeping his heading. The compass needle swung wildly as the cruiser smashed through another big wave and the propeller raced as the wave dropped below the stern. The boat headed down into another trough and the sea rose, curling over to meet him. Tanner's knuckles turned white as he gripped the wheel tighter and he realized he was staring up into a huge wind-ravaged wave. The launch shuddered under Tanner's feet when the big wave slammed onto the bow. Water sluiced down the foredeck and rose against the windscreen. The light in the cabin turned sickly green. He glanced sternward to see the deck awash with foaming seawater.

He turned his attention back to the chart and located the harbor. "I have to drive right at the rocks and make a sharp dogleg to the left between the lights. That'll be nasty in this stuff." Spray blew through the cabin, spattering Tanner's face and the chart. More waves pounded on the cabin roof and poured over the open back of the cockpit. The windscreen rattled. Water surged across the deck and plucked at his feet. The noise grew louder.

He dropped the chart and shouted at the windscreen, "Okay! We're gonna make it!" The danger, the exhilaration of confronting a visible force after weeks of hunting an elusive, unseen, quarry, helped Tanner rally his mind and his energy. Pounding through the rough water, he roared into the narrow harbor entrance on the crest of yet another big wave. Directly ahead was the rock-filled breakwater that formed one side of the harbor. Sharp-edged basalt and granite boulders reached, snaggle-toothed, for the little cruiser. He thought, for a heart-stopping moment, that he was moving too fast and would smash to bits on the rocks. At the last moment the wave died. Tanner spun the wheel to the left and skidded his boat through the dogleg turn past the outer breakwater. He flashed into the harbor, and dropped his engine speed to idle.

Tanner arrived in French Creek in the dim uncertain twilight just after low tide. Outside the harbor, the wind rose and spume from wind-pushed waves blew horizontally across the barrier rocks that surrounded the little refuge. This was no natural harbor, built around an indentation in the shoreline. This harbor had been built by men out of huge rock and concrete breakwaters that jutted out into the sea on three sides.

Tanner idled to the gas dock and roused the harbor master

from his tiny, snug office to help replenish his gas and water supplies. The man told Tanner he could tie up anywhere there was room. There were no open slips, so Tanner rafted to a sleek 42-foot sloop, carefully setting extra fenders to protect both hulls and then helped the sloop's captain, a tall, spare man, check his own moorings against the slight extra strain. Tanner thought he saw a glimmer of recognition on the man's face when he introduced himself. When the boats were secured to their satisfaction, the owner, apparently sailing alone, offered Tanner a drink in the comfortable, roomy saloon of his luxurious sloop. It was an offer Tanner gratefully accepted. They drank companionably, talking little as darkness settled around them.

After two drinks, Tanner rose to leave. He had one foot on the companionway ladder when the man said quietly, "Mr. Tanner, I have known the owner of Patience for many years," referring to the ketch Tanner had towed to Martin's marina a few weeks before. "He commented quite favorably on your seamanship and on your general demeanor. I watched you here today, also. You appear to be a careful, thoughtful man, with more than a casual knowledge of seamanship." His thin lips twitched in what Tanner took to be a smile.

Tanner nodded his thanks and waited.

"Perhaps it will help you to know that there are some of us, men who have some knowledge of these waters, who don't agree with the official version that you came to lose your ship through carelessness. We think your version is quite possibly the true one, as you testified. We hope you find that other vessel."

A lump rose in Tanner's throat. He didn't trust himself to speak at that moment so he only nodded his thanks and made his way topside.

The wind buffeted him severely when he reached the open deck. The breakwater protected the ships in harbor from the violent waves, but the wind had free access to the rigging and to anyone on deck, especially now, on the risen tide, which exposed more of the ships to the snarling weather. Tanner felt the sting of salt spray flung across the harbor, and he heard it rattle on the deck. It mixed with his tears and wet his cheeks. He was not a pariah among the boating community. It was enormously encouraging to learn that others believed him. For the first time he realized how isolated he had felt. Tanner laid a steadying hand on the mast of the sloop and stared at the spray in the lights of the harbor. It gleamed with other-world colors from the red and green beacons that tirelessly flashed their signal to passing vessels. Here is safe harbor. Here is sanctuary. Here is hope.

Wave after wave crashed against the rock-filled barrier. Tanner watched as a larger wave spilled its foaming weight over the top of the breakwater and ran down the inner side in miniature white-water rivulets. It was as if the sea and the wind conspired in howling fury at the intrusion of this harbor and were determined to destroy it.

The cold wind raged against the steel and aluminum rigging of the sailboats moored in their slips. The boats' movements were erratic and skittish like thoroughbreds before a race as they tugged against their mooring lines. The sounds of loose gear banging, the vibrating of stays and halyards mingled with the sounds of the sea and wind in a hellish cacophony. But the surface of the harbor remained calm.

Tanner turned his face to the wind with new resolve. He would continue his search a while longer.

11

He was never sure what roused him. Shivering, Tanner rolled out of his sleeping bag and thrust his feet into his yellow and blue sea boots. A moment later wrapped in his bright yellow rain gear, he stood in the Boston Whaler's cockpit looking at a world gone mad. Pushed by the storm, the tide had raised the level of the water higher against the breakwater. Huge seas crashed one after the other over the rocks, spilling streams of water into the harbor. Fishing trawlers, moored along the outside wharves were being overridden by the waves. Big worklights along the processing plant's dock flickered on to show rain and sea spume filling the air.

Tanner saw a small flat-bottomed barge that had broken loose from its mooring lines at one end smash into the wharf and then swing crazily out into the open water of the harbor. Back and forth, back and forth it swung. Timbers heaved and buckled from the pounding. Men swathed in foul-weather gear lumbered along the dock, reaching out to capture flogging mooring lines. Tanner leapt ashore and ran around to the commercial side of the harbor. As he ran past the harbormaster's shack he saw the barge swing back and smack a hard glancing blow to the prow of a big fishing boat. It left a long bright scar on the steel hull. A direct hit, he thought, and some fisherman's means of making a living would end up on the bottom of the harbor.

Tanner stumbled over a big coil of mooring line on the wharf. He grabbed it up and looked to see that one end was tied to a big bollard on the wharf. The loose barge swung back, slammed into the pilings. The blow shivered the dock under Tanner's feet. As the barge reversed its swing, Tanner flung himself onto the open well of the barge. The shock of landing jarred his bones and he lost his footing. The barge rose and shifted. The movement threw Tanner onto his back into a foot of dirty, oily water, that sloshed over his head. Spluttering, he rolled over and onto his knees. Opposite him, a big man stood on the dock and raised his arms. With every ounce of strength, Tanner threw a coil of the mooring line at him. It unsnaked and dropped at the man's feet. Tanner threw two loops around a big round cleat on the edge of the barge and made it fast.

The other man, bent against the wind, grabbed the line and whipped it expertly around a mooring bollard on the deck. Another man came forward and the two on the dock began to draw the line tight, struggling against the power of the sea and wind. Tanner found the loose end of the mooring line that had parted earlier and flung it to the dock. One man grabbed it and carried it to a dock cleat. The barge was almost under control. Tanner located a huge round orange fender that was lashed in the bottom of the barge. Plunging his arms into the cold greasy water, Tanner struggled to untie it. At the last minute he was able to free up the fender's tieline. He secured it over the side between the barge and the wharf. Tight against the damaged wharf, the barge rode easier and the danger passed. Tanner looked around the harbor to see other hunched figures going from boat to boat, checking and retying mooring lines. He reached for a handhold on the dock and started to climb out of the barge. His legs were trembling so he could hardly get up the greasy ladder. Willing hands reached for his shoulders and helped him to the dock.

The big man took Tanner's arms in a grateful squeeze and shouted, "By God, we win again! Thank you, my fren'!" Tanner nodded and tottered off to his cold bunk.

By morning the storm over French Creek had blown itself out. Tanner finished his cold breakfast and walked along the harbor breakwater to take a look at the sea. The sky was overcast and the air was thick with moisture. The smell of salt was strong. He couldn't see the mountains across the strait. Although they were quieter now, waves still spoke in loud and angry voices as they smashed against the breakwater and rolled onto the rocky shore. Tanner looked at the lumpy waters of the Inside Passage. He knew his light-weight cruiser would give him an unpleasant ride if he ventured out that morning.

Don't need the punishment, he mused. Uncharacteristically, he decided he could wait. He walked up the street into the little town, built along the sloping hills that overlooked the water. To his left was a small shopping mall with grocery, liquor and hardware stores, and two tiny nondescript shops. There were few cars on the street and only one or two older people were out that morning. Beyond the shopping center, he encountered homes and short cross-streets which ran for only two blocks across the hill. All the homes were neat and appeared wellkept in natural wood trim weathered to silver. Heather and gorse grew low to the ground around some houses. A few purple flowers quivered in the fitful gusts of wind.

In the harbor a dozen big, ungainly looking fishing boats filled three-fourths of the available moorings, their scarred sides dripping rusty stains. Tanner saw that the barge and other boats along the commercial wharf that had been threatened by the storm were all still afloat. The barge was down at the stern from the weight of the water it had taken on.

Two hundred yards south along the paved street that roughly paralleled the shore and connected the town and harbor was a large, modern-looking building of glass and stone. Tanner walked down the road and discovered the building housed a bar and restaurant. The neatly hand-painted sign on the big, dark wood doors said "CLOSED UNTIL 4 PM." Tanner skirted the building on a stone path and saw a large two-story-high window that faced the water. He leaned his head against the glass and peered in at the dark interior. Nothing, except a few dim lights glowing over the bar. He shrugged and strolled back to the harbor.

As he approached the dock, Tanner noticed that the owner of the sloop he'd rafted to last night was standing on deck, examining rigging at the mast. He wore bright blue offshore slicks. When Tanner boarded the boat with a friendly hail, the man turned and smiled around the pipe clenched in his teeth.

"Ah, good," he said. "Glad you've turned up. We've decided we can delay no longer, so we're heading down to Victoria."

Tanner nodded. "Looks a little lumpy out there."

"Yes, well, we've sailed in worse, though I don't make a habit of it. However, I've just been informed that I'm desperately needed back at the firm. Damned nuisance, really." He turned and called down the open hatch beside his feet.

"I say, Margery, come topside. Here's someone I want you to meet." A tall, spare, blond woman in dark red foul weather pants and a bright blue sweater appeared in the cockpit. Smiling, she extended her hand.

"Ah, of course, Michael Tanner. My husband said he met you last night." Tanner nodded and shook hands. He must have had a quizzical expression on his face because she nodded and said, "We didn't meet last night because I've only just got here. Drove up with friends who've gone on up-island, you see."

Tanner helped the couple loose their mooring lines and then dragged his own boat to the dock in place of the departing sloop. He stood watching as the couple from Victoria motored out to the harbor entrance. He could tell they worked well together. The way he and Beth had once been a team at the agency.

The man turned from his position at the wheel and raised one arm. "Success, Mr. Tanner, success," he called. The graceful sloop motored out through the harbor entrance.

Michael waved back. For a moment he watched the masthead swing wildly in the choppy waves. Then a triangle of sail crept into sight, inching up to the masthead, and she steadied down. Tanner went into his tiny cabin for a nap.

The overcast remained mired overhead. In the afternoon gloom, Michael walked back to the restaurant. There were several cars in the graveled parking lot, but when he went into the building, a closed sign stood in front of the stairs to the second-floor restaurant.

In the bar three men sat in one corner, away from the big window, talking in low tones. They were hunched over a small round table, each with a bottle of beer in hand. All three looked up briefly when Tanner came through the door.

To his left, a long, polished bar ran the length of the room, ending at the big window that filled the entire east wall. A waitress sat perched on a bar stool beside the wait-station, midway down the length of the bar. Her slender, slack-clad limbs were wrapped intricately in the legs of the stool. The bartender, tall, blonde, encased from chest to ankles in a wraparound white apron, looked up from his close conversation with her when Tanner slid onto a padded bar stool. The bartender walked over and placed a small cocktail napkin precisely in front of Tanner.

"What can I get you?" He had a flat, neutral voice. It didn't go with his warm smile.

"Labatt Blue, please." Tanner fished some Canadian bills out of his jeans.

The man drew a tall glass for Tanner. He tilted the glass just enough to create a one-inch head of foam. Then he placed the glass before Tanner with just a hint of a flourish.

"Buck and a half."

Tanner gave him two singles and waved off the change. Tanner took a long swig. He nodded, appreciating the service and the temperature of the beer. His expectations were raised for the restaurant meal to come.

"How's the food upstairs?" He pointed at the ceiling.

"Nothin' fancy," chimed in the waitress, "just plain, good, home cooking."

Tanner nodded his thanks and went back to his glass. He nursed the beer for a long time, idly gazing out the window at the sea. A few boats passed, battling the wind and waves as they struggled north. The water was still lumpy, and speckled with foamy crests. While impatient to get on with his search, Tanner decided that he was glad to be where he was, and not out on the seaway. After an hour, he felt insistent stirrings of hunger and went up the wide carpeted staircase to the restaurant.

It wasn't large, and the kitchen took up fully half the space. Each table was covered with a smooth white cloth on which the waitress had placed silverware, glasses and white cloth napkins. Fleetingly, Tanner wondered if his bulky fisherman's sweater and wrinkled jeans would be acceptable, but he saw others already seated who were dressed in similar fashion. Cooking aromas drifted by and sharpened his appetite. The waitress placed him near the window so he could continue to watch the water while the light slowly faded. He ordered a broiled steak, salad, and fried potatoes. The simple food was well prepared, and the waitress was pleasant and efficient.

Comfortable and warm, Tanner returned to the bar where he ordered another beer. By now a small crowd had gathered and a second bartender worked beside the man who'd served Tanner earlier. The room was about two-thirds full. Two waitresses handled the seated crowd, made up of fishermen, townsfolk, and transient vacationing boaters who had decided to wait another day before leaving the shelter of the harbor. Weather reports augured well for the next day.

The man next to Tanner at the bar had the look of an experienced fisherman. He was big and clean-shaven with creased, leathery skin and washed out eyes that had come from years of squinting into sun reflected off the ocean. Tanner struck up a conversation and they shared observations on the recent weather, the provincial government, and local fishing conditions. When the opportunity occurred, Tanner launched into his oft-told tale of his search for an unnamed, large, modern white motor yacht.

The man listened patiently and then shrugged and shook his head. "'Fraid I can't hep you, son." He stared into his beer quietly for a moment and then asked, "How were you lying? Did the other yacht have time to avoid you if they were lookin' out? Where did they hit you? How did you come here to French Creek?"

"I rented my employer's Boston Whaler." Tanner explained he was working at a marina in the San Juan Islands.

"Learned to sail in the states, did you?"

"That's right. First sailing with friends, then a school on Lake Washington. But our sailing trip last year, and then working this season at Martin's, they've been a real education," he finished.

The man nodded silently.

What, Tanner wondered, was the man's sudden interest in the details of his boating experience?

"Eddie," the man said, and crooked a large finger at the bartender. The man leaned over and talked quietly in Eddie's ear, too low for Tanner to hear. They stayed that way for some minutes, ignoring nearby calls for service. The bartender straightened, swiveled his eyes and stared briefly at Tanner. Then he shrugged and nodded. Eddie turned back down the bar and Tanner saw him speak to another man at the very end. The second man left his stool and walked with a rolling gait down the bar. He stopped beside Tanner.

"My name is Pierre Bonset. I live here in French Creek for many, many years." He extended a large horny hand and peered more closely at Tanner. "Ah," he said. "You came to help with that barge last night. I thank you. It was my fishing boat you saved." Bonset's English carried French overtones. He was about Tanner's height but many pounds heavier. His graying hair was long. It straggled out from under the black watch cap Bonset wore and hung to the collar of his jacket.

Tanner shook Bonset's hand and shrugged. "I'm glad I was there to help."

"My friend Eddie here, he tell me you have a bad experience on the water last year." Tanner nodded slowly.

The man on Tanner's other side smiled at Bonset and said, "Pierre and I go back a long way. Tell him what you told me.

Maybe he can help you." Then he rose and left Tanner alone with
Bonset. Tanner realized he didn't know the man's name.

Tanner again briefly sketched the tragedy of last summer.
Bonset nodded and took Tanner's arm. He led Tanner toward a
large table of boisterous drinkers at the back of the room. Bonset
introduced him and explained Tanner's mission. It was clear from
the way those at the table quieted and listened that Pierre Bonset
was a respected man in the community. Disconnected murmurs
arose when he stopped. A voice from someone Tanner couldn't
see suggested that it was an insurance matter. Tanner didn't
correct him. Table conversation broke out as several people
compared notes on vessels that might fit Tanner's description.

Then one man leaned toward Tanner and said in a loud
voice that overrode the din. "What about Goldenrod, eh? She's
about ninety feet long, real slick boat. White, I think, over a
cream-colored hull."

Others nodded agreement. Tanner felt his heart speed up.
"That's right," a dark woman across the table said, "Goldenrod
could fit your description. And they're not very friendly, either."
Her thin lips turned down in a disapproving look.

"Oh no," objected another woman, shaking her tight curls.
"We know some people who've been guests on Goldenrod, and
they just rave about how nice the crew is, and how careful they
are when they're under way. Isn't Goldenrod owned by some big
company in California?" There were nods of agreement.

Tanner's emotions rode a rollercoaster. Elation climbed
as he tried to follow the ebb and flow of conversation about the
table. Goldenrod! Here at last was a real possibility. But his
reason cautioned that it was, after all, only a possibility.

"Does Goldenrod often show up out here? Where does
she stop? Do any of you know the captain?" Questions tumbled
out. But there were no more answers. Finally Tanner thanked the
men and women at the table and returned to his stool at the bar.
He turned to Pierre to thank him for making the moment possible.
By doing so, he missed seeing two men who had been sitting
quietly in a far corner of the room, observing his conversations at

the large table. They rose from their table and disappeared from the bar through a side door.

Bonset looked steadily into Tanner's face. "Listen, my fren'. You must be more careful. If those people did this thing deliberately, they 'ave commit murder. You must watch your back at all times."

Tanner looked at his new friend and his breathing quickened. In the excitement of the minute, he'd forgotten how dangerous his quest might be.

With no other names in hand, and with only his sketchy description, Tanner was tempted to fasten on Goldenrod as the vessel he sought. His more rational self urged caution. He soon left the bar to return to his boat for the night. The seas continued gradually to subside, and fog appeared. The scattered street lights along the walk gave off ghostly glows. His footsteps crunched on the gravel and he pulled his jacket close around his neck to keep out the damp. No one else was about. A feeling of exposure and vulnerability came over him. He looked around. God, if somebody jumped me out here, I'd be practically defenseless. He picked up his pace.

When he reached the now-quiet harbor, Tanner stopped abruptly and raised his head. From the dark water on his left, beyond the breakwater, came the sound of the heavy engines of a large boat. The sound floated there on the edge of his consciousness, then grew louder and deeper as the unseen vessel passed, perhaps forty yards offshore. And then he knew. With a certainty that stunned him, he knew.

It was a sound imprinted forever in his brain. It was the distinctive sound of the engines of the white yacht that had rammed the Queen Anne. He was hearing that sound again, for the first time since that awful day. Tanner leaped forward, running, stumbling through the dark toward the harbor and his boat.

With a shout, he dropped to the deck of the Boston Whaler and threw off his mooring lines. The motor caught and Tanner gunned the boat dangerously away from the dock and across the harbor, careless of the noise and his wake. The red and green entrance beacons scattered hazy light across the breakwater.

No time to think about risk.

He spun the wheel and slewed too fast through the dogleg harbor entrance, scraping the hull on a sharp rock. Then he was into the strait. His target was so close! The spotlight on the cabin roof of his boat sent up a huge bloom of light, nearly blinding Tanner with reflections off the fog. He switched it off.

Outside the harbor, the fog was even thicker. Tanner ran south at high speed along the shore, risking the boat and his safety peering ahead. He saw nothing. A few minutes later he slowed his boat to a fast idle. Still nothing. No motor vessel, no other boat nearby.

He killed his engine to listen. The unseen chop rocked and slapped against his hull. Faintly, from uncertain direction, Tanner made out the sound of the diesel engines of his quarry.

"Dammit!" In frustration he beat his fist on the boat's console. Anger rose in his throat like bile. "I know it's the same ship. So close, so close."

Tanner knew that if he got further from French Creek, he'd lose his bearings and have to wait until the fog lifted to find his way back. More rational thought intruded. What if he had found the ship? Tanner realized he might have jeopardized his life while fruitlessly alerting his quarry.

Damn, he thought. If only I'd left the bar earlier. At least I could have run past her stern and got the name and home port. Exhilaration and hope began to ebb away like the outgoing tide. He gave up the chase for that night and returned to French Creek, following the dim glow from the town through the fog.

"D'you see a light over there. Starboard side?"

"Where?" the other man looked away from the compass and through the right hand window of the bridge. It was dark and pale tendrils of fog streamed across the window. "Don't see nothin'. Must be French Creek. According to the chart, we should be just south of it." The other man grunted and went back to his reading.

The object of Tanner's search was one hundred feet of creamy white steel hull under yards of rich, gleaming teak. Above the main deck, her artfully designed superstructure of aluminum and fiberglass revealed the latest in high quality materials and luxurious design. Her interiors were lush and comfortable. The bridge boasted nearly every known navigational aid, from an up-to-date satellite link to modern, sophisticated radar and sonar systems.

"What you looking at, George?" The burly man at the wheel glanced at his companion. They were still running southeast along the western side of the Inner Passage.

"Ahh. It's another change notice. Company's just purchased a new radar unit."

"What, again?"

"Yeh, I hardly got used to the last one. Now we got to tear out this console and put in the newer model. It's just nuts," he snorted.

"Well, at least you didn't have to live through the rerouting of all that air-conditioning this spring."

Fully air-conditioned, the big luxury yacht also boasted bow thrusters and stabilizers. The crew and passengers experienced little discomfort while they smoothly plied the waters of the Inside Passage and beyond.

Her cabins were spacious, with whisper-quiet heat and air-conditioning to reduce any possible discomfort to the barest minimum. In the owner's suite, a large white bathtub crowded the private bath. On the other side of the master bedroom a door led to the communications center. Facsimile printers and computers, connected via satellite to private datalinks, together with high quality VHF, short wave and radio-telephone systems, afforded nearly instantaneous communication with important financial and business contacts world-wide.

Twice each year, the president of the data communications manufacturing and development corporation in California which owned the yacht, played host to week-long excursion parties of his executives and top sales personnel, together with their husbands, wives and companions. At other times Goldenrod moved serenely up or down the Inside Passage with smaller numbers of passengers. These were usually important business contacts, but frequently were well-connected, wealthy members of Seattle's or Vancouver's society. Sometimes a helicopter rested like some large insect on the platform over her afterdeck. Sometimes she was seen to rendezvous with a single-engine float plane.

Occasionally, for no discernible reason, the big vessel shifted her anchorage or motored through the strait of San Juan de Fuca into the rolling Pacific Ocean. She made port infrequently and then only for brief stops. No one kept track and no one asked questions. It wasn't good sailing etiquette to be inquisitive and there was no reason to be so. The captain made sure of that.

"Where we headed?" asked George, absently, immersed in a technical description of the new radar system.

"Does the captain tell me?" The other man snorted. "'Make course for Sydney,' he says. When we get there, he'll give us a new heading or destination. An' I don't ask. Ever since we rammed that sailboat last summer, things have been a little tense, in case you haven't noticed."

"Yeah," said George. "They keep reminding us when we go to town not to talk to anybody. Personally, I think that's going to call more attention. But I ain't in charge."

"You sure got that right."

When the white yacht appeared at the marina at Nanaimo or Campbell River for fuel and supplies, the crew swiftly and efficiently brought her to the dock, paid cash and rarely used credit cards. No one could remember seeing her crew in local bars, even the rare times Goldenrod moored overnight in a remote marina at Lund or Rendezvous Bay.

Most boating folk are friendly and cooperative. In bad weather, when anchorages can be crowded, boats raft together, as Tanner had done during the storm at French Creek. Sailors commonly request permission to cross other decks to reach their own, permission always granted, but the conventions are still observed.   A captain, roused from his bunk by a shift in the weather to check his lines or fenders, will routinely examine those of nearby boats and make small adjustments, or alert their crews.

But this ship was different.   Her crew did not invite friendly overtures. She never anchored in a group of other vessels and friendly hails rarely brought a response. Goldenrod avoided most contacts and so, in her turn, came to be avoided.

12

August became September and Tanner left French Creek. He knew the weather was about to turn colder and winter winds would soon blow across the sea. The little cruiser that had been home these past weeks was not designed nor equipped to shelter him from the winter. Pierre Bonset had met him that last morning at dockside.

"I think, Michael, that this season is over. That yacht you seek will not spend winter in these waters." Bonset, bundled in a heavy wool sweater, cap and gloves, waved at the strait.

"You're right, Pierre. Besides, I'm running low on supplies and funds. But I'll work my contacts in Seattle, and I'll be back next year."

Bonset's smile enhanced the deep wrinkles in his face. Then his smile faded and he said, "If you do not find what you seek this winter, come again to French Creek. There are many eyes here on this water." He lifted a hand and turned away. Tanner stared after him and slowly this time, motored out of the harbor. He headed south, toward the San Juan Islands and home. He had heard his enemy again and he had a new name to check out.

Tanner now knew there was a large white or cream colored motor vessel, named Goldenrod, which often sailed these waters. He also knew there could be hundreds of other yachts of various descriptions, with GOL in their names, that listed a home port near or on the Georgia Strait.

Later that day he anchored in a small cove on Newcastle Island north of Nanaimo. After the stormy and cold morning the day had turned hot and sunny. Clouds cleared away and the night was unusually warm and still for early September, the air a soft caress on his body. Naked, Tanner slipped into the cold water, steeling himself against the icy shock and swam the short distance to shore where he stretched and worked his muscles, a routine he tried to follow whenever possible. Moonglow behind the mountains to the east dimly illuminated the shape of his boat a few yards offshore. He turned and jogged silently down the narrow strip of exposed beach that would be under water in a few hours when the tide reached flood stage. Twenty yards along he saw the dark notch of a path into the trees. He jogged closer and then followed the path a short way into the brush. After relieving himself, Tanner returned to the beach. At that instant his dark quiet world exploded into the white-hot, searing flame of burning gasoline.

With a thunderous roar, the Boston Whaler vanished before his eyes. The blast flung Tanner to the ground and scattered debris over a wide area. He was momentarily stunned and by the time he roused himself and ran up the beach to the closest point to his mooring, nothing remained but a few shapeless pieces of wood from the cruiser's cabin. Some, still smoking, lay on the sand, others he could see bobbing on the restless water. The scene stank of burned, wet wood and fiberglass. Everything was gone, including his clothes, except for the watch on his wrist. The shiver that shook his naked body called attention to the cooling night air. A freak accident? Tanner thought about that, while he pondered what to do. He had never been careless around gasoline. He always vented the bilges before he started his boat's engines, and he refused to let passengers or crew remain aboard any boat he was refueling, unless they were standing by with fire extinguishers.

How had this happened? And what had caused the incredible devastation, the violence of the explosion? It was as if all the gas fumes from a year of refueling motor boats had collected in the bilges, waiting to explode at that precise moment. Would it have happened had he been aboard?

Had the boat exploded while he was aboard, it was clear he would now be dead. Tanner had saved his own life by deciding, on a whim, to swim ashore. It was a chilling thought. His shivers increased, and it occurred to him that the cruiser might have been deliberately blown up, possibly rigged to look like an accident, in an attempt to get rid of one Michael Tanner.

Jesus, he thought. The only reason anyone would want to get rid of me is because of my search for that damn motor yacht. Martin and Bonset are right. From now on I'm going to be a lot more careful.

If the people he sought would attempt such a move against him just because he continued to search, what else might be involved here?

He squatted on the rocky beach and wrapped his arms around his knees to conserve body heat. Clearly, he thought, there's something going on with that yacht that I don't understand. This is far more serious than just trying to avoiding a confrontation with me. His shivers increased. Although the explosion had failed to kill Tanner, there was a good chance the elements would. Tanner rubbed his arms and hugged himself tighter, conscious of the chill night air. His options were running out.

The sound of a marine engine and the lights of an approaching vessel brought him to his feet at the edge of the narrowing beach. For a moment he wondered if his enemies were returning to check on their success. But he didn't recognize the sound of the approaching craft. Tanner began to cast about for some way to signal the oncoming vessel. A bright light sliced through the night and illuminated the beach. In the spill from the spotlight, Tanner recognized the rakish outline of a Canadian Coast Guard cutter.

The welcome sight cheered him with the hope of immediate rescue. He jumped to his feet and hailed the ship. The searchlight picked him out and the cutter heaved to. The crew in the hastily lowered tender brought blankets and boots.

"Well, Mr. Tanner," said the ship's captain, Lieutenant Stark, "we meet again. Yet another boat lost. You can be thankful the explosion was seen by a passing ship. They radioed us and here we are. Otherwise you might have had a long and uncomfortable night out here. And you aren't exactly dressed for it."

Tanner forced a smile of thanks. Interesting, he thought. I don't recall seeing another boat right after the explosion. But why would he say that if it wasn't true?

When they brought him aboard, Tanner kept his suspicions about the explosion to himself. He had no proof his boat was deliberately blown up and he didn't know what to make of the appearance of the same Canadian Coast Guard cutter that had rescued him from Lasqueti Island.

A rating found Tanner a heavy ribbed wool sweater to wear and an old pair of faded dungarees that were too big around the waist. A bit of scrap line threaded through the loops served as a makeshift belt for the trip to the nearest port.

Tanner stood on the bridge with Lieutenant Stark, holding a steaming cup of hot coffee. Lieutenant Stark directed his ship down the coast to Nanaimo. "I'm surprised to find you out here," Tanner said.

Stark looked over at him. "This is part of our patrol area. We're out here to look after you chaps, after all."

"Sure, but the coincidence is just a little surprising, that's all."

"The circumstances, perhaps, Mr. Tanner. But if you're a regular in these waters, as we are, you tend to see us often." He seemed about to say more, then turned away to check the heading.

"Do you know of the motorship Goldenrod?"

Stark thought a moment. There's a schooner out of Victoria. Or is that the Golden Fleece? And I believe we've occasionally sighted a U.S. ship with that name." He shook his head. As I'm sure you've been told, there are over a hundred ships in these waters with similar names. Any particular reason for asking about that one?"

"Just something I heard a few days ago."

"Do I take it you are still determined to seek out the vessel you say ran you down?"

"I'm not sure," Tanner dissembled.

"Sir," said the man at the helm. "Nanaimo harbor dead ahead."

The crew of the cutter brought their ship smartly to the transient dock and Tanner stepped off onto the planks. He thanked the crew and promised to return the borrowed clothes. As he turned to go, Lieutenant Stark stepped out onto the wing of the bridge.

"Mr. Tanner," he called. Tanner looked up. "Be careful, man. There are odd sorts along this passage who won't take kindly to a stranger poking into their business." He waved a casual salute to Tanner, the cutter revved its engines, and curved out and away into the dark.

Tanner caught a ride down the island to Victoria and then a ferry south back to Martin's in the San Juan Islands. John Martin was understanding about the loss of the Boston Whaler and more concerned about Tanner's health. Tanner arranged a loan from his bank to pay for a replacement cruiser. He made a mental note to arrange for the sale of some securities when he returned to Seattle. He was starting to miss the big commissions he frequently collected from new clients he brought to the agency.

Tanner paused in the door to his room at Martin's when he returned. There was something he couldn't quite identify in the atmosphere. He felt a certain disquiet.

Had someone been in his room? He looked at the small bureau and examined his folded shirts and socks. Then he pulled open the door of the tiny closet. A shirt lay on the floor. It looked as though it had slipped off the hanger. He went back to the bureau and opened the drawers again, looking for anything that might explain his unease.

Nothing was missing but he wasn't the most meticulous housekeeper and he couldn't be certain his clothes had been rearranged. What could an intruder, if there'd been one, be looking for? Evidence that Tanner was searching for the unknown yacht? He didn't have anything like that in his room. On the other hand, it would have been easy for anyone to enter and leave the place without being noticed. John Martin came by while he was still sitting on the edge of his bed thinking about it.

"John," Tanner said, "I think my room was searched while I was gone."

"Searched! What for? Did they get anything?"

"No. You know all my valuables are in your safe."

"Place looks okay to me. Damn, I don't want to have to start locking all the doors around here."

"Yeah, that's part of the charm of this island. An ordinary thief would have probably left a mess. This place looks like whoever was in here didn't want me to know it."

"What for?"

"Don't know. Damn! It's just one more odd thing, John." He turned and looked directly at Martin. "I didn't mention it before, but I think the Boston Whaler was blown up deliberately."

"Wait! D'you think it's connected to your search for that white yacht? You better run the whole business by me again."

Tanner went over everything that had happened and what he had learned. It didn't take long.

"Man, you better go straight to the Coast Guard with this."

"Look John, it'd be a repeat of last year. I don't know if that yacht named Goldenrod is the right boat."

"Well ..."

"I'm not sure the letters on the stern of that boat were the beginning of a word, the first word, second word, middle." Tanner flapped a hand in frustration. "I don't know if the boat I heard at French Creek was Goldenrod. I just know it was the boat that ran us down. I have no proof the explosion wasn't an accident, or that this room was searched."

"But there's a pattern here."

Tanner chuckled sourly, "Yeah, and it could be interpreted as evidence of mental breakdown on my part. Next thing, little green men."

Martin nodded. "Don't forget the Coast Guard. In spite of what your Lieutenant Stark said, I find it a bit odd they turned up both times you lost a boat." The two men stared at each other in the yellow light of the bedside lamp.

13

Winter came. A Seattle winter. Raw, windy, bone-brittle cold, and no snow. It was the second winter since Beth and Alice were murdered on the Inside Passage.

Tanner had resumed his full-time career after John Martin extracted a promise that he'd return to the marina, at least for a long visit, the following season.

His reentry into active work at the agency was met with smiles and cordial cheers. Tanner discovered that after just a few days, all his old instincts returned as sharp as ever. He was grateful that his partners' forbearance had allowed him to work through most of his personal turmoil. His first day back at Tanner and Associates he'd taken his partners into his confidence.

"Perry, things look pretty healthy around here. Maybe each of us should take an extended leave every couple of years."

"Not such a bad idea, Mikey." Perry Barstowe was the only one who ever called Tanner by the diminutive of his given name, and then only in private. "Frankly, while you were out of our hair for a while, we fixed a few things too."

Tanner smiled. He knew Barstowe wasn't criticizing him. "Yeah, I was pretty messed up, wasn't I? My time in Mexico really helped me straighten up and deal with my demons. That and last summer at Martin's in the islands. It was good for me and for business as well."

"Any progress in your search?"

Tanner sighed. "Not really. A few threads to pick at, but I can't even call what I have so far a lead. I heard about

Goldenrod at French Creek that night, and I'm sure I heard the same ship that rammed us going by. Some people will say that's a big coincidence. Or, that there must be lots of big yachts out there that sound just like the one that rammed the Queen Anne. I never got close enough to see the one I heard at French Creek, so I don't know for sure if Goldenrod is the right name." Tanner shrugged elaborately and leaned forward. I had the maritime registry run a computer check you know. It came up with twenty-four ships that carry the name. So far I've only located three of them."

"Was that a national list?" asked Christian.

Tanner shook his head and leaned back in his chair and glanced at his partners. "Listen guys. Be very careful who you talk to about this. I'm convinced that the explosion that wiped out the Boston Whaler at Newcastle was no accident. Even though I can't prove it," he said wryly. He stretched his arms overhead, looking more relaxed than he was. Even now, a year later, talking about the tragedy tied his stomach into knots.

Barstowe stiffened and looked at his friend and partner for a moment. "Jesus, Michael! How can you just sit there and casually drop this on us! Are you trying to tell us you think somebody tried to take you out? With a bomb?"

Tanner nodded. "Correct. A bomb. I have to be more circumspect from now on. You could kill me with an injudicious comment in the wrong place. I'm going to take other precautions as well."

"I suppose you told all this to the police." Barstowe started shaking his head, and grimaced at Tanner. "No of course not. Listen, buddy, I think you're making a big fat mistake here. Not telling the cops your boat was blown to hell." Christian nodded his agreement.

Still looking at Tanner, Barstowe realized he wouldn't change his partner's mind so he abruptly changed direction. "Well, your free time is your own. I don't have to restate the obvious." He glanced sideways at Christian. "Okay, if the business press comes around, our official position is that Tanner is back in the biz full time and there's no indication he's still obsessed about some unknown yacht. Agreed?"

Both men nodded. "And as far as any casual comments, essentially the same thing, except in much more informal language. There's nothing to show you're still looking. Gotta keep the target audience in mind, right?" Barstowe smiled briefly, thinking. "That's better than denying we know anything at all."

"Exactly," Christian chimed in. "Everybody knows we share everything. Perry, that takes care of any public statements, but we ought to know about it if someone comes nosing around. I'll figure out a reason to query the staff periodically about any idle questions that come their way. Maybe someone will ask the wrong question and give us a lead. I better look into the cost of ratcheting up security around here."

Tanner walked into the agency the next Monday to the sounds of several telephones ringing, voices of staff members raised in cheerful disagreement, and his secretary waving a fistful of message slips at him.

"Michael, you were gone all day Friday, and I see you didn't get in on Saturday to return these calls!"

He smiled widely at her. "Well, you know, I had some important errands to do and I just didn't get around to the office. Did you notice what a nice day Saturday was?" He took the messages and went into his office. Quickly sorting them by importance, he sat down to a morning of callbacks.

Later, when he'd caught up, Tanner looked out at the city from his big, dark leather chair, and recalled his Saturday "errand." He'd driven to an old, established, marina across the water from Tacoma, at the southern end of Puget Sound. For a couple of hours he'd wandered the weathered docks and talked to sailors working on their yachts, to tradespeople in several of the stores along the marina walks, and to men he encountered in nearby bars.

He had reorganized his life to give him time to visit

marinas and the commercial harbors around Puget Sound. Tanner was discovering that not every task that came to him had to be completed immediately. He found he was meeting deadlines and accomplishing almost as much professional work as before and he still had time for himself and to continue his search.

It's interesting, he mused. When I reduced my work schedule, I began to discover a lot of important things in life I'd left behind without realizing it. He recalled conversations with Beth about how one day they had to reorder their lives to allow time to enjoy what success had brought them. Sadly, it was too late for Beth.

Tanner pushed into yet another seamans' bar near the water. He smiled internally. I seem to be spending a lot of time in bars. If I'm not careful, I'll turn back into a full-bore lush.

Tanner concluded it would take him months, if not years, to visit all the marinas and harbors scattered up and down Puget Sound, but he kept steadily going. Like the tortoise, he thought ruefully, all patience and persistence. He hung a large map on the wall of an empty bedroom in his apartment. On it he carefully marked the places he visited. Gradually his search plan was taking on a more coherent shape.

Weeks passed and Tanner continued to make discreet inquiries about the Goldenrods on the registry list. Several questions remained. Had it been one of the ships named Goldenrod he'd heard that night in the fog outside French Creek? Tanner was certain in his heart that the unseen yacht was the one that had run him down.

His ruminations, as he stared out at the Seattle skyline were interrupted by Jeremiah Christian, who entered his office softly. "Michael, your return from your summer sabbatical," he started with no preamble and no small talk, "has already raised our billings nearly twenty percent for the quarter." Christian consulted a slip of paper in one hand and came forward to the edge of Tanner's desk. "So you see, we do need you to stick around and pay attention to business." Tanner nodded and smiled. "Two more quarters like the last one and we'll be able to repay your loan for the loss of Orienta."

Tanner put his finger to his lips and strode quickly around the desk to close his office door. "Jeremiah, remember that loan business is strictly between us. There's no need to let the rest of the staff know. And I don't care how you cook the books to cover the transaction. just try to keep it legal."

Yes, well," Christian responded, "until the annual audit, that's no problem. Of course, if the IRS asks for another audit, it'll be a different matter."

"Is there something else? You have me all to yourself, for at least an hour." Tanner's eyes flicked to the art deco clock on the opposite wall.

"Your return has greatly improved the agency's bottom line. It has certainly quieted the speculation in town about our imminent demise." Tanner could hear the satisfaction in Christian's voice. "But my analysis indicates we still aren't getting your maximum output." Christian's Adam's apple bounced in his narrow neck, a sure sign he was uncomfortable.

"Spit it out, Jeremiah," urged Tanner. "We've always been straight with each other, haven't we?"

"You've renewed your personal contracts and the new business you've generated is obviously more than welcome, but I've observed something about you. You seem to have ... I don't know ... less drive, I guess I'd call it. And I'm not the only one to see it, others have noticed it too. Are you well?"

"Oh, I get it. You think I'm still obsessing over Elizabeth's death and it's hurting my productivity, is that it? I guess you're too worried about the bottom line." The telephone beeped but Tanner ignored it. "Jeremiah, did you notice what a nice day it was Saturday? And Sunday wasn't too bad, either. How long has it been since you've gone to the ocean, or just sat in the sun for a while? Or gone to a movie?" The other man looked blank.

Tanner shrugged and leaned back in his big chair. "As I told you the last time the subject of Goldenrod came up, I'm no longer obsessed about my search, but you're right about my priorities. They have changed. I'm not paying twenty-four-hour attention to the business the way I used to. What's more, I'm going to continue to live this way. Elizabeth's death has made me see some things about the way we used to live; it's reminded me of conversations she and I used to have about what we'd like to do if we weren't spending so much time on the business. There was too much missing. So, I'm changing things a little. I've decided life is too short not to follow some of my other interests." He smiled at the frown on Christian's face. "I know, that's your all-time cliché, right? For me, it's starting to have real meaning.

"This is not a retirement speech, Jeremiah. I just want, no, I need, more personal time. I want to rebuild my life in a way that allows me time for personal stuff, not just on the agency, business dinners, and client cocktail parties." Tanner leaned forward and put his hands flat on the desk. "Jeremiah, I want to give freer rein to some of the great talent we have here. If the agency grows more slowly because I invest fewer hours, well, we'll just have to live with that, I guess. But I suspect things will be better in the long run. What's more, I'm going to start insisting my partners do the same."

He paused for a long moment, mildly embarrassed at his vehemence, while he and Christian looked at each other.

Christian sighed, then he brightened and said, "I take it then that our people can spend less time searching databases for large white ships named Goldenrod?"

Tanner nodded. "Your idea was a good one and it helped. I don't want to take away agency resources, but I'll still appreciate hearing about anything Research turns up." Christian nodded, obviously pleased.

"Now. There's a big cocktail party tonight that we agreed to co-sponsor for some of our local environmental groups, remember? I'll be there, of course, because I set it up and the environment is important to us." He winked at Jeremiah. "But don't expect me to stay to the very end. And no more late night pissing contests around the bar at these events with our competition down the street, about who landed the biggest contract last week. I don't do that anymore."

Christian looked at his friend and partner with well-concealed amazement. This was certainly a change in Tanner. He didn't entirely approve, he decided, and he doubted it would last. At least, Jeremiah mused as he smiled his way out the door, Tanner was no longer fixated about finding that damned white yacht.

Tanner's adjustments to his life style didn't disappear. As he immersed himself in the agency's daily business, the sharp memories of his loss faded in the minds of friends and colleagues. Business associates began to remark about his more serious demeanor, that he was drinking less and spending less time at social or business functions.

But Tanner continued to think about Goldenrod and he continued his search. He made frequent weekend visits to harbors and marinas, watching and listening. Always listening.

He was still uncomfortable among Beth's family and spent the Christmas holiday visiting close friends and special colleagues. He also spent time alone in his apartment reviewing and refining his search records.

In early February, Tanner got a call from a woman who identified herself as a staff member in the Seattle office of the U.S. Coast Guard. "Mr. Tanner. We've been able to come up with a short list of some additional vessels that might be of interest."

"Possibilities that fit my description?"

"That's correct.

"I certainly appreciate your help. How'd it happen?"

"I don't understand."

"I thought I already had a list of all the ships in your database. How is it there are more now?"

"Gosh, Mr. Tanner, I really can't say. Perhaps these are new registrations. Sometimes the computers miss files, you know? I'll fax you the list if you wish. These are all in Southern California."

"Thanks for your help. I really appreciate it." When the

list arrived minutes later, Tanner studied it.

Two were in San Diego, three others in the Port of Los Angeles, at Long Beach. He decided to fly to California. He would look for himself.

14

The change in weather was startling. From a rainy, raw February day at Sea-Tac, the big international airport south of Seattle, Tanner emerged from a United flight into a sunny, warm day at the San Diego airport. He was reminded of his healing trip to Mexico the previous year. Here in San Diego, there was a slight mist in the air and the temperature was in the high seventies. Like several other passengers, he shucked his jacket while walking to the car rental counter.

"I'll only be here a few days," he told the pretty woman at the hotel desk when he registered. "Can you suggest a couple of restaurants and some sightseeing I might enjoy?" She could and did.

That evening he dined alone in the hills behind the city at a small, excellent restaurant. The Presidio was situated on the grounds of the San Diego Zoo. Built at the turn of the century, the building had been through many metamorphoses, even serving as a barracks and staging area for troops training for the Pacific Theater in World War II. The mission-style architecture of heavy, age-darkened wood beams, and massive stuccoed arches suited his mood that evening. His meal of a seafood salad followed by rich, tender sea bass, was perfectly prepared.

Tanner inhaled the scent of late-blooming hyacinth. Small candles on each table lent a warm golden glow to the skin. All the men were handsome and the women beautiful. Tanner relaxed with his wine and pictured Elizabeth in this setting, there across the table. He visualized her glossy auburn curls, her dark eyes shining in the candlelight. They'd be discussing his latest public relations campaign, or her current editing project. Tears glistened, unshed, behind his lashes. For a time, Tanner forgot his reasons for being in San Diego and drifted in the memories of a happier time.

The next day, armed with powerful binoculars and a small tape recorder, he toured San Diego Bay. The day after that, he drove to Mission Bay, another sprawling port on the north side of San Diego. He peered at millions of dollars worth of seagoing fiberglass, aluminum, steel and wood, ranging from luxurious to spartan. None of the vessels matched his quarry.

What the hell? Tanner puzzled. He'd already found two of the three ships listed for San Diego. Now he was staring at the third, thinking somebody had made a mistake. "This can't be right," he shouted over the rumble of the big Mercury outboard.

The man whose cruiser he'd rented for the day glanced back at Tanner standing in the open cockpit. "Sorry?"

Tanner raised his arm and pointed, stepping forward beside the driver. "According to my list that slip is leased to a physician who owns a sixty-foot yacht named Golden Scalpel. But look at it."

The object of their scrutiny was a tired, dirty sailboat, no more than thirty feet long. The mast was lying in a cradle of two-by-fours that had been set up at each end of the boat. There was no name on the unkempt transom.

The boatman shrugged. "Transient maybe? No, that thing doesn't look like she's been out of the slip for months. Look at her mooring lines on the deck, there. They're grotty." Tanner looked through his binocs. Dark matter had collected in the grooves of the lines around the cleats. The lines were dingy and discolored from the air pollution and lack of care.

"Must have been a hiccup in the computer," Tanner muttered. He scanned the row of ships, adjusting the focus on his binoculars. His shifting view went past the shoreside dock. Two figures on the quay flickered in and out of view. Tanner scanned back and sharpened the focus. One of the two men was looking right at him through his own binoculars. Then he pointed at Tanner.

While Tanner watched, both men dropped down a short ladder into a motor boat tied up at their feet.

"Shit. We're about to have some unwelcome company."

"That runabout?"

"Yeah. I don't want to talk to them now. Can you get me ashore quickly?"

The boat man nodded. "Hang on," was all he said, and laid his hand on the controls. Tanner was thrown back against the seat behind him as the man pushed the throttle forward and the little boat roared into action. They made a tight turn and almost flew out of the marina.

"Where's the nearest landing?" Tanner yelled.

"Yacht club. Just over there." He pointed and made a long curving wake through the sea.

Tanner looked back over his shoulder. His pursuers were still out of sight behind the long finger docks. Who were they? If they were really chasing him, how had they found him, Tanner wondered? He'd told no one where he was going.

The boat jockey expertly brought the craft to a full stop beside the boat ramp and Tanner hopped out. "You can catch a taxi just across the parking lot," the man said.

"Thanks." Tanner shook the other man's hand. "If anyone asks, just tell 'em where you dropped me. You don't want to get on the wrong side of those people."

A block from the yacht club he hailed a cruising cab and went to his hotel where he checked out.

Two days later, Tanner took a seat on a rickety stool in a tiny bar on the seamy side of Los Angeles harbor, in Long Beach. Next to him a grizzled old man perched, half dozing, a smeared beer glass clutched in one grimy hand. There was a small puddle of spilled beer in front of him. Tanner eyed the sign on the wall and ordered a bottle of lager. He waved away the none-too-clean-looking glass and glanced around. Scarred tables were scattered along the length of the room. The back bar was three unvarnished wood shelves holding partially filled bottles of inexpensive bourbon and rye. Irregularly spaced mirrors carrying the slogans of beer or whiskey distilleries glinted back at him in the dim light. It was just after noon and the bar was almost full. Tanner gazed around, wondering why he was here.

In Long Beach he'd hired another man and his launch to tour the harbor amid the oil rigs standing on manufactured islands with their concealing artificial palm trees. The stinging smog was so thick, they'd had to run close in to many of the mooring areas so Tanner could make out the names of vessels he thought were of similar shape to the one he sought. He'd decided the list was useless, but since he was here anyway, he took the opportunity to visit local marinas. Later, in the artificially cleaned air of his hotel, he stripped down to take a shower. An odd smell came to his nose. It was a noxious mixture of methane, crude oil, and dust. His clothes stank of it and he realized it was smog that had permeated his clothes.

Long Beach boasts one of the largest pleasure boat marinas on the West Coast and Tanner spent two boring days searching, only to come up empty once again. Now, a few hours before his scheduled flight home, here he was in yet another grubby bar, asking his questions about a luxury yacht named Goldenrod.

Someone punched up the juke box at the back of the room and Randy Travis blasted into the conversational burble. There was a crash of chairs going over and heads swiveled toward the back of the bar. Two burly men in the heavy boots and clothes of oil rig hands were squaring off, shouting and pawing at each other. Both seemed to have friends in the crowd, and raised voices flashed and spattered around the room. Older, tired looking men edged their way along the walls, sliding out of the fight path, protecting their bottles and glasses with the hunch of their bodies.

Tanner went back to his beer and realized he was being

pressed all around by the crush of those straining to see the fist fight. He pushed his way off the stool and turned to wedge a path toward the door. There was a sudden surge to his left and an anonymous arm swung a beer bottle up and over toward Tanner's unprotected head. He saw it coming but he couldn't duck out of the way, jammed together as they all were. Time seemed to slow, even as the shouting and the noise from the juke box rose to an incredible din.

The hand holding the long-necked brown beer bottle descended in a long arc toward his face. Tanner twisted, struggling to raise an arm to ward off the coming blow. His body cringed and adrenaline surged. His breath came in ragged gasps as he fought to avoid the blow. Foaming beer sprayed out of the open neck of the bottle.

Just as he was about to be smashed full in the face, a windbreaker-clad arm shot forward over Tanner's shoulder and slapped the bottle away. It sailed in a sparkling arc across the bar where it smashed against the wall behind the bar. In a great turmoil of shoving and cursing, Tanner fought his way toward the door. The tightly-packed crowd surged back and forth. He got his arms free and deflected anonymous fists and arms as the fight enlarged and swirled through the barroom. Seams in the crowd opened and closed and Tanner stumbled and pressed his way toward the entrance. Near the door the press of bodies slackened. He stumbled into a casually dressed man in a tan jacket whose gaze just touched Tanner's face, then flicked over his left shoulder. He couldn't be sure, but Tanner thought the man in front of him had sent an unspoken message to someone just behind him. His savior? Tanner wondered. The arm that had deflected the beer bottle had been clad in a windbreaker. But it couldn't be the same man who now stood in front of him. He struggled to turn, trying to see his benefactor. There was no one behind him wearing a windbreaker. When he turned back the other way, the second man was also gone. Tanner slammed through the door and into the street. Neither stranger was on the street.

Later, Tanner reflected that the man he'd seen had looked out of place. Like Tanner, he'd been too neatly dressed, too clean-shaven. They were both out of place in that seedy waterfront bar.

15

While Tanner traveled the smog-filled streets and waterways of California, or searched and shivered in icy rain and sleet, exposed to the raw winds and dampness of the Seattle winter, the Goldenrod he sought rested comfortably far to the south in the blue ocean and temperate conditions just outside Mexican territorial waters. Occasionally, small high-speed launches scurried between her pristine hull and the Mexican shoreline, while black-suited scuba divers busied themselves in the warm water around her bow and along her sides.

In the luxurious main saloon, three men in expensive white tropical linen sat at ease in soft chairs.

"Captain, I've discussed this Michael Tanner person with my people. We agree with you the encounter with that fisherman in the bar at French Creek was unfortunate, but we doubt he's made any real progress since."

"I guess you're right, Talley," responded the captain. "But just to be safe, I've arranged a little meeting. The man who fired that shotgun at Tanner's boat is going to run into him somewhere so we can see if Tanner recognizes the guy."

"And if he does?" Talley flicked an ash from his cigarette as he asked the question. He was a colorless individual, his face nearly always devoid of expression.

"We'll be ready to take him out right then. I still think we were right that day we sank his sailboat. The only mistake was not finding him after we rammed him."

The other man in the cabin, silent throughout the

exchange coughed and in a hoarse rasp said, "We've been through all that. Everybody has agreed we'll just keep track of Tanner and there'll be no more free-lance actions like blowing up his boat at Newcastle Island. Clear? We don't like messy situations. In the future, if there's a problem, just tell us and we'll decide what to do. With this Tanner or anyone else."

"You have to expect he'll run across us if he keeps on looking."

"Look, Captain, the man is going to stop looking for you. Before long, when he doesn't find anything, he'll just quit. We've been shut down now for several months and you've mostly kept Goldenrod out of the Inside Passage. But we have clients to service. They expect us to be back in operation as soon as the weather gets better. We stalled some of them with excuses about the weather, but any more delays and we'll start losing real money. You never go to Seattle, so I don't think he'll ever see this boat again. Or anyone associated with us."

"Except for having my crew run into him," responded the Captain. The other two nodded, a little reluctantly.

On deck, crew members also talked about Tanner.

"I don't see what they're worried about," said one, jerking his thumb at the cabin. "That guy, Tanner? There was nothin' in his room at the marina when I looked. But I say, if he keeps pokin' his nose in where it don't belong, just kill 'im." He grinned at his companions and slowly drew a finger across his throat.

Late one afternoon a month after he returned from California, Tanner walked through the door to the Sailors Rest in Tacoma. Darkness was just over the mountains.

The bar was long, narrow and dark--like a lot of bars I've been in recently, he thought.

When he opened the street door, the stench of the place smacked him in the face. It was an unholy combination of stale tobacco smoke, too many days and nights of unwashed bodies, and unmopped floors. He shouldered his way toward the bar.

The room was crowded with sailors, roustabouts and out-of-work hangers-on from the maritime trades. The dirty linoleum floor clung to his shoes. Several other men followed Tanner into the bar. He found an opening, and a stool, and wedged himself in. As was his habit in these places, he ordered a bottle of beer. Tanner took a long swig and turned to survey the crowd. As he did so, his arm was jostled by a big rawboned man in an old peacoat and a dark-billed fisherman's cap.

"Hey!" exclaimed Tanner. He narrowly avoided slopping beer on himself. "Watch it, mister."

The man, who'd stomped by without pausing, turned sharply and confronted Tanner. "You wanna make somethin' of it?" His heavy mustache twitched. He looked Tanner in the eye and gave him a belligerent look. The nearby drinkers paid no attention. Petty confrontations like this were part of everyday life in these parts.

Tanner looked back steadily, not wanting to start a fight and said, "Since you got my attention, maybe you'll answer a question."

"Why?"

"I'm looking for a pleasure yacht. A particular yacht, about ninety feet, white or cream, with the letters GOL somewhere in its name. Maybe Goldenrod."

"You must be crazy."

"You didn't answer my question."

The man shrugged and turned away. Behind him, Tanner now noticed another man who had been standing quietly watching their minor confrontation. The second man followed the other down the bar. A short time later, they slipped out together through the back door.

The pungent smell of stale beer and an uncleansed mouth washed over Tanner. The old geezer on the next stool leaned closer. Instinctively, Tanner pulled back.

"Y' say yer looking for a boat? 'Minds me of a time when I wuz still goin' t'sea."

Tanner just looked at the man and breathed through his mouth.

"GOL in her name, still out there too. The Golden Hind, she was, a great ship." The man nodded slowly and winked at Tanner. "Afore that, I wuz with Jason in the Golden Argonaut." He nodded and swigged at his beer. Tanner could see the man's attention drifting away. He put a dollar on the bar by the man's tattered elbow and went away from there.

16

In May of the second spring after the sinking of the Queen Anne, Tanner returned to the small marina in the San Juans and his new friend and employer, John Martin. Martin was glad to have him back. He was still enjoying increased business as a result of Tanner's advertising designs and other suggestions. Besides, Tanner had become a reliable efficient worker.

When he stepped off the ferry and saw Martin standing at the office door, Tanner understood for the first time how eagerly he'd been looking forward to returning to the marina.

"Well, John," he smiled, firmly grasping Martin's outstretched hand.

"Well, Mr. Tanner," responded Martin, grinning with pleasure. "Here's the important Seattle executive, back to humble himself once more with ordinary manual labor." Tanner smiled again and glanced around. He liked the marina and the physical labor that was an integral part of the job. He felt comfortable here, like he fit in. Not that he would abandon his life in Seattle, but he now could visualize a future for himself that blended the high-energy, sometimes frenetic excitement of the public relations world, with the more peaceful joys of harmonious existence with the island, the marina and the sea.

Tanner stretched and worked a kink out of his shoulder. "Yep. Don't quite understand what the attraction is. It can't be you." He poked Martin gently in the belly. "I guess it's this place, out here at the edge of the sea." Tanner soon found the rhythm again, and the days flowed warmly one into the next. Yachts came and went and Tanner watched and listened, but there was little difference from the previous summer. He was able to eliminate a few more vessels from his list. There were changes in the sailing scene, however.

"John," Tanner remarked one day while he measured some new planks for one of the finger docks, "did you see that big Gulfstar that stopped briefly yesterday? It had an all-female crew and captain."

"Yep. Not the first one, either," said Martin, standing on the plank to hold one end of the tape measure. "And it won't be the last. We've had several boats through here recently with mixed crews. 'Bout time, too. I never held much for that old saying 'bout women being bad luck aboard ship. There's no reason at all why women can't sail as well as men. I've seen several who did better."

Tanner was becoming convinced that the crew of Goldenrod was doing something illegal. He had no hard evidence but if he could catch them at it, he could alert the authorities. If he could see them arrested, he'd have some satisfaction at least. This summer he brought with him a camera with a telephoto lens and a videocamera.

He had only vague memories of the three figures he'd glimpsed on the bridge that awful day. He couldn't identify any of them. Although he didn't know it, Tanner owed his life to that inability.

The crew member who had fired the shotgun into the cabin of the Queen Anne was the same man who'd jostled Tanner in the small Tacoma bar. The man swore later to his captain that there'd been no glimmer of recognition from Tanner during their brief encounter. The other crew member who'd watched them agreed.

Mary Whitney arrived at the hotel next to the marina a week after Tanner took up his duties.

"Hi, stranger."

"Good morning, Ms. Whitney."

"Please, it's Mary, remember?

Tanner smiled at her and nodded. He realized as he gazed up at her on the dock above his head that he'd been hoping she would return to the island. He thought she looked good, standing there in snug powder-blue slacks and a white blouse with loose sleeves buttoned at the wrist. A matching blue scarf fluttered at her throat.

Later in the week he encountered her again on the dock near the harbor-master's shack.

"Mary. Hi. Anything I can do for you?"

"For a while, I thought I was going to be stranded here."

"I beg your pardon?"

She laughed. "I hope you can abide assertive women, because I've come to invite you to supper tonight as my guest at the hotel. It's outdoor grill time and I understand they've collected some pretty good eating fish."

Tanner knew about the annual fish fry to welcome the summer season. He was pleased with her invitation.

"Gosh, I'm not sure. Do I have to dress?"

She threw her head back when she laughed, a full-throated sound. "You'd better, or they'll throw you off the island."

That evening, a large happy crowd of islanders, hotel guests, staff, and yachties gathered on the beach in front of the hotel. Two beds of glowing coals under heavy sheets of steel sent fragrant smoke drifting up into the darkening sky. The smoke mixed with the odor from slabs of fresh-caught, sizzling salmon steaks. Martin played smiling bartender, dispensing cold beer and white wine supplied by the hotel.

Later, Tanner and Mary Whitney sat side by side on a log. "Boy, that was some feast." He felt relaxed, pleased to be there in the company of this woman.

"Look there. A shooting star." Mary's dreamy voice filtered softly across his consciousness. "Uncle Mack and I used to lie on the deck for hours when we sailed to Desolation Sound.

Watching the stars, looking for meteors."

A hotel guest brought out her guitar and soon old camp songs floated across the little bay.

It was approaching midnight when Mary said, "Walk me to the hotel." They stopped at the foot of the steps to the veranda, just out of the pool of light. Suddenly an awkward feeling came over Tanner.

"Thanks for inviting me," he said. "I had a good time."

"So did I." A slight hesitation, then she leaned forward and her lips brushed his cheek. "Find peace, Michael Tanner," she whispered, and ran lightly up the steps.

They saw each other more frequently after that night. Still, it was clear to Tanner that Mary Whitney was popular and had an active social life, and he was only one part of it. Sometimes, depressed and missing Elizabeth, he felt disloyal.

It was the Memorial Day weekend, a long busy time for the marina workers. Tanner was refueling yet another large ocean-going motor yacht southbound for Seattle from Princess Charlotte Strait, which lies just north of Vancouver Island.

"She was a real beauty, but I dunno what the hurry was. Somebody aboard sure must have wanted to get up-island real quick," said the crew member standing beside Tanner. Deep-tanned sinews on the man's arms stood out against his crisp whites.

"Yeah, that sucker was really moving," agreed the second crew member. He kept a careful eye on Tanner as he disconnected the fuel pump hose from the through-hull filler pipe to the yacht's tanks. Tanner gestured to the other man to use his deck key to screw down the cover on the filler pipe while Tanner reeled in the pump hose. Careful as always, Tanner handled the hose and nozzle to avoid scraping it across the gleaming deck or spilling any fuel. The crew member nodded his appreciation of Tanner's care.

"How come you remembered her?" Tanner asked.

"Who? Goldenrod?" said the man.

Tanner's heart bumped. "Yeah."

"Couple reasons, I guess. She was such a beauty, all that creamy-white hull and smoked superstructure. That boat's got really nice clean lines. But she was in such an all-fired hurry." The man went on to describe the peculiar sound of her diesels.

"Where was she?" Tanner was having difficulty keeping his voice casual.

"Oh, up the strait near Texada. She was goin' north at a great rate. Plus," he continued, "she coulda been the one mentioned in that complaint." The man explained to Tanner that a sailboat charterer, a 'ragman,' as they were disdainfully called by some powerboaters, had complained recently about a near miss with a big creamy-white motor vessel somewhere in the San Juan Islands.

Tanner's excitement grew, but he forced himself to remain outwardly calm. "Anything come of the complaint?" he asked, relieved at how casual he sounded. He used a piece of soft waste to polish the cap on the through-hull while he chatted with the men.

"Nope," the crewman continued. "The Canucks couldn't decide which boat had the right of way. Maybe Goldenrod didn't have a lot of maneuvering room. Prob'ly another guy who knows the rules only by the book. Hell, if I was on a sailboat, I'd give a vessel like that a wide berth all right, rather than chance gettin' run down." He spat over the side.

Tanner waved off the big motor yacht, then turned to the owner-captain of a 44-foot ketch that had just slid neatly into the other side of the gas dock while still under sail, and without using its engine. It was against the rules of the marina to sail up to the dock, but like most sailors, Tanner appreciated seeing a yacht wellhandled in such tight quarters, so he merely grinned at the captain and started filling out a charge slip for fuel and water. But he continued to think about this latest information. Instinct told him he was drawing closer to his quarry.

17

After he serviced the ketch and it departed, Tanner had some time to himself. He cleaned and straightened up the harbormaster's area. The sun streamed down on his shoulders. Head bent, he swept the piers and hosed down the gas dock. He moved almost mechanically while his mind picked through what he knew and what he had just learned about Goldenrod. It was the second or third time Goldenrod's name had come up in a context that seemed to fit a profile he was developing. He remembered how close he had come, that night last August in French Creek, to identifying once and for all the killer yacht. Now the crew member's description of the sound of her engines had Tanner convinced that Goldenrod was the yacht he was looking for. But he had to see Goldenrod for himself. He toyed with the idea of chartering a plane to fly directly to Goldenrod's last reported position.

Good sense prevailed. To identify Goldenrod from the air, he'd have to get near enough so the crew would realize they were being closely observed. By the time he could get to a marina, charter a boat, and return, Goldenrod could disappear again. He had to find a way to see the name and listen to the engines without alerting anyone aboard her.

John Martin appeared at Tanner's elbow.

"I been watchin' you from the window. You gonna become a real curiosity around here, you stand there like a statue much longer."

Tanner explained his dilemma. "What do you think, John?"

Martin sighed and scratched his belly. "I think you ought to get a boat and run up there, see what you can find out. The rest of the week will be slack, always is. Besides, that's the deal we made, you and me. Take the rest of the week and next weekend. You want the new Boston Whaler?"

Tanner shook his head. Privately, he thought he might be gone longer than just the rest of the week, and he wanted a bigger, more comfortable vessel, one that could shelter him for a longer time. "I'll see what else is available. But thanks, John."

The tide was in. Tanner knew he should wait for low tide to get extra boost from the current generated by the inflowing current. That gave him a few hours before he should leave. Just enough time to get organized.

He made several useless and increasingly tense calls to contacts on the island, trying to charter a boat. Finally, Tanner trotted across the road to the resort office. "I want to charter a sailboat. Do you know of anything available?"

"One of our guests owns that 34-foot Tartan out there. The one docked on the east finger?" remarked the man at the desk. Tanner nodded. He knew the boat. "She sometimes rents it out, short-term. That's all that's here ..."

"Who's the owner? I'll call her," interrupted Tanner, beginning to wonder if he was going to lose his chance for lack of a boat.

"She's not around, but Mac handles things for her. He's in the office," gesturing behind him.

Tanner, having lost two boats already, hesitated long enough to call Mary Whitney on the house phone, and to marshal his arguments for Mac. Mary didn't answer.

Mac, a little, round, bouncy man in his mid-fifties, had never acted particularly friendly toward Tanner. Word had gotten back to Tanner that Mac wasn't too pleased with Tanner's attitude toward some of his guests during his first season on the island. In an environment where customer satisfaction is paramount,

Tanner had sometimes been too forthright when questioning the abilities of certain guests to safely handle their boats. So far this year, Tanner had neither heard anything negative, nor, as he thought about it, had he seen much of Mac. He wondered if his effort to rent the Tartan was a waste of time, but Mac readily agreed to the charter and handed him the keys to the yacht named Sea Queen. Mac told Tanner that no one else had asked to charter Sea Queen. Chartering had been slow this season, so he wasn't concerned if Tanner was a few days late returning.

Tanner single-handed her from the slip to the gas dock where he topped up her diesel and water tanks. Sea Queen was an elegant, well-fitted-out Tartan sailboat. He was surprised and pleased to find that she had a hefty engine and an oversized prop that would drive her at good speed through the water. He found few supplies aboard, but the alcohol stove reservoir was full and a quick look around assured him there was a complete set of sails, several nearly new from the look of them. The standing rigging appeared well cared for. The deck gleamed and the rich mahogany trim was clean and well oiled.

"Your owner," Tanner mused, running his finger lightly over the smooth hand rail beside the companionway ladder, "really keeps you shipshape. You and I will get along just fine."

He examined the Tartan's rigging and layout closely. Since he'd be sailing alone, he wanted to be sure he could handle her in a sudden change of weather. And he wanted to sail her, not just motor the entire time. He wanted to sail for the satisfaction and joy of sailing, but there were practical reasons as well. The distances involved made it impossible to rely on the engine alone, unless he occasionally broke off his search to enter a port for a new supply of fuel. Sea Queen was rigged so that single-handed sailing would pose few problems.

He had been moving quickly, ever since he decided to go north, and now that he had a few hours before the tide changed, he relaxed and wrote out a list of provisions he would need. He looked at the weather, the sun on the sparkling blue waters of the harbor, the fluffy white clouds skating past overhead. He became more aware of the comfortable temperature, of people going by on the connecting docks, of people watching him prepare the yacht.

He noted that several individuals were observing his activity. Why was that? Was it casual appreciation of his boat-handling skill, or was there something more? I'd better be a little cautious, here, he decided. He recalled admonitions to watch his back. A white-hot explosion that had destroyed the Boston Whaler off Newcastle Island also came to mind.

From the harbor master's shack he again called Mary Whitney but there was still no answer.

"Damn," he muttered, recalling that they had tentatively arranged the day before to have dinner that evening.

Where was she? Time was running on and he finished provisioning Sea Queen with the necessary essentials. Mary Whitney was still among the missing. Questions to other employees at the marina were of no help. Tanner sold gas and water to two more transients. He had to help them maneuver their yachts around Sea Queen at the gas dock, but his skill and care in helping the boaters quickly soothed any minor irritations.

With the golden light of late afternoon casting benign shadows across the harbor, Tanner sat on the sun-warmed dock, staring almost vacantly at Sea Queen's waterline. He felt a gentle tap on his hand. He brushed it away, but it came again, insistently. He looked up and saw the slackened stern line now rested across the back of his hand. The tide had turned and Sea Queen was no longer pulling at the line. She was telling Tanner it was time to go.

He switched on the bilge blower and took a few minutes to walk to the phone booth at the end of the dock, where once again he tried to reach Mary Whitney at the hotel. There was still no answer from her room. "Can you tell me where I might reach her?" he asked when the manager came on.

"Sorry, sir. Miss Whitney comes and goes pretty much as she pleases. There's nothing here to indicate where she went or when she'll be back."

"Thanks. Leave a note, please. Just say something unexpected has come up. I apologize for missing our dinner date, but I'll explain when I return." He walked swiftly back to Sea Queen. As he hopped aboard, he realized he was upset at missing her, at not being able to explain in person why he was canceling their date. But how would he have explained?

There was no more time for delay. Tanner cast off the bow line, stepped back aboard and pressed the engine starter. As before, the big diesel under his feet responded instantly and he let it warm up while he mentally ran through the steps he would take to cast off and get clear of the dock. He shifted to reverse, engine running dead slow. The tide, now flowing out of the harbor, gently pulled Sea Queen's bow toward the dock. With bow line loose and stern line taut, the engine nudged the stern tighter to the dock, and forced the bow away, countering the gentle force of the tide. Tanner gauged her swing, shifted to forward and loosed the stern line. Sea Queen slid forward a few feet off the dock, all mooring lines clear. He looked all around for possible hazards and throttled up, angling away from the dock.

He reached the end of the long dock, turned to port and headed straight for the harbor mouth. As he passed the end of the dock he saw John Martin standing at the door to his office with an arm raised in farewell. Tanner waved back and inched the throttle lever forward. Sea Queen motored into the open water of the harbor. He felt the breeze on his back and, uncharacteristically, hauled the big genoa jib he had previously secured to the forestay up to the peak of the mast. It snapped out to port and Tanner quickly controlled the set of the sail. He took the breeze over his right shoulder and, with the added lift from the genoa, motor-sailed briskly out of the harbor and into the seaway.

Once clear of the harbor mouth, Tanner set a course and shackled the wheel with a pair of stout shock cords. He nipped below, grabbed a beer, binoculars, and tuned the VHF radio to the weather frequency.

"...winds southwest at five to ten knots with a one-foot chop," said the announcer.

The combination of three knots of favorable tidal current and the breeze sent Sea Queen swiftly north toward Desolation Sound. Shortly after leaving the harbor, with a clear path ahead, Tanner raised the mainsail. For a few minutes he played with the mainsheet and the traveler to set this second sail for the best slot and maximum drive as he reached up the passage. Then with a relaxing sigh he shifted the engine to neutral and switched it off.

18

With the engine off and the wind at his back, Tanner could hear the creaking of the rigging and the water creaming around Sea Queen's bow. The sloop took the wind and seemed to lift in response to the breeze, with a slight heel and pressure of the rudder against the wheel. Tanner automatically shifted his stance on the tilting deck. Although the day wasn't hot, sailing downwind as he was, the air seemed almost still and the sun warmed his back. Sea birds cried sounds of welcome as the Tartan rushed northward under a deep blue sky. For a time, as the sun sank toward the Pacific Ocean behind Vancouver Island to the west, he could almost forget his grim quest, and respond to the rhythm of wind and waves, and deal solely with his yacht and the natural forces that carried him north.

Leaving the Gulf Islands well to port, Tanner encountered few other boats. Most had already found safe harbor for the night. Tanner thought ahead to no snug anchorage. He intended to sail through the night, reaching Desolation Sound as soon as possible. Darkness fell, the winds continued, and Sea Queen, as if glad to be released from her mooring lines, rushed on, cleaving a long, straight wake behind her transom.

With nightfall, the temperature dropped. Tanner again secured the wheel while he went below for a sweater and another beer. A handful of trail mix lessened his hunger. Real supper would have to wait.

Hours later, hungry, eyes gritty with tension and lack of

sleep, Tanner changed course to a more northerly track while the wind still held from the southwest. He watched over the starboard side as the lights of the city of Vancouver slid by. He held his course and felt the wind beginning to freshen. Now the low chop became more apparent as he sailed by the wide entrance to Vancouver's harbor. Weather radio reported stronger night winds in the north.

Tanner realized then he should have prepared for a sail change if the weather made up. Normally an ordinary task, here he faced the night and an unfamiliar boat, in addition to being alone. There was no one to steer while he ran forward and changed sails. He thought about dropping the main while he changed the jib, lying dead in the water, but that would cost him too much time.

Damn, he thought. Too eager to get going, I guess. I should have had the small jib up on the rail at the bow.

Still, he knew he must change down to a smaller jib now, while the wind was relatively light and steady. Tanner shrugged into a life jacket and then a safety harness. The chop wasn't rough, but even a small misstep on a strange boat in the dark could pitch him over the side. With no one at the helm, Sea Queen would simply sail off and leave him.

Nothing for it now, he told himself. Easy does it, though. A screw-up here would cost a lot more time than a little patience.

It could have been Beth whispering in his ear. With a sigh he released the jibsheets. The sudden wind-driven flapping of the sail sounded like rifle fire. It was as if the sail was about to be torn in shreds from the mast, an illusion, Tanner knew, unless he left the sail unattended for a long time.

He secured the wheel again and hooked his safety harness to the lifeline. He tied the free end of the jib halyard to his belt. Then he crabbed forward, setting each foot carefully on the rocking deck as he made his way to the bow. He lowered the bucking, flailing, sail and gathered it quickly on the deck.

Not bad. Kept most of it out of the water.

Tanner lashed the genoa to the lee rail and returned to the

cockpit. Again he took a long look around to be sure no traffic was approaching. With a hand-held compass he took two bearings and verified his approximate location off the north side of Vancouver. Then he made a quick notation in the ship's log. From the sail locker under a cockpit bench he dragged a sailbag holding the smaller jib. Tanner carried the sail to the bow. Already, wind-driven waves were causing the bow to rise and fall an alarming amount. Squatting there at the bow in the dark, with nothing but black water in front and close on either side, it seemed to Tanner he was in the midst of a major storm. Intellectually he knew that wasn't the case and then his stomach turned.

"Uh, oh," he muttered to himself. "Let's not be sick out here."

Ignoring his sudden queasiness, Tanner secured the jib to the forestay, the wire cable running from the bow to the top of the mast, from which the foresails were hung. Then he connected the shackle on the jib halyard to an eye in the top of the sail. Finally he was able to scuttle back to the security of the cockpit where the motion was considerably less. He hauled on the halyard, turning slightly into the wind as he did so to ease wind pressure and making it easier to raise the sail. Once properly set, Tanner corrected his course again to take the wind nearly dead aft. He sailed on north and northwest, up the east side of the Inside Passage. Puffing slightly from his exertions, he glanced at the sails, then checked his speed indicator, the knotmeter.

Not too bad. Sure would have helped if Beth had been here, though. Took too long to change.

He forced himself away from that line of thinking. Beth would never again join him on night sails.

Dawn came to a clear, gusty day. Tanner sailed on up the passage and by moonlight the next evening, exhausted after two days and a night with no sleep, he admitted he could go no further without rest. He was becoming dangerously uncertain in his judgment. The anchor chain rattled over the bow roller and echoed off the nearby shore. The anchor bit into the bottom and

Sea Queen nodded quietly at rest, swinging gently on the tide.

The next day, after a few hours anchored in a small, exposed cove at the edge of the mainland, Tanner sailed on. The afternoon sun was sending Sea Queen's shadow further off to the right when Tanner finally saw the fjord-like openings in the coastline that meant he'd arrived at Desolation Sound. But his hurried efforts to reach his destination were of little value. Goldenrod was nowhere to be found.

Days later, with still no sign of his quarry, Tanner cruised north toward Port Hardy, a small coastal town near the north end of Vancouver Island. Hardy is surrounded by a multitude of small islands, deep channels and inlets, an area in which a whole fleet of yachts could be hidden. More time went by and he knew he'd have to go to his alternate plan soon.

Tanner had been in touch with a charter seaplane pilot who was based in Comox on Vancouver Island. They could cover a lot of territory by air and the seaplane would allow him to land nearby, if he spotted his target. Gradually that idea had faded and for some reason he didn't entirely understand, Tanner decided to do it this way, on the water. Now, frustration was becoming Tanner's constant companion in Sea Queen's cockpit.

How much time should he spend looking for Goldenrod? Was she even here in these waters? He was also keenly aware he was looking for a yacht that might not be the right one. Tanner sat staring into nothing, thinking. Not too long ago he'd have motored off, tried to force the issue, make something happen. Patience had never been one of his strong virtues. Tanner realized he was becoming a different person.

He worked his way south from Port Hardy and was now anchored in a small bay off a main channel on East Redonda Island. He was studying charts of the area when the sound of big diesel engines reached him. By the time he raised his head out of the companionway, Tanner knew he had found the object of his search. The sound of her engines was a sound he would never forget. When he saw the white yacht steadily cruising by, and her name, GOLDENROD, clearly lettered on the stern, any lingering doubts disappeared. Tanner stared after the passing yacht. Now that he was this close and knew this was the yacht he'd been searching for, the pain, the agony, and the terror he'd kept inside him all these months poured out. The memories of that terrible afternoon returned full force. Again he saw the dark figures on the wing of the bridge calmly watching; he heard again the boom of the shotgun and felt the numbing shock as the little yacht was crushed under Goldenrod's onrushing bow.

Goldenrod rumbled by in the bright sunlight, sending off sparks of reflected fire. Tanner stood unmoving. Scarcely breathed. He stared after his enemy. The killer yacht. Tanner's fingers were so tightly clenched on the sides of the companionway that they seized up and sent sharp spasms into his wrists. Painfully, bent over as if suffering from stomach cramps, he climbed the ladder and slumped down in the cockpit. Tears of anger and loss coursed down his face. He curled up on the cushion and voices came to him. Alice, screaming. Beth, alarm coarsening her sweet voice.

Deep inside, a kernel of resolve hardened and grew; a resolve born of rage and frustration. Now, finally, Tanner knew his nemesis. He would finish his task. He would, somehow, discover why Goldenrod had sunk his boat and bring those responsible for the death of his beloved Beth to some kind of justice.

Tanner raised his head and wiped his face. Now he'd found Goldenrod, could he gather enough evidence of wrongdoing to go to the authorities? He would. He must. Tanner sat and watched Goldenrod slowly disappear up the channel.

Or should he devise a suitable revenge?

He could try to follow Goldenrod in Sea Queen. He'd have to keep well away. Since they'd already seen his boat moored in the cove, they would likely wonder why he was persistently off their stern, shadowing them. Following a ship in these waters for any distance and concealing one's true intentions required at least a second pair of eyes and hands and a lot of luck.

The task was virtually impossible.

Tanner wondered at Goldenrod's destination. Maybe they were looking for an anchorage for the night. It's late enough. Tanner pulled out a chart of the area and found his location. Right. A couple of nice little bays just up the line there.

Unless Goldenrod was going someplace in particular, they would likely anchor in this channel. The minutes were passing and Goldenrod was getting farther away while Tanner pondered.

He went below and dragged an inflatable dinghy out of its storage compartment under one of the forward bunks. He was grimly pleased to find a pressurized gas bottle packed with it so he wouldn't have to pump up the dinghy by hand. It took only moments to fill the dinghy's flotation tanks from the gas bottle and secure it over the side.

Minutes later with a small outboard motor attached, Tanner motored up the coast in Goldenrod's wake. He stayed close to shore, varying his speed from time to time, to cast an illusion of casual sightseeing, in the event someone aboard Goldenrod heard his motor. Zipping around the second bend in the channel, Tanner discovered that the captain of Goldenrod had found his anchorage in a cove near the entrance to Toba Channel. The big white vessel lay quietly across the channel from Tanner's location. He saw the vessel from nearly a mile away, marked her position and turned back to Sea Queen.

He made a hot supper and decided to approach Goldenrod after dark. When the darkness was complete, and the sky had turned black, Tanner loaded trail mix, a windbreaker and the jacket to a wetsuit he found aboard, along with a flashlight and a large container of baby powder into the dinghy. He turned on his anchor light and after some thought, left other lights burning in the main cabin. He didn't want to give anyone who happened by an impression he was trying to conceal Sea Queen.

An inner voice counseled caution. He ignored it and yanked the starter cord on the dinghy's outboard motor.

19

Tanner motored slowly up the channel, staying just off the western shore. Once he stopped, curbing his impatience to get closer. He knew that anyone aboard Goldenrod who was listening would hear his outboard. Sound travels great distances across the water. He calculated, however, that unless he approached very close, the sound would not alarm them. Residents on the islands, as well as visiting fishermen, often used small runabouts or inflatables to get around, even at night. He didn't plan to get very close to Goldenrod using the motor, and he'd approach on a roundabout course.

Tanner used the oars the last mile, thankful for the conditioning brought about by his work at Martin's marina. Although he saw several places to beach the dinghy and get ashore, the rocky, overgrown slopes of the mountain made an overland approach impossible. He decided to swim to the yacht after approaching in the dinghy as close as he dared. Tanner hoped the wetsuit would give him sufficient protection from the cold sea. He beached the dinghy as full night raced across the water. He located a piece of driftwood to support himself in the water when he needed to rest. It was large enough for that, but small enough to be easily maneuverable. He'd intended to wait until after midnight to make his surreptitious sortie, but it was only a little after ten when Tanner grew tired of inaction and stripped off his clothes. A liberal application of baby powder made easier the job of wriggling into the foam and neoprene wetsuit. He wasn't wearing socks, so the swim fins were uncomfortable on his feet.

The sea was colder than he expected. For a moment it took his breath away. He soon found the water seeping into the suit was warmed by his body and made conditions more bearable. It also helped ease the fit of the wetsuit. Taking care not to splash, he paddled steadily toward Goldenrod. Tanner rested twice on his swim across the small bay.

Draping his arms over the chunk of driftwood, Tanner breathed through the snorkel tube and rested with only his eyes out of the water to present as small a target as possible, should anyone be watching. He looked at Goldenrod across the narrowing strip of water, measuring her sleek lines with his eyes. He was aided by the slight tidal current that flooded up the channel, toward the big motor yacht. The night was very still. Faint music drifted across the water, punctuated by occasional louder bursts when someone opened a cabin or passageway door to the deck. As he neared the ship, individual voices became discernible. Apparently there were both men and women aboard. It sounded like they were all having a very good time.

Tanner knew the closer he got, the greater the risk of discovery. He didn't care. There was in him an insistent need to get as close as possible to his target. Perhaps he'd even manage to get aboard and locate something to explain why Goldenrod had run down his boat and killed his wife and friend. More than that, he needed to put his hands on Goldenrod.

He knew he wasn't being entirely rational. But for Tanner the very act of secretly touching Goldenrod, of going aboard her, unseen, had become vital. That would somehow breach her armor. It would mean Goldenrod was vulnerable. It would mean he might reach her masters.

Tanner paddled slowly to the anchor chain off the bow and hung there in the cold dark sea for a time. His breathing was slow and steady. His mind ticked over, weighing risk, figuring odds. Now that he had a hand on her anchor, had touched the very bow that penetrated the Queen Anne's hull so many months ago, a calm descended on him.

He hung there listening, peering upward at the empty rail. The absence of a moon and the thick clouds reduced night light to a minimum, especially for those moving in and out of the lighted saloon and cabins on the decks above his head. With infinite care, Tanner swam entirely around the yacht, touching it as he went, gliding his hand along the smooth white hull.

He avoided swimming through occasional patches of light shining from doors and portholes that reflected off the sea. He saw nothing out of the ordinary except an over-large swim platform at the stern which could be raised and lowered as needed. He didn't know quite what he expected to find, but whatever it was, it wasn't in evidence, or he failed to recognize it. When he reached the bow again, he rested, clinging to the taut anchor chain.

For several minutes, Tanner stayed where he was, listening to the footsteps and snatches of casual conversation above him as people passed back and forth. Occasionally he heard a familiar-sounding voice, but dismissed it. No one he knew could be aboard or had any connection with Goldenrod, of that he was confident.

He was not as uncomfortable in the water as he had expected to be after the shock of his initial plunge. With great care, moving slowly to avoid splashing, he removed fins, gloves, and snorkel tube and mask. Tanner tied them to the piece of driftwood and to the anchor chain with a piece of twine attached to his mask.

Fortunately for Tanner, the captain of Goldenrod believed in using plenty of anchor chain when he had swinging room, so the angle from the water to the bow was not as steep as it might have been. He was able to sling himself easily by hands and feet from the chain and then shinny hand-over-hand up the chain until he could grasp the coaming at the edge of the main deck and peer carefully about, feet still hooked over the chain. Even with the chain angling down to the water, it was a difficult piece of work. After a long look, seeing no one, he slid noiselessly onto the deck and rolled to the edge of the forward cabin bulkhead. He lay there for a moment breathing through his mouth. His heart pounded so loudly in his ears, he was sure anyone passing within ten feet would hear it. But no one did. So far so good. As he lay there pressed to the deck, he looked up at the bridge. It was a solid wall of dark glass. There was just the smallest glow from working instruments. Tanner sensed that at least one crew member must be on duty.

I certainly would have somebody there, even at anchor with this party going on, he mused. His gaze traveled from side to side along the bridge, alert for any movement on deck or on either wing of the bridge above him. Adrenaline surged through his body. His tongue began to dry. Tanner's nerves became so sensitive he thought he'd be able to see from the ends of his fingers if he pointed at the brightly lighted portholes nearby. He smelled teak oil and some kind of perfume. Cooking odors drifted by. Was that a béarnaise sauce? The texture of the deck beneath his hip seemed as precise as the edge of a razor.

Finally he moved and started a slow crawl aft on the port side. Tanner found a door and cracked it, rose to his knees, risked a quick look. Empty. Then he carefully leaned his head and shoulders inside. The dimly lit passage appeared to run almost the entire length of the vessel, right down its centerline. To Tanner, the passage seemed endless, narrowing and disappearing into the gloom, and it felt like a trap. He crouched half in and half out of the door, his fingers trembling slightly on the door jam, sweat beginning to trickle down his face.

What in God's name am I doing here? His silent question received no answer. He knew his next step might be his ultimate mistake. A long moment of hesitation, breath drying his mouth, then he crept in, bare feet noiseless on the carpeted passageway. Pause. Every moment he lingered increased the possibility he'd be discovered, but he knew somehow he had to take this terrible risk. He also knew that the people who had already murdered at least two people close to him, wouldn't hesitate to eliminate him if he was discovered. He took a deep ragged breath, stepped forward again and closed the door behind him. The latch made a soft snick when it closed. In Tanner's ears the sound was the boom of an iron door slamming shut behind him.

Ahead of him, music swelled. Down the corridor a few steps, he found a stairway to a lower level. The more utilitarian decor below the main deck indicated crew's quarters. A little way along, Tanner found an unlocked door. Inside a very small cabin, no more than a large storage locker, he found nine complete scuba-diving outfits and wetsuits, together with several racks of air tanks. Along another wall were three large black steel cabinets. He tried the doors. Two were locked. Inside the third Tanner found three shelves filled with brown, wax-coated pasteboard cartons. There were no markings and the boxes were all tightly sealed with strapping tape. Each shelf had a high lip, so the boxes crammed on the shelves were secure. He wondered what was in the cartons, but he didn't dare open or try to remove one. In the bottom of the cabinet was another carton. This one was open. In it, he found several World War Two vintage .45 caliber semi-automatics smeared with a thick coating of grease and wrapped in oiled paper. The weapons looked well used.

Now why, he wondered silently, would a luxury yacht carry a large quantity of old weapons? Very odd.

Tanner checked three other doors along the passage. None was unlocked. His fear of discovery was rapidly increasing. Although he had learned next to nothing, he broke off his prowl and retraced his way toward the main deck. Just as he entered that long, main corridor, a door opened toward the aft end and voices floated out. People were coming into the corridor! He ran, bolting through the door and out on deck. Tanner felt a tug at his wrist when he burst through the door but he went on without pausing or looking back. He dropped into a crouch against the bulkhead and checked the surroundings. He saw no one.

Starting toward the bow at a careful trot, he stopped short. Twenty feet away, two figures, outlined against the night glow, stood leaning on the rail right at the bow. Tanner looked to his left in case he had to jump for it, to see the rail eight feet away. The two men at the bow had a flashlight pointed at the water.

"See there," he heard. "I thought I felt something on the line. There's a piece of driftwood rubbing against the anchor chain."

Yeah. I see it. It's not big enough to worry about," said the other, snapping off the flashlight and turning back to the other side of the yacht, away from where Tanner knelt in the darkness. Instinctively he kept his head down so his white face wouldn't be visible.

Besides, the tide will carry it away pretty soon." They moved slowly down the deck, and one waved toward an unseen watcher on the bridge. The voices that had sent Tanner running to the deck were still behind him and getting louder.

Christ! he thought. They're coming out on deck!

Tanner silently willed the two crewmen to move faster down the other side of the yacht while he scuttled forward at about the same pace. He made it to the bow undetected, praying that whoever stood behind those dark windows on the bridge above him was looking elsewhere. His back itched and he felt horribly exposed. When he leaned down to go under the rail and grab the anchor chain, his left wrist hit a large cleat on the deck. He heard a soft thunk as he swung out and grabbed the anchor chain. It hung straight down. In the few minutes he'd been aboard, the tide had slackened and Goldenrod had ridden up over her anchor. Tanner went down the line into the water. With the chain hanging straight down, the link where Tanner had tied off his fins and snorkel was nearly two feet under water. Only a few inches of the board he'd brought still showed above the surface. Working quickly, almost soundlessly, he freed the wet knot and retrieved his gear from the chain and the piece of driftwood the crew members had been examining by flashlight. He was fortunate they hadn't noticed the line securing the fins and gloves to the driftwood. With a rush Tanner realized that if Goldenrod hadn't come up toward her anchor, his gear would have been in plain sight.

About to push off, Tanner became aware that two other

people had come forward and were standing at the rail near the bow, talking softly. Both were women and with a chill, Tanner recognized the voice of one, the voice he had heard earlier. It was Mary Whitney! Tanner almost lost hold of the driftwood. He felt as if he had been kicked in the stomach. Why was Mary Whitney aboard Goldenrod? How well did she know the owners? The captain? Was she a spy? After a few minutes of quiet conversation, while Tanner hung motionless below them in the water, the women moved away, voices fading. Alone again, Tanner groaned softly with a mixture of relief, anger and disbelief, then carefully paddled off, pushing the log before him. A hundred questions, all unresolved, went with him.

His return swim to the beached dinghy seemed to take forever. Twice Tanner stopped to rest, hanging in the sea, arms draped over the driftwood. After a while he began to wonder if he'd missed the little beach and was swimming into the channel and away from shore. Finally he came to a place where he recognized the faint profile of the hills and dragged himself, chilled and weary, over the gravel into the relative comfort of the dinghy.

20

Mary Whitney led her companion, Leticia Barnes, into the long main corridor and then stopped. Leticia, too close behind, bumped into Mary.

"Oops, sorry, Mary. You should signal when you stop so abruptly. Is something wrong?"

No. My mind is wandering, I guess. I just thought--" she smiled at her companion. Mary didn't voice the rest of her thought, but she couldn't have said why not. "I could swear somebody was just lurking in the passage just now. People pass back and forth in that corridor all the time, so what if there was someone?" She shrugged. But it felt wrong, as if whoever it was shouldn't have been there. But the passage was empty, so Mary dismissed her feeling as just another odd event on this trip.

A few minutes later, when she and Leticia strolled up to the bow of the vessel in hopes of seeing stars or the moon, Mary stepped on something small and hard. Already a bit unsettled, she checked her natural impulse to pick up the small object. The two women soon went back to the other guests in the main cabin.

Mary Whitney's feelings of unease persisted and now she'd stepped on something on the deck. It was unusual for anything to be lying loose on the deck. The crew of Goldenrod seemed almost obsessive about keeping the ship meticulously clean and well scrubbed. That even included the hull. Earlier in the trip, after she'd stumbled on that small room with all the scuba gear, she'd asked the steward about the large number of tanks and wet suits they carried. He merely shrugged as if he didn't know or care what she was talking about. Yet an hour later at lunch, here came Captain Trawley to her table.

Ah, Ms. Whitney. There you are." The captain smiled down at Mary and took the empty chair beside her. "I understand you've been wondering about our scuba gear."

Well, I suppose so. You seem to have a lot of it on board."

He laughed, completely at ease. "I guess it may seem so. To some."

A little condescension there, Mary wondered?

We frequently have guests aboard who want to scuba."

Mary couldn't remember it happening even once on the other trips she'd taken aboard Goldenrod.

"And the owners insist we keep Goldenrod's hull really shipshape."

What he was saying made sense; Mary knew a clean hull meant more speed and more efficient use of fuel. But frequent scrubbing seemed excessive. Most boat owners, herself included, only had the hull cleaned once or twice a year.

Captain Trawley was a large, bluff individual whose ready smile and courtly manner didn't extend to his cold appraising eyes. He suggested that Ms. Whitney might wish to be present the very next morning when the crew was scheduled to scrub the hull, right down to its keel.

Indeed she would, decided "Ms. Whitney" and at six next morning she was on deck in the chill sunlight to see four crew members, two of whom she was sure she had never previously laid eyes on, dangling over the side in pairs of bosun's chairs. Each held a bucket filled with some kind of sudsy liquid and a short-handled brush. Two others, working in the sea right at the waterline, were wearing scuba gear. The mate stood by on deck. When Mary approached, he eyed her warily. Mary got an impression that none of the men cared for the task.

Tonight, standing just inside the main saloon door, Mary recalled those earlier events. Now she'd stepped on something lying on deck. Her problem was how to retrieve it without calling attention to herself.

Excuse me, Ms. Whitney? Are you enjoying the party?"

Mary looked up and blinked back to the present. One of the ship's crew, resplendent in pressed whites, stood in front of her. He carried a tray of three cocktail glasses which he offered.

She smiled and shook her head. I can't just waltz back out there, she thought. I need an excuse. Mary crossed to the bar and got a drink from the bartender who looked a bit puzzled. Adroitly she fended off two insistent male guests who'd had too much from the well-stocked bar. After an hour, the excuse she sought was supplied by her friend.

"Listen, Mary," murmured Leticia Barnes. "I'm getting tired of beating off Handy Andy over there. Walk me to my cabin, will you?" The women said goodnight and left the party.

When they reached their side-by-side cabins, Mary started to fish her key out of her purse, then paused. "I'm starting to get a headache, Letty. I'll just take a quick walk on deck for some fresh air before I turn in."

Leticia Barnes nodded sympathetically. Mary went down the passageway and out onto the starboard deck. She passed a ladder leading to the next deck and looked up at Goldenrod's bridge. She could see a faint glow on the glass from several instruments and once, a dark shape passed across the windows. She knew that the bridge was manned night and day, whether under way or at anchor. An overriding concern for passenger safety, she'd been assured. At the time it had seemed reasonable, but she wondered whether watchful security might not be part of their concern.

When Leticia Barnes had called her with a last-minute invitation to join her on this early-season trip, Mary had agreed because it occurred to her that Goldenrod fit Tanner's description of the yacht he was looking for. So she'd flown to Nanaimo and joined the cruise there. It was an opportunity for her to eliminate Goldenrod from Tanner's list. Mary was not meddlesome by nature, but something in her had responded to Tanner when they first met, and that attraction was steadily growing. She didn't believe Goldenrod was Tanner's target, so she'd accepted the last-minute invitation.

For reasons she couldn't even explain to herself, she hadn't told those on board that she was acquainted with Michael Tanner, or that the "killer yacht" he had been describing sounded like Goldenrod. It certainly didn't occur to her that she might be in any personal danger. Tanner hadn't told her that a crew member had fired a shotgun at close range into the cabin of the Queen Anne. More than once.

She'd come aboard prepared to eliminate Goldenrod from Tanner's list. But she was discovering some things that didn't add up, like the extra scuba gear.

Mary stopped after walking slowly along the rail, breathing deeply, drawing in the tang of the sea air she loved. The salty air was mixed with the scent of pines growing along the shore. There wasn't the slightest breeze. No branches rattled on the shore, overhead the stars were blanketed by the overcast. She leaned over the rail and looked down at the black, quiet water. Only the mutter of a small outboard motor somewhere down the channel disturbed the night. She moved on again toward the bow, acting like a bored guest just out for a little fresh air. When she reached the rail at the very bow, her foot struck the same deck cleat Tanner had smacked, less than an hour before. She looked down and saw a small dark object lying beside the cleat. She leaned toward it and a voice came out of the dark.

Miss. Excuse me, are you all right?"

She straightened and turned toward the voice of the crew member standing at the door to the open wing of the bridge. "Yes, thank you," she called back. "I just needed a little fresh air. I'm fine now." Her fingers relaxed and her small purse plopped to the deck at her feet. Sure that the man couldn't see exactly what she was doing, she exclaimed, "Oh, I dropped my purse." She bent further and turned her body to shield her actions from the man. She scrabbled on the deck with both hands and swept the small object into her open purse.

The man hesitated. His order to never leave his post was explicit. Did the woman need help?

"I found it. Fortunately nothing spilled out." Mary noticed that her fingers were trembling slightly. Why is that, she wondered silently? She turned from the bow and retraced the steps back to the doorway behind the ladder to the bridge. Mary held the purse up so the man above her could see what she held. She smiled slightly.

"See? I feel much better now, thanks." Without breaking stride, she went through the door into the main passage, and on to her cabin.

For Tanner, the exhilaration of his night prowl was only now beginning to ebb. Climbing back aboard Sea Queen in the faint light that presages dawn, Tanner looked at his right wrist. "Damn!" The watch he prized so much, the one Beth had given him two years earlier, was gone. Then he remembered how he'd cracked his wrist on the door frame aboard Goldenrod and then hooked it again on something just as he was dropping down the anchor chain. He supposed the watch had fallen off on his swim back to the dinghy. A glance over the side confirmed that it wasn't lying on the bottom of the dinghy. Shivering from cold and still wondering about Mary Whitney's presence aboard Goldenrod, he went below and fell asleep in his bunk.

Safely inside her comfortable cabin, Mary Whitney examined the object she'd retrieved. It was an ordinary black-strapped digital watch which had obviously had hard wear on the arm of an active man. The pin that held the plastic strap to the watch case had been torn loose. She had seen other watches like it. She turned it over to look at the steel back. Then her head came up and she stared blankly at the bulkhead. The symbol etched on the back was familiar to her. It was the logo of Tanner's public relations firm. Where had it come from? Did Tanner wear such a watch?

Still, Mary reasoned, there were many similar watches. She knew from earlier experience that Tanner's firm sometimes gave similarly engraved watches to employees, and to clients for promotional purposes. It was hardly possible Tanner had been aboard Goldenrod and dropped this particular watch. Unless he had learned something new since she'd last seen him at Martin's Marina. Had he figured out that this was the yacht he sought? Was it possible the presence she had felt--or thought she felt--earlier in the passageway had been Tanner himself? It didn't seem possible. But if so, he was out there somewhere right now. But why? How had he come here? She sighed in frustration. There were no more answers to be found that night. She turned in, first burying the watch at the bottom of her luggage, inside her dirty laundry.

The next morning at breakfast, the first mate announced an abrupt change of plans. "I'm sorry and the captain apologizes, folks, but Goldenrod's owners have unexpectedly called us away." Mary glanced at Leticia Barnes, who raised an interrogative eyebrow. She didn't believe the mate's expressed sorrow, either.

"We'll drop you all at Campbell River. If you'll just put your names on these slips of paper and where you want to go from there, the Captain will make the necessary arrangements."

When Goldenrod passed Sea Queen on its way back down the channel, Tanner was still asleep. On Goldenrod's bridge a crew member noticed Sea Queen at anchor and pointed her out to the first mate.

"Yeah, I see it. I'll mention it to the Captain. Right now, we've got to be sure the air tanks are all checked and topped up. And for God's sake, keep the damn door locked."

In her cabin, Mary Whitney packed her belongings and wondered about the sudden change of plans. She glanced out the porthole occasionally, always appreciative of the magnificent scenery they were passing and saw the sloop anchored against a high bluff on the western shore of the channel.

"Now there's a good-looking Tartan," she thought. Then she started, recognizing Sea Queen, last seen lying quietly in a slip at Martin's marina, many miles to the south.

Twenty minutes passed and Mary felt Goldenrod's engines

slow to an idle. Curious, she went on deck to see one of Goldenrod's powerful motor launches hanging in a davit on the port side. Two men went over the side and stowed canvas duffel bags in the bottom of the boat. The first mate stood at the davit controls and, while Mary watched, lowered the launch into the sea. The two burly men unhooked the shackles and started the engine. With no conversation and no farewell wave to the mate, they headed out in a long curving path to the west. As soon as they'd gone, Goldenrod got under way again and resumed her course toward Campbell River. Mary went to the saloon for coffee. Had she watched a while longer, she might have seen the powerboat continue its curving path until it was headed back up the channel from whence Goldenrod had come.

21

Refreshed from his long sleep, Tanner fixed his first meal at noon and pondered his next move. He'd identified Goldenrod as the yacht that
ran him down, but he still had no proof of illegal activities. He knew the authorities wouldn't investigate without something more substantial than his accusations.

At least I know my target now, he mused. I can get some information in Seattle about the owners and crew. He stared at the bulkhead for a moment. What about the owners? Perhaps they had no idea what their crew was doing--whatever it was. If that was the case, Tanner knew his approach would have to be different. Any accusation now would only alert them that he was getting closer. He stood over the stove, frying a hamburger and thinking hard.

It was odd that the yacht carried that carton of old automatics though. Was ammunition stored in those other cartons? And why was Mary Whitney aboard Goldenrod? How did she fit? Was she a friend, or an enemy? All sorts of possibilities flitted through his mind from the paranoid to the frivolous.

He was still unaware that Goldenrod had slipped away from him and was even then crossing the Georgia Strait toward the harbor at Campbell River. Finally, Tanner decided to motor by Goldenrod's anchorage and find another place to stop, well west of her location. From his new vantage point he would watch her, and try to learn more about her activities.

But Goldenrod was gone.

Damn, he thought, gazing at the empty sea.

Tanner decided to return to the San Juan Islands and Martin's Marina, that he'd done as much as he could for now. He turned Sea Queen's bow about and motored slowly west along the channel. There was little wind, but he raised the mainsail. The farther west he went, the more wind he encountered. Soon a big light-air genoa strained from the forestay. Tanner worked his way under sail along Pryce Channel, still considering ways he could make a case against Goldenrod's crew.

Maybe I can find someone to introduce me to the owners, he thought. It's possible they don't know what's going on. Approached in the right way, the owners might be of more help then the authorities. Tanner sprawled in the cockpit, one leg cocked over the near coaming, his hand resting lightly on the wheel. He concentrated on the constantly shifting breeze and his thoughts about Goldenrod. Every few minutes he raised up and looked all around for possible hazards.

Maybe I could sue the owners in civil court, he mused, just to see what that might shake loose. Tanner was used to confronting problems head on in his business. When a situation arose, he would examine it and work out an appropriate solution. Here, the natural solution, an approach to the authorities, hadn't helped. He heard an engine approaching.

Looking ahead, Tanner saw a small motor launch with two men aboard, coming north across the wide channel directly toward him. Automatically he checked the depthfinder, the compass, and then his distance to the nearest land. Finally, he glanced at the sea behind him. Sea Queen and the approaching launch were the only craft in sight, and both had plenty of maneuvering room.

The motor launch from Goldenrod came on. It was

traveling at high speed, sending out a wide frothy rooster tail wake behind it. Tanner watched it approach, first with concern, now with growing anger. The launch driver didn't slow down.

What the hell? It's obvious they see me. Damn fools!

The two men in the boat stared at him across the narrowing strip of water. They didn't wave or acknowledge his presence. Tanner leaped to his feet and grabbed the pulpit rail to brace for a collision. At the last instant the man driving the launch twitched the wheel and altered course slightly. The change was just enough so they ran close under Sea Queen's bow. It happened so fast Tanner had no time to change his own course. The wake from the motor launch rocked Sea Queen. Her genoa collapsed and then filled again with a crack. Angrily, Tanner waved them off. The maneuver had been a direct challenge. He'd heard from other sailors about occasional abrasive encounters between sailors and powerboaters who resented each other for many reasons. But this seemed more aggressive than usual.

The powerboat cut sharply to the right between Tanner and the shore and ran in the opposite direction for a few moments. The sun came out from behind a small cloud and sparkled on the spray and the waves created by the launch. Tanner continued on his course, still watching as the powerboat turned like a bee circling a flower. Much faster than the larger Sea Queen, the launch ran across his stern, then circled again to draw up to Sea Queen's left rear quarter.

Now what, Tanner wondered?

The launch ran alongside the cockpit and the man at the wheel cut the power so his boat dropped suddenly off the step and then, by playing his throttle, neatly matched Sea Queen's speed. The bellow of the engine dropped to a tolerable mutter. Tanner couldn't see any numbers or name painted on the sides or stern of the boat.

"Ahoy, mate," came the hail.

Tanner raised a hand, not bothering to conceal his

annoyance. "Cutting it close there, weren't you?" he snapped.

"Aw, sorry, mate, just havin' a bit a fun." The burly man sounded faintly English, or perhaps Australian.

"What can I do for you?"

"We're a little thirsty, got a cold beer about?" Tanner noticed that the second man said nothing during this exchange, but his eyes were never still, examining Tanner, scanning the deck of Sea Queen all the way to the bow, and then back again to Tanner in the cockpit.

The hair on Tanner's neck prickled. This encounter was more than coincidence. He forced a neutral tone to his voice. "Sorry, fresh out. Just drank the last one." He held up an empty can to add emphasis. His unease grew.

"Well then," said the first man, "how 'bout a cool glass of water? We'll just tie off here and come aboard. You can keep right on goin' down this channel like you are. We won't delay you none."

"Sorry, I never allow strangers aboard while I'm at sea."

The little launch began falling behind.

The man at the wheel revved his engine and said something to his companion that Tanner didn't hear. He brought the craft right up against Sea Queen so their hulls banged together. The second man reached out a hand to grasp the scupper rail that ran along the outside of Sea Queen's deck.

"Hey there," Tanner cried. "Bear off. You'll gouge my hull." The two men ignored his protest.

"Be reasonable, mate," the man at the wheel shouted over the engine noise. "Just let us come aboard for a drink of water!"

Tanner waved them off again and shouted back, "Back off! I'll pass you the water jug!"

He knew that if he left the cockpit, they could climb aboard before he could return from below. It would be almost impossible to keep them off if they made a determined assault. Why were they hesitating? Maybe, he thought, they aren't sure I'm the only one aboard.

He reached to his feet and found the plastic gallon jug of water he had filled the night before to carry in the dinghy. The water would be tepid and a little stale, but at that moment, Tanner didn't care. He decided he wasn't going to let either man aboard without a fight.

The launch driver again shifted to neutral, idling his engine. The second man changed his grasp on Sea Queen's scupper rail so he could reach up with his other hand. Tanner passed over the jug, carefully keeping his hand away from the man's grasp.

"You sail out here much?" asked the driver.

"Some," said Tanner, taking a quick look to be sure his course was still clear. There was a wide expanse of intensely blue water ahead and no other boats in sight.

"You men from that yacht I saw yesterday? Goldenrod?"

"Why d'you ask?" said the man at the wheel.

"No particular reason. Good-looking vessel."

"Well, take care," said the man with the jug. He wiped his mouth with the back of his hand. "These can be dangerous waters. Lots of shipwrecks hereabouts." He waved his arm in a random sweep. "You sailin' alone?"

"No," Tanner lied. He tried to keep his voice even and casual. "One of my business associates is in his bunk, sleeping off a late night."

"Must be a pretty hard sleeper, not to hear our engine out here," said the driver.

Tanner shrugged.

The breeze had steadily increased and he was forced to pay more attention to his helm. The big genoa luffed and then filled again, sending a shudder through the Tartan. He glanced at the sail and back at the launch, trying to split his attention so he didn't give away even a small advantage to the men in the launch. It was becoming harder for the second man to keep his hold on Sea Queen. Tanner judged that it wouldn't be long before he'd have to let go or be dragged over the side.

At that moment the wind dropped.

Tanner had a sudden premonition that an unspoken message had passed between the two men. They'd decided to board Sea Queen and jump him. He glanced about. There was a winch handle in easy reach, but it made an awkward weapon. Then he remembered the flare pistol. He reached into the small cubby hole beside his left knee and fumbled open the signal flare case stored there. The bright orange flare launcher was shaped like a pistol. Tanner knew he wouldn't be able to load it with one hand, and Sea Queen was straining against the rudder. The pistol fired a 12-gauge shotgun shell with a special load. At close range it would seriously injure a man. They wouldn't know the pistol wasn't loaded but it might intimidate them long enough so he could maneuver some distance between the boats. He was pretty sure that if he could get his engine going and get up some speed, he could maneuver Sea Queen to keep the men from boarding, unless they had grappling hooks or strong casting tackle. He didn't dare provoke the men by starting the engine while they were still attached to the hull like a leech.

"Through with my water jug?" he asked evenly, staring down at the men.

"Sure, man," said the driver. His companion stood and reached a hand to the lifeline above his head. It looked innocent enough, as if he just wanted to steady himself, but Tanner knew the man was about to swing himself aboard. Sweat ran down his nose.

He hunched over slightly and took the flare pistol in one hand. The launch driver suddenly rose up on his toes and looked ahead. At that moment, all three men became aware of a thrumming in the air, which rapidly became the sounds of several large marine engines. Around the gentle bend just ahead came six big cabin cruisers. Arrayed in a casual vee behind the leading cruiser, a power squadron swept down on Sea Queen and her harasser.

The second man in the launch grunted something

unintelligible and tossed the water jug into Sea Queen's cockpit. Tanner straightened and revealed the flare launcher in his hand. The man beside the driver let go of Sea Queen and for a moment the two boats hung there side by side, then slowly the wind drew the yacht away.

Tanner altered course slightly, seeing the gap the powerboats had created in their formation to allow Sea Queen to safely pass through. They drew abreast and the lead cruiser throttled back to reduce his wake. The man at the wheel, high on her flying bridge, waved at Tanner. He waved back, thinking, boy am I glad to see you guys. I'll never complain again about engine noise.

Tanner looked down and, saw that the launch had fallen behind Sea Queen. The men stared sullenly at him, and at the bright orange flare pistol in his hand. Abruptly their boat lunged forward, raised up on its step and charged down on Sea Queen, narrowly missing her and again rocking the sailboat with its wake. The pilot of the nearest power cruiser, seeing the near collision, sounded his horn in raucous warning. Other cruisers took up the cry as they passed and for a moment, Tanner and Sea Queen were surrounded by waves, roaring engines, and the hooting bellow of electric air horns.

Tanner waved again at the passing powerboat skippers and then trimmed his sails for more speed. The power cruisers continued along Pryce Channel, rounded a curve and passed out of sight. The echoing sound of their engines was soon smothered in the forests on the mountain slopes. The wind held and Tanner continued on course, west along the channel. The launch also continued west at high speed until it was a tiny black speck on the sparkling sea and eventually was lost from sight. Tanner checked his chart of the area and once more swept the channel with his binoculars.

"Good, they're out of sight. I hope they stay that way," he muttered and changed course, now angling across the channel to bring him nearer the south shore. It occurred to Tanner the launch might return when he was once again alone.

But he reasoned that the two men had now been seen by several other people. If Tanner and Sea Queen disappeared, someone on those launches would remember seeing Tanner and the two men in the launch. He continued to watch carefully through his binoculars, trying to pick out any sign that the motor launch was returning.

After a few minutes sailing along the south shore, he came about, reversing his direction. A short time earlier he'd passed the narrow opening to Waddington Channel that separated East and West Redondo Islands. It was his most direct route south and he hoped that by sailing down Waddington, he would permanently lose the motor launch. He sailed east with the wind now on his left side and the opening to Waddington Channel soon appeared. With a last look back from where he had come, he turned south. When he entered the narrower channel, his sails were blanketed by the mountains. Tanner dropped them to the deck, started his engine, and motored swiftly on, the sound reverberating between the green, heavily timbered hills.

A few miles south, according to his charts, lay Allies Island, sheltering three small coves often used for overnight anchorages. Tanner hoped he'd find some company in those coves. An occasional glance behind him showed only empty blue water. The launch did not reappear. When he arrived at Allies, he was pleased to see three boats in one bay, two motor cruisers and a small sloop.

22

Tanner cruised slowly into the bay off Allies Island and surveyed his options, like any prudent yachtsman entering an unfamiliar anchorage. He wanted to anchor where it would be hard for someone to reach Sea Queen without passing close by other boats in a dinghy. But he also wanted to be far enough from the shore so no one could board the boat except from the water. He felt protected from the men in the launch as long as there were other boats around. He was sure that whoever they were, the men in that launch didn't want to be seen with Tanner by anyone who might turn into an embarrassing witness. In this anchorage, the crew from Goldenrod posed the biggest threat after dark, and that could be a very tricky business.

He found a place to his liking and with the motor in neutral, drifted over the spot. He trotted forward and dropped the hook, snaking the anchor line through a block at the bow. Then he dragged the line back along the deck to the cockpit, so he could control it from the wheel while he backed away. Once he felt the Danforth anchor take hold in the bottom, Tanner slowly motored back and paid out the line. When he reached the spot he wanted for Sea Queen, he snubbed off the line, shifted to neutral and rested for a few minutes. Then he went below and got a cool beer, smiling wryly as he opened it. At Sea Queen's navigation station he checked the book of tide tables to be sure the outgoing tide wouldn't set him aground. Back on deck, he took a long swig of beer and glanced casually around. Sailors on other boats were sitting in their cockpits. Tanner waved at those who seemed to be watching and then opened a locker under one of the cockpit benches. He hauled out a second, smaller anchor and laid it on the deck. Then he motored back until Sea Queen's stern was a couple of feet from the sheer rock cliff at his back. He dropped the second anchor right off the stern and reversed his direction, dragging the anchor until it caught. Tanner slackened the stern line and pulled in the bow line until he had Sea Queen positioned between the two anchors. He worked cautiously, moving easily in Sea Queen's cockpit. He'd never used the double anchor technique before, but he'd carefully studied it in the sailing books, and he'd watched boats at Martin's Marina set two anchors. With Sea Queen tied off between the two anchors, neither tidal currents nor wind would cause the yacht to swing into rocks or nearby boats and she now lay a considerable distance from the steep, brush-choked, shore of the bay.

Satisfied he was as safe as he could be, Tanner stretched out in the sunny cockpit to finish his beer, finally able to relax and let loose some of his tension after a wearing afternoon. Directly in front of him a vertical cliff of ancient rock rose forty feet in the air. He rested his head on a cushion and felt the sun warm on his face. It was an almost perfect afternoon.

"Nicely done, sir. My compliments."

The voice came from behind and slightly below him. Tanner sat up quickly. He'd dozed off in the sun, and hadn't heard the approach of the man paddling the little rubber dinghy.

"Thank you," he responded, looking down at his visitor.

"I take it you're sailing single-handed. Most people wouldn't go to that much trouble to anchor, even with crew to help."

"I know, especially not in such peaceful conditions." Tanner saw from the name neatly lettered on the side of the dinghy that the speaker was from the sloop anchored at the outside edge of the little bay. "I like to practice routines like that whenever I can so I remember the drills when they're needed." Tanner smiled at the ruddy-faced man. "But it is more work."

"George McReady here. Out of Vancouver. I do a bit of construction now and again."

"Michael Tanner from Seattle. Public relations is my game." McReady nodded. Tanner couldn't see any particular reaction to his name. Either McReady didn't know about Beth Tanner's death and the subsequent investigation or he was a terrific poker player.

McReady nodded again, waved and resumed his solitary paddle around the little bay. A few minutes later he drifted by again.

"Ahoy again, Mr. Tanner."

"Yes?"

"I've just had a word with my wife, Polly."

Tanner raised his eyebrows. McReady grinned and showed Tanner the walkie-talkie in a holster under his jacket.

"We've a couple of very nice steaks I'm planning to grill this evening," he went on, "plenty for three. Since you're alone, perhaps you'll join us?"

Tanner grinned. He'd just been thinking about whether to open a can of stew or pork and beans. Tired of his spartan meals, he accepted with alacrity. "Thank you very much. I'll be pleased to join you"

"Done. See you about six-thirty, then."

After McReady paddled back to his sloop, Tanner stripped and dove into the sea. He swam briskly twice around Sea Queen, and then climbed back aboard and went to the shower. At six-twenty he paddled across the bay to the McReady's sloop. He tied up to the ladder and handed up a bottle of merlot he'd found in one of the galley lockers.

"Ah, very nice. Welcome aboard," said McReady, giving him a hand.

"Thanks, I was getting tired of my own cooking."

McReady, a big, raw-boned man with a seamed, leathery face and the hard hands of a man who spent time working outdoors, turned back to check the steaks already sizzling on the grill hanging off the stern of their vessel.

"Mr. Tanner. I'm pleased to make your acquaintance. I'm Polly McReady."

Tanner turned to see a tall slender woman with lustrous

dark hair emerging from the companionway carrying a large wooden bowl filled with an assortment of greens. She set the bowl on the cockpit table and extended her hand. Tanner shook, discovering she had a strong grip. She smiled into his eyes.

"I hope you can forego starch this evening. We've run out of decent potatoes, so I decided that steak and a fresh salad would do."

"That'll do very well. I haven't had a good salad in several days."

"It's such a nice evening, I thought we could eat on deck, though it's a bit crowded in this cockpit."

"Fine with me." The arrangement would also allow Tanner to keep an eye on Sea Queen. No other boats had entered the little bay after Tanner arrived, and he'd seen no one aboard the forty-five-foot Hattaras motor launch anchored close to the shore, so he was relaxed, but he couldn't avoid remaining alert.

McReady liked his steaks on the rare side which suited Tanner. The salad, which Polly McReady served, was fresh and the tangy herb dressing nicely complemented the red wine and the steaks.

"How do you keep salad greens so fresh," asked Tanner?

"I bought the lettuce this morning from a fisherman we encountered. The rest we picked along the shore when we stopped for lunch. Some of those greens you're eating are frequently called weeds. I've been a student of natural foods for many years. I can always find the odd grass or other plants that are safe and provide a tasty counterpoint to more usual greens."

"You know, George, I was thinking about what you said. And I put it together. You're THE George McReady of McReady Construction, the biggest construction firm in British Columbia."

George smiled and nodded.

"George tends to be a bit modest when he meets people outside the business," smiled Polly.

"We've never met before, Mr. Tanner, but I recall that your firm bid on an annual report project for us a few years ago."

"I guess we lost the bid."

McReady laughed. "Yes, we decided it would be better

to go with a Canadian company, although I liked your proposal very much."

As the evening went along, Tanner floated a few questions about Goldenrod, and then about the Whitney family, eventually getting around to Mary Whitney. The McReady's acknowledged that they knew Mary Whitney but had no personal insights to offer. Tanner sensed that neither of the McReadys was prone to gossip.

No direct mention had been made of Tanner's loss or his search for the killer yacht. The trio finished the bottle of wine and Tanner said goodbye. Polly and George McReady stood close together and watched Tanner paddle slowly across the water, following the beam from the masthead light and another in the cabin shining the way to Sea Queen, "Poor blighter," murmured McReady.

"I think he's a good man," said Polly. "I wonder if he thinks Goldenrod is the ship that ran him down."

"Doesn't seem likely, but there's always been something odd about her. He seems quite interested in Mary Whitney, doesn't he?"

"Mmm. Of course, we don't know Michael Tanner at all, but my instincts about men are pretty good and--"

"Right you are. After all, you chose me."

"--and I think Mary Whitney could do worse, a whole lot worse."

In the early morning, Tanner followed the mist and slipped out of the little cove to motor south. Several hours later he entered the harbor of the little mainland hamlet of Lund. The public docks stood out clearly, the government-painted bright red railings, visible from a distance. Tanner moored Sea Queen in an empty slip. The harbormaster suggested that since it was late, he replenish his fuel and water in the morning.

Tanner walked up the hill to the lone restaurant in town. A large sign on a knoll overlooking the harbor proclaimed Lund the end of the highway. Behind the town he glimpsed an empty, two-lane blacktop road that wound its lonely way back into the wooded hills of British Columbia.

In the crowded, noisy restaurant, he found a seat at one of the long plank tables with several locals. There was no menu; one ate whatever the meal of the day happened to be. The food was plain, well-prepared meat and potatoes with thick brown gravy, and an overcooked side dish of canned green beans. It all tasted delicious.

He talked with his table companions, asking questions about Goldenrod.

"She sounds familiar, the way you describe her," one man remarked in a husky voice. Others nodded. "She's probably been in here a time or two. But I can't say much more than that. We get quite a few stopping by for fuel or water and the odd bit."

Another man recollected he'd helped service one of their motor launches and found the launch driver surly and untalkative.

"I'm pretty sure her home port is San Francisco," said a woman at one end of the table. "I watched her leave the harbor a couple of months ago, and I recall thinking how much money was tied up in something not so useful."

Tanner smiled, knowing that most of the people in the room would also consider his sailboat as "something not so useful."

Conversation in the restaurant turned to other topics. "Well, Yank, are you pleased with your new president?"

Tanner shrugged. "I don't know yet. Sometimes the man grows into the job. I think he needs more time. Then we'll see."

"Ah, politicians, they're all crooks, you ask me," from a bearded giant down at the other end of the table.

"How's the fishing?" asked Tanner. He found himself relaxing. He enjoyed being with these people. A torrent of complaints and firmly held opinions followed his question.

"They put any more limits on us, we'll all be out of work and starving. Then what?"

"Well, Jock, if we over-fish the strait and the salmon are gone, what then? Same result, eh?"

"Never happen," said another. "The fish, they always come back." The arguments, obviously familiar to all, raged contentedly around the room.

Lund owed its existence primarily to the continued good health and abundance of salmon. Decades of persistent over-fishing had caused regulations to be imposed in order to maintain the long-term health of the industry. Those regulations required shorter fishing seasons and smaller catches. That in turn meant less income for the fishermen.

Early the next morning, dawn sent streams of light down the mountain to play languidly across the quiet harbor. Silvery wisps of mist curled across the water and wound their inquisitive way through the trees. It played among the masts. Tanner awoke to a stillness that penetrated everything. The birds were silent; it was as if all of nature held its breath. Tanner moved carefully about Sea Queen to avoid disturbing the natural tranquillity. He looked, delighted, around the little bay. He saw others doing the same. Even a huge black Labrador, standing rigid in the bow of a departing fishing boat seemed to sense the special feeling. It was a stolen moment, frozen in time. For just those few seconds, the mystery and the threat of Goldenrod seemed inconsequential.

23

Two days later, having made his peace with a mildly disgruntled John Martin, Tanner was back at work in the marina. Today he was standing on a ladder suspended over the water, five feet below the deck level, replacing worn dock fenders. He glanced up to see a pair of female feet firmly planted before his eyes. Following the sharp creases of her tan slacks upward, he saw a serious-faced Mary Whitney.

"I haven't seen you around in a while," she said. "I find I miss our conversations."

Tanner raised his eyebrows and smiled at her. Until that moment, he had wrestled with whether to confront her with the knowledge of her presence aboard Goldenrod. Unable to decide, he'd avoided her. But he found that he missed her, too.

"How 'bout dinner tonight?" he asked.

"Oh, good," she smiled down at him. "I just knew I could maneuver you into an invitation if I worked it right, Mr. Tanner." He noted her slight emphasis on the mister. Mary smiled again and went off down the dock. Tanner followed her with his eyes, still wondering how to ask her about Goldenrod.

That evening in the dining room of the resort, their conversation lacked its usual raillery and time passed in fits and starts. They both felt an uneasy strain.

"What've you been up to?" Mary finally asked over her after-dinner brandy.

"Oh, you know," he hedged. "Working. I took a few days off and rented the Tartan for a little sail up the passage."

"I know," she said. "How do you like her? The Tartan, I mean."

"Nice boat. Well set up and well kept. Her owner must know boats and have some money. Someday I'd like to own a boat like Sea Queen."

"Oh? I though you were just a casual sailor, basically an urban type."

"A couple of years ago I would have agreed with you, but working here these two seasons and this business about finding Goldenrod--" Tanner stopped abruptly and looked down at the white tablecloth. Damn! He hadn't meant to name the vessel he was searching for. Silently he cursed his slip and then looked up, warily watching for Mary's reaction.

She frowned at him. "So, now you're sure that's the name of the yacht you've been looking for?"

"Oh," he waved one hand in a meaningless gesture. "I'm not positive. It just slipped out. But that name has cropped up a couple of times, and she sounds like a possible fit." He hoped he sounded casual enough. "Why?"

"Coincidence, I guess." Her smile came and went like a light bulb flickering in a bad socket. "I was aboard her last week for a few days."

Her bald admission startled him. "You were?"

"Yes. My former husband was once on the board of the corporation in California that owns her. They still invite me on cruises. Even after the divorce, I am after all a Whitney, you know." She raised her chin and stared down her nose at him in a parody of a socialite. "These little trips are partly business related. I'm sorry this latest cruise came up after you and I had made dinner plans. Weeks ago I'd accepted for their next outing. But at the time the dates weren't firm. And then when my friend called to plead with me to join her, I flew to Nanaimo. You got my note?"

Tanner shrugged. Because of his own abrupt decision to sail north, he hadn't received Mary's note until he'd returned to the marina. The note had done little to calm his concerns.

"It was a little odd this time, though," she went on. "We expected to cruise for two weeks around the northern islands, but after a few days they told us there'd been a sudden change in plans. I guess the owners needed Goldenrod for other business. They hustled us ashore at Campbell River. The captain apologized, but I think they were actually glad to get rid of us."

Tanner sensed she was studying him for a reaction. He frowned at the tablecloth.

"Sounds like something serious came up," said Tanner. The silence stretched out. When Tanner looked up again, Mary was looking at him intently.

"What?"

She blinked. "What time is it?"

Tanner reached to shove back his sleeve, then remembered. "Uh. I don't have a watch on. Sorry." There was another lapse in their conversation.

Mary Whitney shifted in her chair and said, "I guess I'm not very good company tonight. Let's call it a night."

Tanner gaped at her. He'd never seen her change moods so abruptly. Then she leaned forward and touched his hand.

"I'm sorry. It's not you. It was a lovely dinner. I guess I'm more tired than I thought I was. It isn't your fault."

Tanner wasn't convinced.

Mary Whitney rose, touched his hand again and left the room without a backward glance. As she walked out of the dining room, her fingers touched the small package in her purse. Why didn't I just give him the watch, she thought? As soon as I was sure it was his, I should have just handed it to him and told him where I found it.

Tanner sat and replayed the conversation in his mind, like it was a video presentation to one of his clients. What was going on? Mary had seemed ill at ease the whole evening. His concerns about her came back to him. Was she a plant? Was she staying at the marina to keep tabs on him? It didn't seem possible. He paid the dinner tab and stopped in the bar for a drink.

He strolled back to his room in the cool evening air, hoping there was a logical explanation for her presence. When he turned the corner of the upstairs hallway, he saw that the door to his room was ajar. There were no locks on the doors, so valuables were carried by the occupants or left in Martin's safe. But he was sure he'd closed the door when he left.

He pushed the door open and stood there a moment looking in. Nothing. He could see the whole room from the door. It was empty. Beside the bed was a little side table and on it a small brown paper sack that hadn't been there when he left for dinner with Mary.

Tanner sat on the bed and picked up the sack. Gingerly he opened it. Inside was his missing watch and a folded piece of paper. He recognized the marks and scratches immediately.

The paper was a note from Mary Whitney. Thanks for dinner, she'd written. I noticed you didn't have your watch on today. If you've lost it, here's a replacement. It isn't new, but it has special meaning for me and I'd like you to have it.

Tanner exhaled noisily. He didn't know what to make of it. He strapped on the watch, his mind busy with new questions. Why hadn't she given it to him at supper? What did the note mean? Of course he'd wear it. But how did she come by it? Did she find it on Goldenrod? Of course! That must have been where he dropped it. But why was she returning it in such an odd way? Maybe she wasn't sure it was his, or was she using the watch as a warning to him to stay away from Goldenrod? He rose off the bed to go down the hall to the phone to call her. At the door he stopped. No, he decided. I'll talk to her tomorrow face to face. But what would he say?

Puzzling over questions and fragments of information that tumbled through his mind, he stripped and went to bed. For a long time he lay in the dark while sleep eluded him.

24

The next morning when Tanner called the hotel, Mary Whitney was not in her room and no one seemed to know her whereabouts. For two days Tanner went on with his routine work at the marina and wondered where Mary Whitney was hiding. If she was hiding. He was once again repairing dock fenders, a constant necessity, when the object of his concern walked down the dock toward him. He looked up at her and held up his wrist.

"Thanks for the watch," he said evenly. "I lost one just like this last week. I appreciate the gift."

"You're welcome." She sounded normal. Nothing in her manner or expression seemed the least bit unusual. She watched his eyes closely.

"Kind of an odd way of delivering it, though." He studied her for a reaction. "Where did you get a watch with our logo on it?"

Mary's expression smoothed out and became almost bland. Her experience in board rooms helped her mask the uncertainty she was feeling. There was an awkward pause. "Yes, well ... I'll talk to you later. Got some errands to run." Uncharacteristically ill at ease, Mary turned and walked off the dock. She'd thought a good deal about her surreptitious visit to Tanner's room to leave him the watch. It wasn't something she would normally do. Why she'd done it was still an enigma to her. This is crazy. I'm attracted to him, she thought, but I don't know how to deal with the presence of his wife. It's almost as if she's still alive in his mind. Maybe if I can help him answer questions about Goldenrod, and find the real yacht that ran him down, we can develop a relationship. She realized then that Tanner was the first man since her divorce with whom she was interested in developing a serious relationship. Shaking her head, Mary walked swiftly off the pier.

Damn, Tanner thought, watching her go, that was a stupid thing to say. I should have just accepted the watch and thanked her for it.

Tanner thought about what Mary had said about the guests' abrupt departure from the yacht and decided that the captain of Goldenrod must have acquired some new information to so suddenly ship his guests ashore, and that their change of plans had nothing to do with his clandestine prowl. He figured that if a crew member of Goldenrod had found his watch, they would already have taken aggressive action against him. The men in the launch had been a little tentative in their approach, as if they were looking for something. Or maybe his easy lie about not being alone on board had put them off.

If Mary was part of whatever illegal business they were engaged in, returning his watch was her own initiative. It continued to bother him that she'd been aboard Goldenrod. But he knew he would still pursue the elusive yacht.

Tanner finished with the fenders and went looking for Martin. He found him bent over the engine of his old truck, out behind the office. "John, I've got to go back up north again, and soon. I have to find out what the operators of Goldenrod are doing. That's the only way I'm ever going to learn why they sank my boat. I know this is kind of sudden, but I'll make it up to you."

Martin raised up and looked at the younger man. He slowly wiped his greasy hands on an old towel. "Okay, Tanner. I figured this might happen. I don't suppose I have to tell you to be careful, and remember that you haven't even a shred of real proof that Goldenrod is the right ship." All you've really got is your memory and a gut feeling." He wiped a smear of grease off his face. "I still think your plan to scope out her owners is better."

Tanner shrugged. "I had a call this morning from one of

my partners in Seattle. He had a lot on the data communications company in California that owns Goldenrod, but nothing to suggest anything illegal or even questionable. I've got him doing more research on the individual directors, but my gut feeling is there's nothing to find. I suspect Goldenrod's crew is running a rogue operation."

"Whatever is going on, it must involve Goldenrod's captain," Martin commented.

"Sure. The obvious possibility is drug smuggling. Her sailing patterns are odd from what I've been able to learn. Lots of isolation, aimless wandering. Of course, I still don't have the whole picture. Damn it! This is frustrating. I thought about filing a civil suit, but as you pointed out, I still can't prove Goldenrod is the right boat." He paced up and down beside the truck. "That's the main reason I'm going again. If I can catch them in something illegal, maybe then I can get the authorities to take a closer look." He shrugged

"When do you leave?" Martin asked quietly, smothering his concern.

"I've requested more money from Seattle, so I'll go tomorrow after it comes. On the late tide. Besides, I want to replace the dock fenders on a couple more of the fingers."

Martin laughed and waved him away.

That evening, Tanner and Mary again had supper together, this time in a small inland bar on the island. The place had a well-earned local reputation for fried clams.

"I'm glad we came here," Mary was putting away her plate of clams with steady efficiency. "These are really good!"

"I like a woman with a healthy appetite." He grinned. "I'm glad we came here, too," he said, "it's just the kind of place one likes to bring a friend." He inhaled deeply, savoring the mixture of beer, cooking aromas and sea food.

Mary looked across the oilcloth-covered table at him. The table was littered with the residue of their meal. "I hope we are friends, Michael Tanner. I'd like that."

He considered her answer. Yes, he'd like that too. He'd

never looked at another woman while Beth was alive and since her murder, his alcoholic binges and self-abasement had depressed any interest in women. But he was aware of changes. Since cleaning up his life, and in spite of his near-obsession with finding Beth's killers, his interests in other aspects of life were growing. Mary Whitney was an important part of that growth.

"Mary, I'm leaving again and I've chartered the same boat I had the last time. I expect to be gone even longer than before. Probably for several weeks."

"Are you going after Goldenrod again?" She frowned at him.

He ignored her question. "I'm leaving tomorrow afternoon with the tide so we won't see each other for a while. I know we talked about some outings, but this is something I have to do. I'd have left tonight, but I'm waiting for mail from Seattle." He stopped and licked his lips. "I'm going to miss you."

Mary just looked at him and then she said, "If you leave on the flood tide you'll go around supper time?"

"That's right."

"Sailing all night?"

"Sure, but I've discovered that I like to do that, and I'll get up to Desolation Sound quicker and easier going with the tide."

"Your clams are getting cold," she said. "I volunteer to help you shop for provisions. But Michael," her fingers were warm on the back of his hand, "if you're going to try to force a confrontation with Goldenrod, forget it. I've been aboard her, remember? They have a big crew--all very capable looking."

"Well." Tanner hesitated, still wondering if he could completely trust her. Anyway, there was no reason to involve her any further. "I appreciate your concern, but confrontation isn't the idea. I haven't had much time to sail this summer and I find I miss it." Tanner stopped and looked at Mary Whitney in the warm candlelight. He didn't like lying to this woman sitting across from him. Then it struck him there was a lot of truth in his statement about sailing. He did miss it. It brought a kind of calm and relaxation he hadn't known much of. If he could combine his search with sailing, so much the better.

The morning ferry brought an envelope with his requested cash, and a short written report on the directors of the corporation that owned Goldenrod. The report repeated what Tanner had learned on the telephone with a few additional details. There was little new information in the pages. Mary helped him shop for provisions as she'd promised and together they carried them aboard Sea Queen. They stood close together in the cockpit.

"I'll come by later to see you off," she said. She raised her head and looked him in the eye. "Be careful up there," she said. "I wouldn't want to lose a new friend."

Tanner had a sudden impulse to kiss her on the cheek. He suppressed it and the moment passed. She looked at him as if she knew what was in his mind, then turned and hopped ashore.

"Remember, I go with the tide, about six." He watched her go, appreciating the image of her lithe figure striding down the dock. Tanner turned to storing the provisions. Then he went to his room and packed his duffel. He settled affairs with John Martin, promised to call occasionally, and sat down in the sun on the warm dock to wait for the tide.

Mary did not return.

By four-thirty the sun had started its retreat and the tide was nearly at its lowest ebb. A tiny niggling worm of worry began to gnaw at Tanner. Where was Mary? He didn't want to delay his departure. Was she even now trying to reach a contact aboard Goldenrod with a warning? He hated the thought, but his doubts refused to fade. In spite of his doubt, he realized that he wanted to see her one more time for more personal reasons before he sailed. He knew he would miss her.

The sun slid faster toward the horizon. The harbor master closed and locked his tiny cubicle, waved to Tanner and sauntered off. He wouldn't return until morning, unless there was an emergency at the marina. The tide was on the verge of turning and soon would create powerful north-running currents that he would use to reach Campbell River as quickly as possible. That was where he intended to base his renewed search, continuing until he located Goldenrod.

He ran down the dock and tried Mary's room from the pay phone at the end of the wharf.

There was no answer.

Tanner took one last look around the harbor, cast off and began his journey north.

Several hours later, the wind rose in the dark night just as it had on his first voyage aboard Sea Queen. The moon sailed serenely through scattered clouds. In its first quarter, it radiated little light.

This time Tanner was better prepared. The small working jib was ready to hand when he dropped the big genoa. He went to the bow to change sails. He'd just about completed the job and was hooking the halyard to the eye in the head of the sail when he heard a loud bang, somewhere below.

He froze, listening. After another sharp bang, everything was quiet below deck. He strained to hear. The noise had sounded like a door slamming against a bulkhead, but how could that be? He'd checked that everything was secure before he set sail.

There were no more sounds except the creaking of the rigging and the normal sounds of the sea as Sea Queen sailed serenely northwest up the passage.

Had a drawer or hatch come loose? I better take a look, he thought to himself while he finished rigging the sail. Crawling back aft, the halyard in one fist, he reached the mast. He raised his head and looked toward the cockpit. In the starlight he saw the silhouette of a seated figure. He was no longer alone.

Casting about for some kind of weapon, he put his hand on the winch attached to the mast. In a holster just below the winch was a large handle used to crank the sails up. Tanner pulled the winch handle free and started slowly aft, praying any noise he made would be covered by the sounds of the yacht and the sea. He bent low to remain as invisible as possible while he crept slowly toward the cockpit. The dimly seen figure, seated to one side of the wheel didn't move, except to sway with the rocking, plunging yacht.

Plunging.

Tanner became aware that the sea was getting choppier as the wind continued to rise. Sea Queen needed a hand at the tiller. But who was in the cockpit? He reached the edge of the cabin roof and began to raise the winch handle above his shoulder.

"Michael? Where are you? My eyes haven't adjusted yet."

God, it was Mary Whitney! Tanner's breath exploded noisily and his arm fell limply to his side. "Whatinhellareyoudoinghere?" he yelled at her, voice rising.

"Just protecting my investment," she called back. "Now come down here off the cabin roof."

"What investment? He clambered into the cockpit just as a big wave rolled up on the stern and sent cold spray into his face. "Here," he sputtered, "keep her steady while I get that jib up."

Sea Queen responded immediately to the hand on her wheel and the set of the jib, and settled down to a rolling, quartering tack, the big following seas that blew up behind the yacht no longer threatening to swamp the cockpit.

"You take the wheel now and I'll make some coffee," Mary said, as if it was the most natural thing in the world for her to do.

"Coffee? Forget coffee. I want to know why you're here."

Mary just turned and went toward the hatch. She waved a hand and disappeared below. Tanner stared at the dark hatch and realized that he was glad she was aboard. All thoughts about finding a convenient place to put her ashore faded away. Even with his doubts about her, he was glad for her company. She could help sail the boat, keep watch. Another set of hands would be welcome.

Below in the cabin, Mary switched on red lights so she could see, lights that would preserve most of her night vision. Tanner hadn't known about the red night lights, except over the chart table. Had she sailed before on this boat? And then understanding came to him. Of course. She owned the yacht. Sea Queen was the investment she'd said she was protecting. Sure that Tanner would have refused to take her along if she'd asked, she'd stowed away, gambling he wouldn't want to take the time to put her off. He smiled to himself.

Tanner checked his course on the binnacle compass and settled back as the pleasant odor of fresh-brewed coffee rose from the hatch.

When Mary reappeared with two steaming mugs, Tanner looked at her through the dark and said, "You seem to know your way around this boat pretty well." He struggled to keep the smile on his face out of his voice.

"I told you," she responded. "I'm here to protect my investment. Sea Queen is my boat, and if you're going to use her to look for Goldenrod again, I want to be aboard." Tanner was silent. "I know you have some doubts, but I told you before why I was on Goldenrod," she went on. "I suppose you have a right to be suspicious, but a couple of phone calls to Seattle would've satisfied you that I couldn't be involved with anything illegal on Goldenrod. Always assuming there is anything illegal about its operation, something I really doubt."

"Was I that obvious?"

"Actually, yes, to me. And I don't believe the company in California that owns Goldenrod is responsible for your wife's death. I really went on that last cruise because I thought I could help by eliminating Goldenrod from your list."

"But it is the right boat. I know it is. I recognized those damn engines. I'll never forget 'em. Sometimes I hear them in my sleep." Remembering, sitting there in the dark cockpit, Tanner blanched at the thought of this lone woman poking around aboard Goldenrod.

"There's something else you may not know. The papers didn't print everything I told the authorities. Goldenrod needed two attempts to sink us that day. The first time they tried it they missed and somebody on deck shot at us. With a shotgun! Jesus, Mary! If they'd discovered you poking around they'd have killed you without a thought." Tanner and Mary Whitney considered that in silence.

"Yeah," Mary said softly. "Lost overboard one dark night. So sorry. I guess I did jump in there, didn't I? Sort of like what you're doing now, wasn't it?

There was another silent pause. It occurred to them that this voyage could result in both of them being murdered.

"And what about the watch? she said. "You were there. That really is your watch, isn't it?"

Tanner sighed. "Yeah, okay. Point taken. I was aboard and it is my watch. An anniversary present. From Beth. Later we used the logo on several watches for gifts to employees and clients so there are quite a few of them out there. But none with the particular nicks and scratches this one has." He blew out his breath in a noisy gust.

They sat sipping hot coffee, swaying to the rhythm of the boat, listening to the sounds of the sea and the yacht. Then Tanner leaned forward and touched her hand. "Well, they didn't catch you, and to tell you the truth, I'm glad you stowed away. Did you learn anything useful?"

"I don't know. I don't think so. The only thing of interest was your watch. You can't imagine how I felt when I found it and realized it might be yours. I recognized your logo on the back."

"That was pretty cute, returning it to my room that way."

Mary shrugged. "I planned to give it to you at dinner. I still don't know why I didn't. I wasn't absolutely sure it was yours until I saw it on your wrist the morning after I put it in your room."

"Where did you find it?" Tanner asked. "I thought it fell overboard when I couldn't find it in the dinghy."

"It was lying on deck, right by the bow cleat."

"God, when that cabin door opened and people started coming into the passageway, I thought I was a goner for sure. I must be living right. With all the people aboard Goldenrod, I'm lucky it was you who stepped on it."

"Actually," said Mary, "I was pretty sure it was your watch after I got back to Martin's and learned you'd chartered Sea Queen to go north. When we went down Pryce Channel the next morning I saw Sea Queen moored against the shore. Everybody who was awake must have seen her as well."

"So you didn't notice anything peculiar at all?" Tanner

asked, returning to his main concern.

"Peculiar, yes. They carry a lot of extra scuba gear." Tanner nodded, remembering. "The captain said they had it for guests to use and for the crew to keep the hull scrubbed. They even invited me to watch them scrub the hull the morning after I mentioned the gear to the captain."

"Sort of like a performance?"

Mary grabbed his arm. "That's it! I thought the crew working over the side that morning were irritated at something. You must be right. If the captain lied, he must have decided to give me a demonstration so I wouldn't ask any more questions.

"The other peculiar thing that happened was when we got to the end of Pryce. We stopped for a few minutes while they sent two men off in one of the runabouts Goldenrod always carries."

"What? Wait a minute. The timing is certainly right. What did they look like?"

"Is it important? I'm pretty sure I never saw them before, even on that trip. Two big guys, burly, both white men with dark, short hair. One had a tiny gold loop in one ear."

"Huh. I don't remember that," interrupted Tanner.

"The launch was dark blue. Open. It didn't have a cabin. Big black outboard. Mercury, I think."

"That pretty well matches my friends." Tanner told her about his confrontation with two men in a boat that fit her description. "I've always thought they came from Goldenrod, and you've pretty well confirmed it. If they'd been earlier or I'd slept longer, they might have found me easy pickings.

"Michael, I recall from earlier trips that some guests occasionally practice target shooting off the stern, so they certainly have shotguns on board. Bastards!" she exclaimed suddenly, surprising Tanner with her vehemence. "We've got to figure out some way to pin those murders on them!"

Through the rest of that long night, they sailed north and northwest, spelling each other at the wheel. They drank more hot coffee and talked about Tanner's search and what they might do to get the proof they needed of the ramming of the Queen Anne.

25

A fair wind that night and all the next day carried them swiftly up the Inside Passage toward Desolation Sound. But in the end the wind died and the sea turned to glass.

Tanner and Mary began methodical sweeps of the sea around Desolation Sound, gradually working their way into the sound itself. They motored into hidden coves and scanned the charts to bypass too-shallow inlets. To preserve fuel, they often hoisted Sea Queen's jib, but mostly it flapped listlessly except for the occasional passing breeze.

At night, when they anchored, they tried to find coves that gave them visual access to the nearby channels so Goldenrod would not elude them. Recalling Tanner's confrontation with the two men in the launch, they tried to sleep lightly to be sure they'd awaken if anyone came near.

"Michael, do you think Goldenrod is worried about Sea Queen? About you?" Mary asked at one point. She was standing at the wheel as they cruised along in a fair wind, both sails drawing.

"I expect they may be, even if that confrontation with the men in the launch satisfied their curiosity for the time being. For all we know, someone is keeping track of us right now." Tanner glanced down at her. He was sitting cross-legged on the cabin roof with a sailor's palm, a needle, and some waxed twine, repairing a seam in a sail that was starting to separate. He yawned one of those huge, jaw-cracking yawns, groaning slightly as he did.

"Bored?" she asked.

He smiled at her remark. "Nope. Just a mild case of sleep deprivation. I could be happy for a long time sailing in these waters." With you, he silently added. He looked down at his stitching and then back at Mary. Not for the first time he saw what an attractive woman she was and with mild surprise he felt stirrings in himself. He'd been celibate since Beth's death; it hadn't been a conscious decision after the first year, but no one had captured his interest that way. He went on making neat, tiny stitches in the sail fabric. He finished repairing the sail and looked up, rotating his shoulders.

"How 'bout taking the wheel while I change?" Mary was still wearing her foul weather jacket and heavy slacks although the sun had burned off the mists and the day was warming up.

"Sure."

They smiled at each other and changed places. It didn't take long for us to become pretty comfortable shipmates, Mary thought. We're becoming a team. He anticipates Sea Queen's needs the same way I do. She skipped below, shedding her jacket as she went to her cabin. I like the way he shares responsibility without being asked. Her thoughts ran on while she changed to a light shirt and slacks. I'm beginning to care a lot for this guy. Still, her instincts warned her that Tanner wasn't looking for any romantic overtures until his business with Goldenrod was settled. The death of his wife still affected his relationships with women.

And it could be too late, she thought, if things go badly out here. Mary had no illusions about the dangers riding with them on this voyage.

She went back on deck to see that Tanner had selected their anchorage for the night. He steered sea Queen toward a high sheer cliff that rose straight up from the inner curve of a shallow bay.

"Your turn to sleep in the cockpit, sailor," Mary said, going forward to unlash the bow anchor. One of them always dozed near the open hatchway or slept in the cockpit itself. They were never fully rested, but they ate regularly, kept to their routine, and made meticulous entries in the log. They talked to the few boaters they encountered, but Goldenrod continued to be unreported.

Tanner was convinced no ship had sailed south past them, at least not in the channels they searched. For three more days there was no break in their routine. As the days passed, They became acutely aware of the difficulties they faced, trying to trace a single vessel in the miles of twisting channels and inlets of the Inside Passage. The job was daunting. They needed a flotilla of searchers. Georgia Strait was too wide to lie in wait for Goldenrod to pass, and the many channels and islands made it possible for the big white yacht to go around them unseen.

The days flowed one into the next, becoming, in memory, an almost seamless panorama of hazy dawns, rain, sun, mists and motoring from wooded vista to peaceful channel. From time to time they ventured into the wider reaches of Georgia Strait. There they encountered a steady parade of recreational and commercial traffic. They kept a constant radio watch in hope they might hear something that would provide a clue to their quarry's location. Frustration rose and polite conversation waned. They continued to ask about Goldenrod in brief conversations with men on passing fishing boats.

"Wal, I recollect the boat you describe," one old islander told them. "But I'm blessed if I can remember when I last saw her. Musta been a long time ago, though."

Another stared at them suspiciously. Then he said, "You that feller Tanner I heard about?" Tanner nodded. The man shrugged and turned back to his nets.

"Michael, maybe you ought to lie when someone asks your name."

He looked at her, wordlessly. It came to him then that whatever the outcome of his search, there would always be people along these shores who would think ill of him. Tanner hardened his heart and their search continued.

When they docked at Campbell River for supplies, a man approached them on the pier; told them he'd heard Tanner was looking for Goldenrod, but could only say that he had watched the vessel going out of the marina headed south.

"When was that?" Tanner grasped the man's sleeve.

"Dunno exactly. Few days ago. A week, mebbe?"

Mary was in town for groceries while Tanner attended to fuel and fresh water for Sea Queen.

"Michael, Michael!" Mary called excitedly when she returned. Tanner popped his head out of the hatch where he had been cleaning the galley stove. Other heads turned to watch the attractive woman, trotting down the wharf carrying two big bags of groceries.

"Hey, don't yell so. You'll disturb the fish." Tanner smiled and gave her a hand aboard. She confirmed that Goldenrod had indeed been in Campbell River for a few hours less than a week earlier. Tanner's momentary lift was dashed when she admitted she'd been unable to learn where the ship was headed.

It was then that Tanner remembered his night at French Creek and the French fisherman. He telephoned Pierre Bonset and explained that he was now sure of his quarry.

"That is good, my friend. I will pass the word. We are many and it will be difficult to hide from us."

"Pierre, I don't want you or your friends to get hurt. And we must be careful not to alert Goldenrod."

"Ah, you are right. I will think of something and we will also use the telephone, not the radio. Don't worry, we will find them and get word to you."

"Pierre Bonset promised to put the word out," Tanner explained to Mary. "More eyes will be a big help. I think we can stay here tonight instead of heading out."

"Are we safe in this berth?" Mary suddenly remembered the still unexplained explosion that had destroyed Tanner's boat the previous year.

"I don't know. More and more people know we're looking. Some of them are probably unfriendly. It's too late to find an anchorage now. But I guess we'd better stand watch."

"How 'bout moving Sea Queen closer to the end of the pier?"

"Good idea, but it's pretty crowded."

"I'll talk to the harbor master." Mary went to find the old gentleman. "He says there's no hope of moving," she reported, "unless we leave altogether. Hardly any spots left, anyway."

He looked at her for a long moment. "Mary. You've been great." He put a gentle hand on her shoulder. "But this isn't your fight. The closer we get to Goldenrod, the more dangerous it gets. I think you should get off here."

Her hand came up and touched his cheek and she looked into his eyes. "You are wrong, Michael," she murmured. "It is my fight too."

More than you know, she thought. Tanner looked back silently, then his shoulders loosened. Was he half afraid she'd agree to leave? She wondered.

They ate dinner aboard, deciding that foot traffic was so frequent along the docks and piers, it would be easy for someone to sneak aboard a deserted Sea Queen. Nervous tension joined them in the cabin as the chill night air crawled down the open hatch. After they washed up, Mary went forward to her bunk while Tanner bundled into heavy woolens and sat reading under a dim light in the main cabin.

It was near eleven and he'd nodded off when a sudden hoot from a ship's horn and a bright searchlight woke the sleeping marina. Tanner bolted from his doze and stuck his head out of the hatch. He heard the heavy throb of a powerful diesel engine.

Other crew on sleeping boats grumbled and looked out as a gray Canadian Coast Guard cutter slid slowly into the narrow slot between the pier where Sea Queen was moored and the next pier over. It was obvious they were planing to take the one remaining spot, about thirty feet inland from Sea Queen. It would be a tight squeeze for the big cutter, Tanner saw and went on deck to lend a hand fending off.

"Sorry to disturb you, gentlemen," came a voice from the bridge. Tanner looked up and his eyes met those of the now-familiar Coast Guard Lieutenant he had encountered twice before. The man touched the brim of his cap with two fingers and disappeared. A moment later Tanner heard his voice again as the cutter eased expertly into the tight space across the narrow span of water. "Stop engine. Set the watch, Mr. Davis, fore and aft."

"Sir?" questioned an unseen voice.

"You heard me, mister."

The marina quieted again and Tanner looked bleary-eyed at the cutter. She had two lights burning topside, one illuminating the stern of Sea Queen and the boat just behind. A crew member wearing a sidearm appeared on the cutter's fantail. Tanner felt warm breath on his neck and his pulse increased.

"What's going on out there?" Mary was standing close behind him, a jacket clutched tightly around her. Her voice was a warm, muzzy murmur.

"I'm not sure. Canadian Coast Guard cutter just showed up and squeezed into the next pier. Woke us all up." This guy seems to show up a lot, Tanner thought.

"Well, that guard on the cutter and all the light makes me feel a whole lot safer."

"True, true." Mary went back to her cabin and warm bed. Tanner turned to watch her go, watched her bare slender legs flicker through the light from the portholes. He went to his own cabin and slept soundly the remainder of the night. For the first time in many nights, he didn't dream about Beth.

Next morning, Sea Queen rounded Francisco Point and headed east. Days passed. They docked briefly at Refuge Bay for fresh fruit. Tanner felt the gradual return of the frustration he experienced earlier. There was no word from Bonset and the fishing fleet.

In his high-energy world of public relations, he was used to calling the shots, setting the pace. His two seasons working at Martin's Marina and the sailing had taught him greater patience and an appreciation for working with the forces of nature, but his efforts to resolve the killing of his wife seemed to be stalled. Mary's presence was a great help, but he was again facing the reality of his nearly impossible task.

"I'm getting a sense of *deja vu* here."

"What do you mean?" Mary turned from her stance by the port stays where she was scanning the distant island shores with her binoculars.

"On my previous trip up here I had to fight the same feeling. Frustration. We're spending all this time out here making zero progress."

She nodded. "I understand. There is so much water, so many places to hide. But you are making progress. You know the name of the boat. Your friend from French Creek is helping. We just have to be patient."

"Yeah but if Goldenrod passed us in the night they wouldn't have to be very far away to slip by unheard. And if they run, there's no way we could catch them on Sea Queen." He sighed, squinting up at Mary. "Maybe we should call it off."

"Since we're not sure what to do when we do sight them, you might be right. But let me ask you something, Michael." Mary swung around the stay and walked back toward him. Her auburn hair blew back in the soft breeze. She studied him and wondered if the increasing attraction she felt toward him was reciprocated. Since their overnight stop in Campbell River she'd felt increased intimacy, a subtle heightening of physical awareness. But she knew in many small ways that he still held the memory of his wife very close. Beth Tanner was almost a third member of the crew.

"Deep down, way inside, could you live with that decision?" she asked him. "Stop searching? Many people would never have started, you know. But you did. You wouldn't let it go. I think we should keep on, at least for a while."

Tanner nodded, looked down at his shoes and then put a hand on her arm. "Thank you," he said quietly. "Will you take the wheel while I get lunch?"

Tanner put together thick bologna, cheese and lettuce sandwiches and thought about what Mary had said. He thought about their companionship, how they'd become a good sailing team. And he thought about Mary, the woman.

"Look," she said, pointing, when he returned to the cockpit. He handed her the tray and took the wheel.

A big tug boat was laboring across the sea. "Some of the more interesting traffic out here. A log boom."

"Is that what he's towing? Where is it?"

"Look 'way back off her stern." Mary pointed further aft. "The loggers corral the stuff they cut, and when they have enough, the logs are wired together with cables into a big raft. See the sun shining off the bridle? That's the towing cable."

Tanner squinted and saw a silvery stripe dancing above the water behind the tug. "The boom is so far behind, they hardly seem to be together. Must be almost a quarter mile. How big is that thing?"

"Dunno. Many yards long. Plenty wide, too. Go left a little more, will you? Those things make me nervous."

Tanner adjusted their course to give the log boom a wider berth. "Doesn't have a very high profile, does it?"

The tug and its long, low raft of logs, departed to the south. Mary and Tanner sat side by side in the cockpit, finishing sandwiches, the wine bottle between them on the bench. Sea Queen continued quietly across the calm sea in the direction of Campbell River. It was a cool, brightly overcast day. They gradually became aware of the sound of heavy engines behind them. A large fishing boat was slowly closing on them, heading for the commercial docks at Campbell River.

Mary adjusted their direction just enough to run on a nearly parallel course and both watched with idle interest as the big fishing boat drew closer, huge black net-handling spars and cables giving her a faintly menacing look.

"Ahoy, Sea Queen."

The hail startled them. They'd passed many other such boats with a mere wave, except when they inquired for news of Goldenrod. This was the first time they'd been hailed. They jumped up and waved.

"Michael Tanner," came the call.

"Yes? Ahoy." Tanner stared at the bearded man near the fantail of the fishing boat as it rumbled by.

"Pierre sends regards. He say to tell you you'll find the fishing better in the northern inlets. There's Good Hope and Queen Bess to show you the way." The man waved once more and disappeared off the deck.

Mary looked at Tanner, perplexed. He looked back. Then

he frowned and jumped for the companionway.

"Wait," he said scrambling below. "Charts. If the message is from Pierre Bonset, it must have come by radio. He wanted to tell us what he learned without being too obvious. Damn! We should have had the radio on."

Mary shook her head. It was a sign of their weariness they had forgotten to monitor the radio this day.

Tanner reappeared with a chart of the area in one hand. Navigation charts concentrate on information for the seagoing, but significant land features that provide recognition and navigation aid are also indicated. A few moments of searching and his finger stabbed the chart at a location many miles north of their present position.

"There!" he exclaimed. "I thought I remembered it. Here's a mountain named Queen Bess and right next to it is another called Good Hope."

Mary looked at the chart. "Is he saying that's where we should look?"

Tanner nodded. "Together, those two mountains form the east side of Butte Inlet. He must mean that's where Goldenrod is now."

Tanner looked up at her and smiled. Pierre Bonset's promise of help had not been an idle boast. All the frustration and depression of the past few days sloughed away.

"Seems pretty flimsy to me."

"Maybe so, but here we go." He took the wheel and swung Sea Queen around in a long fast curve to a new course, north, northeast.

"What if it's a trick?"

"That's certainly possible," Tanner admitted, "but I trust Pierre Bonset and it's our first real lead. Let's take a quick look and if Goldenrod 's not there, we'll come back to Campbell River as we planned."

Still doubtful, Mary shrugged, gathered the lunch remains and went below. Tanner checked their fuel supply and throttled up a bit.

Mary's head reappeared in the hatch. "I'm gonna shower

and wash my hair while I have the chance. Give it a little more gas."

He throttled up slightly.

There, that's your best engine speed. Conserves diesel, too." She disappeared again.

For a long time in the bright gray afternoon. they motored north. Tanner estimated it would take about three hours to reach the mouth of Butte Inlet. After that, they would have to proceed more slowly. He hoped they'd reach Butte while there was enough light to navigate safely some distance up the inlet. There were no buoys or channel markers in these waters and the winding inlets were too narrow to risk motoring at high speed in a vessel like Sea Queen.

The sun, long since gone behind a growing cloud cover, was fast losing its power when Tanner saw the entrance to Butte Inlet, a thirty-mile-long winding fjord that carves its way back into the British Columbian coastal mountain range. His first view of Butte Inlet was a three mile fetch to the first bend in the channel.

The mountains were very tall. Tanner looked up and saw flashes of white snow at their peaks. The sky turned a darker gray and the air grew misty. Gray-green pines covered the mountain's flanks, densely blanketing the ground. Closer to the sea, the tree cover was occasionally broken by sheer, dark, rock cliffs, some towering 200 feet above the water. Struck by the powerful physical beauty of the place, Tanner switched off the engine. Sea Queen drifted peacefully on the placid sea. A light, cold breeze from high on the mountain sides sent a rustling, silvery whisper down the channel, and the slender, regal, trees bowed to its passing.

Mary, a towel wrapped around her damp hair, came to the companionway. She looked up, about to ask why they had stopped when she saw Tanner's rapt expression. She smiled and turned quietly back to her cabin.

He switched on the engine.

Now he had to find a safe anchorage. The chart indicated that the mountains rose straight out of the sea. There was great depth of water beneath their keel.

"I'm going to aim for Fawn Bluff here," Tanner said, when Mary came on deck. He pointing at the chart spread on the cockpit bench. "We can make that easily before it gets too dark."

They reached the bluff and found the water deep enough, even at low tide, to anchor against the cliff. To avoid scraping on the rocks or swinging too wide, they set two anchors and hung fenders over. Mary, in a tattered dark blue terry bathrobe that dragged on the deck, and her sea boots, helped set the anchors and adjust the fenders.

"Let go the anchor," Tanner called. He glanced up to see her leaning over the bow. Mary's robe had come undone and hung on either side of her body like a ragged tent. When she turned back, she abruptly clutched the robe around her and Tanner realized she was naked underneath.

Once the ship was tethered to their satisfaction, Mary went below and built drinks. Tanner tarried only long enough to double check the anchor lines and fenders. Then he too went down to the cabin and started dinner.

He pan-fried two thick pork chops while potatoes were boiling, sautéed some sliced carrots in olive oil and garlic. To the drippings in the frying pan he stirred in flour, milk and spices to make a thick, fragrant gravy.

Later, well bundled against the chill night damp, they each had a glass of brandy in the cockpit.

"For a semi-yuppie, you seem to have a real feel for sailboats," Mary remarked.

"It's a learned response," he said, smiling into the dark. "I am--or was, your typical urban product. When the business really took off a few years ago, Beth and I began to acquire some expensive toys. You know, big stereos, elaborate VCRs, sports cars. We had several friends who sailed and we sometimes sailed with them, mostly on Lake Washington or day-sailing on Puget Sound. It was fun. Just expensive pastimes, you know?"

Mary nodded. She did know. "Oh yeah. My ex was like that. I grew up in a family with a seafaring background and I sailed a lot as a kid so it seemed natural to get a boat. I bought

Sea Queen here in Port Washington and we were going to have it delivered to the east coast." She sipped her brandy. "We got divorced before that happened. George never even saw Sea Queen. I love to sail." She stretched and tilted her head back, gazing up at the dark cloud-filled sky.

"Anyway," Tanner resumed, "we have a client in California who has a big yacht docked in San Francisco Bay. We spent a week aboard her a couple of years ago on kind of a working holiday, and that got me interested in cruising. I talked friends into letting me crew for some races. Beth came along to watch me race sometimes and our interest grew." He paused, then said quietly, "Then we chartered the Queen Anne in Anacortes."

Mary leaned forward, a measure of intensity in her voice, even though she tried to sound casual and said, "How do you feel now, about sailing?"

"Oh." He paused, arranging his thoughts. "There's something about it that is so elemental. So clean. You must know what I mean. When you're sailing, you use your skills in concert with nature, not in spite of her. You have to be aware of what the wind and the water are doing. But, no wind, no sailing, so you have to develop patience, too.

"I told myself I'd never get back on a boat after Beth and Alice were killed. But now I love sailing more than ever. I've changed, I think, these last two summers. I remember once Beth and I tried to go somewhere against the tide. We spent hours wasting fuel and getting nowhere. I wouldn't do that now. I'd just stop and wait for the tide to turn."

Abruptly he looked up from his brandy and stared through the dark at Mary in the other corner of the cockpit. "There's something specially wonderful those first few minutes after you leave a harbor. You motor out on the sea and set the sails and switch off the engine. There's a kind of lift, a freeing of the spirit. It's as if both you and the boat are cut loose from everyday concerns. At the same time, your focus seems to sharpen. You get closer to a different kind of reality. It's a wondrous feeling. I think Beth was having the same kind of response."

His voice grew soft in remembrance. "We chartered the Queen Anne for three weeks. It was going to be our trial together, to help us decide if we wanted to buy a sailboat." His voice cracked. "Beth loved the sea." Mary reached out a hand to touch his knee.

"Will you take the first watch?" he muttered, getting to his feet. Mary nodded wordlessly and settled back on her cushion, drew her jacket more closely about her throat. She stared out at the black water as Tanner went silently below.

26

The next morning, when the brisk dawn arrived, Mary and Tanner were already under way. Steam rose in random tendrils from the warm surface of the sea along the shore. Freed again from the bottom, Sea Queen nosed gracefully around Fawn Bluff into the broad reach of Butte Inlet. They began a cautious reconnoiter up the long, twisting, waterway. Above them the towering mountains reluctantly gave up the morning mists that overlaid their gray-green shoulders. There was a sharp September chill in the air. Tanner realized it was just after the second anniversary of Elizabeth's death.

They were alone on the still water, a long v-shaped ripple extending behind them to temporarily mark their passage. Small islands lying close to either shore came into view from time to time. Tanner noted them automatically in his mind. They could provide shelter, should the need arise. After an hour of slow motoring, Tanner spotted a long white streak that fell down the mountain into the sea.

"Look, there's a stream," he said. "Let's refill our water jugs."

They motored as close to the mountain as the shoaling bottom would safely allow and anchored. Tanner rowed ashore while Mary stayed aboard and kept watch. He carried plastic Jerry cans that he filled from the sweet, icy, stream. The day wore on, the sun drove the chill from the air, and they shed their jackets.

"No logging camps up here," Mary remarked.

"Plenty of evidence of it though." Patches of brush and

young saplings dotted the mountain sides, softening the scabs of past years' clear cutting. Frost had not yet touched the lower reaches of the terrain and in many places the greenery extended to the water's edge.

They continued up the gradually narrowing channel. Mary was at the wheel while Tanner dozed in his cabin. A sudden alteration in the sound of the engine brought him upright on the edge of his bunk. He glanced quickly out a porthole to see that Mary had made a radical change in direction. They were now headed back the other way and angling across the inlet toward the western shore.

"What is it?" he called, slipping back into his shoes and heavy shirt.

For a moment there was no answer. Then Mary throttled back and said in a tense, quiet voice, "I spotted a ship anchored just up the channel."

Tanner came topside. "Is it Goldenrod?"

"Don't know for sure, but I think so."

"Let's put her over there, against that cliff." Mary pointed. "The ship I saw is anchored on the other bank."

"Good idea." Tanner looked to fenders and mooring lines.

"After we anchor I think I should row the dinghy up to that bluff at the bend and take a look." Mary pointed and then eased the wheel over, bringing Sea Queen expertly in against the cliff. Tanner threw a line around a rock outcropping to hold the sloop against the cliff.

"I'll go," said Tanner quietly.

Mary looked at him. "Why? Don't you think I can handle it? Or don't you trust me yet?" There was more than a touch of asperity in her tone.

"Of course I think you can handle it. And I do trust you. But this is really my fight and I've already involved you more than I should." He stopped, aware again of other, subtler feelings. "You're perfectly capable of handling the job, I know that. But ..." his voice trailed off and then he tried to smile at her. "Look. I'll just go up there in the dinghy and if it is Goldenrod you've spotted, I'll go ashore and try to climb that bluff. Having a higher observation post might be an advantage."

Only slightly mollified, Mary inflated the dinghy and slid it over the side. She tied the painter, the dinghy's mooring line, to the boarding ladder near the stern. Tanner grabbed a heavy jacket and stuffed a couple of apples and a handful of trail mix into a small knapsack he dropped into the dinghy.

"You'll have to finish anchoring, or tie up to the bluff somehow while I'm gone," he said, climbing over the lifelines onto the ladder. He went down a step and then stopped.

"Look. Promise me something. If they spot me you just take off. Don't wait for me. Those people are murderers. They won't listen to reason if we're discovered."

They were close, at eye level, with only the lifeline between them. Mary took a half-step forward and leaned across the line. She kissed him lightly on the mouth. For an instant, he kissed her back. Then she backed away.

"Be careful, Michael." Her voice was calm and her eyes held his gaze.

"I intend to be," he gave her another small smile that faded quickly. His stomach muscles were tight. "My mission is to observe and report only." He was away, rowing up the coast with strong, regular strokes.

As she watched him go, Mary felt a familiar pressure building in her throat. As a child, she'd had occasional bouts of what one doctor had called "hysterical panic". He had recommended psychiatry. The attacks made her sick to her stomach and sometimes incapable of movement or speech other than what she thought of as a disgusting whimper. More sanguine medical examiners sent her to a specialist who determined that she had a weak muscle in her throat. Sometimes, when she was under extreme stress, the condition allowed stomach juices to be forced back into her throat, creating nausea and dizziness. During her divorce, Mary experienced one incident which incapacitated her for several hours.

Now she stood erect, arching her back and took several deep breaths, forcing the pressure down and watched Tanner row away. Oh God, was she going to lose him before she really had him? Wished she'd purchased a gray or black dinghy instead of the bright red one. Damned dinghy stands out like a sore thumb, she mused.

When Tanner reached the bluff, he saw it would be a tough climb, but the brush and smaller trees would give him handholds where the rocks were particularly steep. Cautiously he rowed on around the rock. There she was. Goldenrod. Even before he took a closer look through the binoculars, he knew it was the right yacht. The ship appeared to be anchored, or was simply stopped just off the far shore, about three-quarters of a mile away. He could make out tiny black figures moving about her afterdeck. The swim platform was hanging just above the waterline. A small, single-engine, floatplane rested nearby on the calm sea. It looked like a Cessna.

His high-magnification binoculars were difficult to keep steady on his target from the bobbing dinghy. Tanner gave up the effort and paddled back around the concealing cliff. When he beached the dinghy, he sat for a few minutes, eating an apple and breathing deeply to settle his fluttering nerves. Then he dragged the dinghy well up on the rocky shingle. He couldn't remember the state of the tide and he didn't want to lose his only practical transport back to Sea Queen. With a sigh, he shouldered the knapsack, waved in the general direction of Sea Queen, just visible against the brush and tree-shrouded shore line, and began the difficult climb up the bluff.

The flat shelf of rock was almost 100 feet above the water. When Tanner struggled through the thick brush at the land-side edge of the shelf, he suddenly found himself looking down on the sea and on Goldenrod. Sweat beaded on his forehead from the effort of his climb.   He crouched down and focused the binoculars. Goldenrod leaped into his field of view.

A wave of pain, of anger, then sorrow, passed over him. A vision of that high white bow as it bore down on them two years ago near Lasqueti Island came into his mind. Somehow, looking down from the little rock shelf, Tanner felt a small lift. Here, now, for the first time he felt he was gaining the upper hand.

Tanner made himself as comfortable as he could manage on the shelf among the small trees and shrubs. He cut a crotched stick and drove it into a crack in the rock, making a simple crutch on which he could steady the binoculars. He dragged handfuls of fallen leaves and lichens into a thin bed on the ground facing toward his quarry's anchorage. Then he lay down and watched the activity on Goldenrod for a long time.

It appeared men were diving. He saw at least two wet-suit-clad divers go into the water off the platform. He saw the same divers or others, at this distance he couldn't tell which, climb back aboard. He could not discern what they were doing. It was an odd place and time for recreational diving.

The sun still shone brightly out of the azure sky. Tanner doubted that after abruptly separating themselves from one group of guests, they'd pick up another group so soon, unless ... unless the owners had required that the crew do exactly that. It was even possible, Tanner admitted to himself as he continued to spy on Goldenrod, that this idyllic scene was exactly what it appeared to be. Possible, but damned unlikely.

Four o'clock came and a buzzing sound attracted his attention, roused him from a brief doze. The propeller on the seaplane was whirling and the little craft was moving slowly across the water, straight toward him. After a few moments, the pilot turned and headed up the channel. With an increasing roar, the plane raced across the water, lifted to the steps of its pontoons, then gracefully rose a few feet above the water. Gaining speed quickly now, it climbed higher and headed north into the mountains.

27

Tanner had spent an entire afternoon watching Goldenrod, and other than his observations of the activity in the water around the yacht, he knew little more than he had when he first crawled up that bluff. Still, all that activity in the water must have some meaning. He slithered back down the steep hill, cracking his shin on a small sapling as he went.

"Ow!" His inadvertent yelp of pain echoed off the mountain sides. He yanked up his pant leg and gently probed the reddening skin. It was tender but nothing was broken. Tanner threw his gear into the dinghy and rowed back down the inlet to Sea Queen. When he reached the yacht, he saw Mary'd been active during his absence. Sea Queen was now tied to the sheer rocky bluff with three fenders out and bow, stern and spring lines looped around the bases of stout trees growing from crevices in the rock. Each of the lines led back to cleats along the deck. The arrangement of doubled lines made it possible to adjust the lines for the rising and falling tide without going ashore.

When he clambered aboard, Mary had a torrent of questions. Tanner had questions of his own.

"How did you get her moored like this?" he asked.

"Well," Mary said. "First I dropped an anchor off the stern out there. Then I hung some fenders along the side and at the bow. I motored right up to the shore, slacking the anchor line as I went. When I had her right against the rocks, I snubbed the anchor line and used the boat hook to work the bow line around that tree. I just left the motor in gear to hold her in place. Of course, once I had a bow line around the tree and back here, I could get the anchor back."

"Of course." He smiled, shaking his head in admiration. "This is great. I wouldn't have thought of it."

"With the anchor back aboard," she went on, "I ran forward, tied off the bow line, and cleated the rudder hard left to help keep her against the cliff. I saw this other good tree right there. I didn't even have to get off the deck. In fact, that bluff is so sheer I don't think you could go ashore here without climbing gear. Anyway, I just backed away to set her between the bow and stern lines. Later I put a spring line out." She stopped talking and they grinned at each other, tension draining away. "I scraped the bow on a rock a couple of times, but I can't see any marks."

Mary had also draped a couple of plastic tarps over the stern and bow to alter the Tartan's appearance and cover the name on the transom. Then she'd cut and strung up a few branches on the mast to blur the precise lines of the yacht.

Tanner scratched his head. "Great job. That was really a lot of work I probably wouldn't have thought of the camouflage, either."

"It won't cover us against a close look, but in the dark or dim light, we might get by." She surveyed him up and down, hands on hips. "Now you. What did you see? What are they doing up there?"

"Diving. Goldenrod is anchored near the other shore. The swim platform was down and I saw divers in the water."

"I thought I heard a big engine once."

"That must have been the seaplane. Small, single engined. It took off around three and went north. It all looked pretty innocent."

"C'mon," she said. "Let's go below. I'll make us a drink while you tell me the rest."

"Okay. And I'll get supper started."

After supper Mary asked, "What about tomorrow? What's

the plan?"

"I'm not sure. I guess I'll go back up the cliff and watch them again. Try to figure out their routine. If I have to go aboard again, knowing their routine will help."

Those were alarming words to Mary. She knew better than he how close he'd come to being discovered the last time he'd sneaked aboard Goldenrod.

Tanner watched all the next day, lying on his lumpy bed of moss and leaves. After the first morning, even the diving ceased. He returned to Sea Queen early on the second day. Mary looked down at him as he rowed up to the boarding ladder and saw the frustration on his face.

"This isn't getting us anywhere. I have to get closer. Try to listen in on them."

Mary had her say. She threw every objection she could think of at him. Finally she said, "All right, damn you!" Exasperation was plain in her tone. "Paddle up there tonight and see what you can overhear. But promise me you won't get too close and you won't go aboard! It's just too dangerous!"

So he promised to stay off Goldenrod's decks and out of her cabins.

The sun was down and the moonless night was inky dark. A good night for skulking. Ideal for Tanner's mission.

Mary came rustling up the ladder to the cockpit. "Here, Michael. Take your rain jacket"

"I don't think so. It's bright yellow and it's very noisy."

"But you know it might rain." He finally agreed to take a dark, olive, cloth ground sheet Mary found in the bottom of the sail locker. He wadded it up in a small bundle and jammed it under his feet. This time they did not touch when Tanner went over the side.

Tanner found, as he rowed the little dinghy up the inlet toward Goldenrod's anchorage, that once his eyes adjusted, he could see quite a distance. Vague shapes on the shore passed in indistinct silhouette. The masses of trees in the forest were darker against the sky. The sounds of the forest, so different from those of the sea, gave him an additional feeling for how close he was to the shore line. Still, when he rounded the curve in the inlet that separated Sea Queen from Goldenrod and crossed to the eastern shore, a sense of isolation and great, empty space enveloped him.

He felt alone in a vast, unfriendly void. The feeling became a palpable weight on his shoulders.

He focused his mind on his target. Somehow, he thought, I have to catch them red-handed. Should have brought a camera. Pictures of innocent-looking activity might help. I should have done more research into smuggling. I'd have a better idea what to look for.

He pursued his thoughts, pushing aside the darkness while he rowed steadily across the bay. Maybe I can provoke them into a public attack. At least I could get them into court. He avoided dwelling on the thought that such a provocation could result in his abrupt demise.

The tide was in his favor so he made good headway without much effort. Tanner practiced rowing hard in absolute silence. He feathered his oars, raising them no more than he judged absolutely necessary above the surface of the quiet sea. After several minutes of steady rowing, mist began to fall. He dragged out the ground sheet and draped it around his shoulders, absurdly glad Mary had insisted he bring it along.

Tanner looked around. He was far from shore and the mist limited his vision. There was nothing to be seen. No shore, no mountains. No Goldenrod. Only blackness and the cold night air.

I should have brought a compass, he thought. At least a compass would tell him he was going in the right direction. He now realized that unless there were lights showing on Goldenrod, or he was lucky enough to catch a glimpse of her superstructure against the sky, he was going to have a tough time finding the white yacht. He was in danger of rowing right by it. Worse, he could hit her hull with an oar, or with the dinghy, and alert the crew.

He rowed on, concentrated on maintaining a straight and quiet course over the water. It seemed all right, but it was so dark he couldn't tell for sure. The mist came and went. It began to seem as if he'd been rowing for hours.

He looked at his watch, shielding the dim light with the ground sheet. It was only ninety minutes since he'd left Sea Queen. He'd checked the tide tables before he started out so he knew he had plenty of time before the ebbing tide began to run strongly enough back down the inlet to hamper him. When he twisted about again to scan the darkness ahead, there she was.

Closer than he'd expected. A few dim lights glowed across the sea, haloed by the falling mist. If he hadn't known better the lights would have been a welcome sign. More tense than ever, Tanner altered his course slightly and rowed on. He dipped water with his fingers to lubricate the oar locks. He adjusted the small cloth sack at his feet to be sure none of its contents would shift noisily.

His course took him in a long curve around the anchored vessel, steadily bringing him closer and closer. The few lights were high up above the main deck, and little light actually reached the water. His greatest danger was that he would row through a beam of light from a porthole just at the moment someone aboard Goldenrod was looking in his direction. After many minutes of steady, cautious rowing, Tanner reached the side of the yacht undetected. His gut was tightly clenched. He put a trembling hand gently on the cold hull and blew out his breath in a silent stream. In spite of the cool night, sweat moistened his hairline.

He wondered about guards. If they were doing something illegal, wouldn't there be guards? There were guards, he soon discovered. Someone at the rail on the deck above him coughed and a brightly glowing cigarette butt arched overhead to fall with a brief hiss into the water.

A voice floated through the dark, "Those unfiltered things'll kill you."

"Ahhhh," responded another disembodied voice, "I dunno why we're out here. No one in a hundred miles cares about us."

"Yeah? Being real careful has kept us out of trouble so far."

Much later, Tanner shuddered when he thought about how

close he had been to discovery at that moment. He strained to hear more.

"Sure be glad when this trip's over," said the first man.

"Yunnh," grunted the second. "Hairier this time. Hope the plane gets back early enough so we can finish and make Campbell River tomorrow."

Tanner surmised the man was talking about the small float plane he had observed earlier.

"You know it's been a pretty good gig all these years an' still nobody has any idea what we're doin."

"Yeah? Lotsa people along the line know. An' I don't trust those cokeheads we ran into in Lund."

There was a soft laugh. Their voices faded as the men shifted back and forth along the deck. "... idea using company guests. Who'd guess broads ... Barnes dame are just cover?"

"... wouldn't kick that one outa bed."

Rain came and pattered on the sea, covering parts of the conversation.

"... last trip this year. I'm not too keen on some of that stuff in the keel pods. I hear it gets unstable ... old."

Another cigarette butt spun like a dying firefly from the deck above. It bounced off the end of the dinghy and landed in the wet bottom beside Tanner's foot. There was a faint hiss and the coal died. Tanner flinched, hoping the butt hadn't damaged the rubber dinghy, hoping the men above him hadn't seen the coal bounce once before it snuffed out.

He clung in place to the side of the yacht by spreading his fingertips against the cold hull. The conversation between the two guards explained so much about Goldenrod's movements; about her private travels up and down the Inside Passage. Tanner remembered the cartons he'd seen earlier on his foray aboard.

After a long period of silence, Tanner heard the men moving down the deck. He breathed softly through his open mouth and began to relax. Then the muscles in his thighs started to tremble and cramps started in his shoulders. His tongue was dry and his lips felt cracked. He was sure if he had to talk he'd only be able to croak.

Silence settled over the scene. What was happening on deck, Tanner wondered?

He heard no further conversation, and he couldn't decide if the two guards were still there or had gone into the cabin. He wanted to get away. He hadn't planned on staying so long and his nerves were unraveling. The longer he stayed where he was, the greater the chance he'd be discovered. He forced his mind away from thoughts of how vulnerable he was in the dinghy, even if the night was pitch black.

He heard a soft squeaking and realized the tide was now running down the inlet, gently swinging Goldenrod on her anchor line and pulling the dinghy slowly along her side.

Tanner let go with a gentle push to separate the dinghy from Goldenrod and they drifted apart. Still trembling, he hunched his shoulders in instinctive and anxious anticipation of a shout of discovery or the obscene crash of a shotgun as the dinghy swung around so his back was presented to Goldenrod. An image of the jagged hole in the cabin roof of the Queen Anne formed unbidden in his mind. His hyperactive imagination projected another image of what that same shotgun could do to his body. The image was too vivid. He forced himself to think of other things.

But no shot came. The dinghy drifted farther from Goldenrod and finally, still breathing through parched lips, Tanner eased his oars into the water and began slowly to row away from Goldenrod and back down the inlet. Wet from the mist and the rain, his strength depleted, distracted by what he had heard, Tanner's instincts took over and sent him in the general direction of Sea Queen, Mary Whitney and fragile sanctuary.

28

Goldenrod's dim lights disappeared. The currents swirled about, carrying Tanner away from his enemies. But he'd stayed too long and now his tired mind and wet clothes drained away his reserves of strength and conspired to impede his progress.

He tried to focus on getting out of danger. His eyesight blurred. The almost continuous outpouring of mental and physical tension over the last two hours had exhausted him. The night chill seeped in bleeding away his remaining stamina. He had to find Sea Queen and warmth.

Tanner rowed on, more slowly now. Gone was the strong rhythmic stroke that had characterized his earlier progress up the inlet. His breath came in ragged gasps. A vague thought penetrated his growing mental fog. He had to cross to the other shore to reach Sea Queen. To the western side. Had he done that already? Tanner tried to remember. His sense of direction was muddled and he was no longer certain whether he was south or still north of Sea Queen. He had by now lost contact with the shore. Around him was only blackness and steadily falling rain.

He crossed the inlet and as he did, the ebbing tide captured the dinghy more strongly. The current swept him against a bluff, banging the dinghy into sharp rocks along the shore. Sweat dripped off his chin and he shivered in the chill air. When he had struggled around a little promontory, he saw a small rocky patch that he seemed to recall lay at the base of his observation cliff. Now he thought he was still up the inlet from the bluff where Sea Queen was moored to the rocky wall. His energy was nearly gone. With the passing minutes Tanner's disorientation increased. He had never before experienced such enervation. Teeth-rattling chills constantly wracked his body and disrupted his rowing rhythm.

I'm dying out here, he thought. Have to keep going. At times, during his erratic progress along the shore of the inlet, he thought he was reaching out to Beth, sometimes to Mary. Even Alice's face rose and wavered before him. Their indistinct images floated in the dark before his bleary eyes, sometimes separate, sometimes merged. He heard laughter, faint, scornful. Tanner scarcely realized that he had been out the entire night and the sky was beginning to lighten as he struggled to reach safety. Rain still fell and the cold water gathering in the dinghy sloshed over his feet.

Dry and warm in her foul weather suit, Mary anxiously kept watch for Tanner's return. As the night wore on she stayed in the cockpit, scanning the dark water. If she hadn't been alert, he might have skittered on down the shore and missed Sea Queen. As his exhaustion increased, his ability to row silently deserted him. It was a sloppy, splashing, uncoordinated Michael Tanner who rowed in a kind of drunken pain over the water, and passed Sea Queen just a few yards away in the predawn light. He was mumbling incomprehensible words to himself when Mary first recognized his approach.

She stood in the cockpit, chilled by the transformation that confronted her. From the strong confident man who had rowed away in the darkness, Tanner had disintegrated into this struggling pitiable creature. As she watched, the shadowy figure continued to row past Sea Queen.

"Michael!" she called, softly at first. There was no reaction. Louder she cried, "Michael Tanner!" Urgency lent unaccustomed sharpness to her tone.

This time he reacted, and with a start she realized she could see him clearly. The dawn was surrounding them with its gray gentle softness. But here, now, she had to hold Tanner's attention. He looked toward the sound of her voice, but he still stroked the oars, widening the distance between them, sliding away on the outgoing tide. The rain began to slacken.

She called again, louder still. "Michael, please. Row over here! Listen to my voice. Come this way!" Her voice echoed and bounced along the shores of the inlet. Gulls cried out in the middle distance, swooping low over the water.

Her voice penetrated his fogged mind and Tanner turned laboriously, as if a great weight were on him. Bleary-eyed, he looked in Mary's direction.

She couldn't tell if he even recognized her. "I'm here, Michael. Come to me. Paddle over here."

Tanner struggled to turn further toward her voice. He looked up and he saw her, Mary Whitney, solid, real, leaning over the lifelines, hands reaching out to him. Slowly he turned the dinghy about and rowed with stronger strokes toward her.

"That's it, Michael," she called, encouraging him. Grudgingly the tide gave up its grasp and the dinghy drew closer to Sea Queen.

Tanner reached out a hand and grasped the boarding ladder almost as if he'd been offered another chance at life. But now that he had the shiny, cold, ladder in his hand, disorientation and fatigue overwhelmed him.

Exhausted, he held on and dropped the oars. He knew he should throw Mary the painter so she could tie up the dinghy, but he hadn't the energy. He couldn't figure out where the painter was. He still had to get up the three steps of the ladder and he didn't know how to begin.

Mary dropped to her knees and leaned under the lifeline, watching him closely. There wasn't room on the ladder for both of them and she knew she hadn't the strength to haul him up the ladder by herself.

"Michael." Mary looked down at Tanner slumped in the dinghy. "Take the dinghy rope. It's right there by your left foot. Tie it to the ladder." She said it twice. Finally, with fumbling fingers after repeated tries, he located the painter and tied it off.

Mary continued to talk to him, forcing him to pay attention to her voice. "C'mon, Michael. Put your hand up and grab the ladder." He reached overhead with first one hand, then the other and grasped the ladder rail. Mary stretched down and seized his wrist. Her warm hand seemed to give Tanner a small infusion of strength.

"Come on, Michael. You can do it. Climb!" As she said it, she looked down and understood that Tanner was about at the end of his resources. If he slipped and fell into the sea, he'd drown.

Mary clung to his arm; turned his hand so his limp fingers fell naturally on her wrist.

"Take my wrist, Michael," she urged. "Squeeze it."

He raised his head. Mary locked her gaze with his, willing her strength into him. He looked back at her dully, but she felt his fingers tighten on her wrist. She leaned back into the cockpit, forcing Tanner to rise to his feet in the rocking dinghy and follow his imprisoned arm up the ladder.

"Raise your foot," she cried. "Find the step. Push down, damn you! Push. Your foot's on the step. You've got to help me! I can't do this alone!" Fleetingly she recalled the man-overboard drills she'd learned from her uncles and her grandfather. Maybe, she thought, she should have rigged a block and tackle with a harness, but it was too late for that now.

Tanner responded to her voice and the strain on his arm. His foot found the first rung and he pushed on it, raising his body and sliding upward along the vertical rails of the ladder, muscles trembling with the effort. Over and over Mary's voice urged him on. Tanner stepped higher and then leaned forward over the lifeline. With a final wrenching tug, Mary upended him into the cockpit. At last he was safe, sprawled on his haunches, head hanging, breathing hoarsely through slack lips.

After a few minutes rest, Mary helped Tanner down the companionway into the cabin. He collapsed on the seat. She filled a kettle and put it on the stove, her movements swift, while she struggled to hold her concern at bay.

She hauled him partly upright and wrestled his drenched outer garments off his nearly inert body. Tanner wasn't quite unconscious; it might have been better if he had been. In a disjointed uncoordinated manner he tried to help, but only managed to hinder her efforts.

"C'mon, Michael. Let's get those shoes off." Mary rubbed his icy feet after she removed his boots, then his hands. Tanner's spasms increased and his shivers were almost continuous. His eyelids drooped and he mumbled incoherently. He's so cold, she thought. I've got to warm him up. He could die right in front of me!

She tried to get him to drink some hot tea, but they spilled most of it. It didn't seem to help. Occasionally he mumbled something. His eyes fluttered open for a moment, then closed. Once she thought he mumbled Beth's name. He appeared to Mary's untrained eye to be slipping away from her into hypothermia.

Finally she ran to her cabin and dragged her big, down-filled sleeping bag back to the main cabin. Heat, I've got to warm him up, she thought.

She threw cushions on the floor and opened the sleeping bag. Grunting with the effort, she pushed and prodded and hauled until she got the rest of his clothes off him. She rolled Tanner off the bench and into the bag. Warmth. He had to be warmed up. Her body was the most immediate source of warmth.

She turned out the lights and pulled the curtains. In the light of approaching dawn, she stripped her clothes off. Naked, she crawled into the sleeping bag and gathered Tanner's inert chilled torso into her arms, pressing close against the length of his icy form. Then she closed the big bag over their nestling bodies. Later, Tanner would have vague memories of smooth skin pressed against him, of warmth, of softnesses, of peace.

Hours later Mary woke and gently removed his warm hand from her breast. Sunlight pushed against the curtained portholes. Without waking him, she slid out of the sleeping bag and quickly dressed. Tanner slept on, snoring gently.

Coffee, she thought. I need a good jolt of caffeine. God, and am I ever hungry. She smeared a stale bagel with jam and wolfed it down. Then she made a big pot of coffee and fixed bacon and scrambled eggs. The sounds and the smells eventually roused Tanner. He blinked owlishly up at her from the cabin floor. Then, without a word, climbed to his feet and staggered into the head. When he returned to the cabin, dressed and washed, the bags under his eyes were testament to his weariness.

"Oh, God, what happened? I feel like I've been kicked by a horse and drunk for a week. Is this some kind of hangover? Have I been celebrating something? Help me out here. I seem to have lost a big piece of time."

Tanner's voice was plaintive and hoarse with fatigue. He slumped down at the table Mary had set. He rested his chin on his hands and peered up at her while she served him soft scrambled eggs and hard fried bacon.

"Don't you remember? I guess we're getting too old for this macho stuff. Now eat." She smiled, her earlier concern fading away. "You were pretty much out of it when you got back here last night, or this morning, really, and you weren't making much sense. I want to know what happened! You were gone practically the whole night! What did you find out?"

"Ohhh," he began to remember then. How he'd felt coming back across the water, how out of control he'd been. His near total collapse. Slowly, between mouthfuls of the hot food, he told her about the night, up to the time he returned to Sea Queen.

"Keel pods!" Mary exclaimed. "That must be why they carry all those diving rigs. I never bought the idea they used 'em just to scrub the hull."

He nodded. "Sure. The divers open the pods under water to store stuff and get it out later when they'd ready to deliver it. But what stuff?"

"What does it matter? It's probably drugs. How big are the pods? Drugs wouldn't take up much space."

"Unless its marijuana." Tanner watched Mary closely. She had a way of deeply furrowing her brow when she concentrated on a knotty problem. He found it oddly attractive.

Somehow in the explanations, they avoided talking about what happened after Tanner had returned to Sea Queen. Mary couldn't decide whether he remembered their hours together in her sleeping bag. She decided not to mention it at all, unless he brought it up.

She looked up. "I read something in the <u>Times</u> once." Her voice trailed off and she stared at the bulkhead, the frying pan still in her hand.

"What?" Tanner waited, fork suspended in mid air.

"It was a story about all the guns the FBI found in that isolationist's compound in Idaho. I think it was Idaho. Did you read about that?"

He nodded.

"Anyway, the story said the government knew there were similar groups in the Canadian and Alaskan Rockies. Could Goldenrod be selling arms to those people?"

"Seems entirely possible." Then he sat up straighter, hunger forgotten for a moment. "Yeah. And that remark I heard about old stuff being unstable. I think dynamite gets real unstable if it gets too old. Maybe other explosives do too."

"How do you know that?"

Tanner shrugged. "I don't remember exactly. When you work for a lot of different clients you pick up all sorts of odd bits of information. That's one."

There were gaps toward the end of Tanner's narrative. He didn't quite remember how he had returned down the inlet and finally located Sea Queen. If he recalled their time together in the sleeping bag, he said nothing about it. Finally he ran out of words and they sat quietly.

Tanner suddenly sat up straight. "Hey! Do you know a woman named Barnes?"

"Leticia Barnes? Sure. She's been a guest on Goldenrod a couple of times. In fact she's the one who called me from Nanaimo the last time I went. Why?"

"I just remembered something else. One of those guys mentioned her name. He said they invite people like her aboard for camouflage. I guess that means you too."

"You mean they were using us to provide protective coloring? Those bastards!"

He looked into her angry face. "I owe you an apology,

Mary. I never should have doubted you."

"Thank you. I'm glad that's behind us. But I can't blame you for being cautious."

"There's more. I think you better have the whole story. At least what I know of the whole story." Tanner related his suspicions about the explosion that destroyed his cruiser last year. He told her about the clandestine searches of his room at the marina. "My risk factor is pretty high, and it's the same for anyone close to me."

"You're not getting rid of me now. Why can't we just go to the authorities and tell 'em what you heard?" said Mary. "Let the Mounties take over."

"The problem," mused Tanner aloud, "is still the same. We don't have any proof. If I could just get aboard again and find something, even if I have to steal it. Canadian Coast Guard won't board Goldenrod on our say-so, especially since I've been kind of a pest the last year." He smiled briefly at the recollection of previous encounters with increasingly exasperated authorities.

"Mmmm. Well, what if I tell 'em? My family's well respected in Seattle. We've been around a few years and money has some influence. I have contacts in Vancouver who might help, too."

"Won't work." Michael shook his head. "Money moves a lot of mountains but not this one. Not without concrete proof to back up your word. And remember, we're in Canadian waters. I'm sure the diplomatic maneuvers would take forever. Plus I doubt we could keep it a secret. Somebody would get the word to Goldenrod and they'd just get rid of whatever they're hiding. What I can do is try to get aboard and find some proof of their smuggling," he said. "Something small I can carry away."

Mary didn't like the sound of that at all. "You're crazy!" she cried. "If they catch you, you'll just disappear. They'll shoot you and throw you in the ocean."

"How 'bout I get a gun and shoot at them? I could do a lot of damage with a good pump gun and some double-O buckshot, maybe even sink her."

"Good grief, Michael! They aren't going to just stand

around doing nothing while you pump a few dozen slugs into them! You know they'll shoot back. And how many shots would it take? Could you even sink Goldenrod with a shotgun? Sure. I'll run the boat and you can shoot at 'em as we sail by. It'll be like an old-time pirate movie." She glowered at him. "And just when things look blackest, John Wayne or Kevin Costner or somebody will lead a cavalry charge to the rescue. Except there ain't no cavalry out here."

Tanner gestured vaguely. "Well, you suggest something then. I know. I'm a pretty good swimmer. I'll make a bomb and fasten it to Goldenrod's hull. Then after I swim far enough away, you . . ."

"A bomb! Out of what? Be sensible! Even if we can get the necessary materials, d'you even know how to make a bomb? How to set it off? God, Michael, use your head."

"I'll buy one," he growled as a tiny smile lifted one corner of his mouth. "I bet the hardware store in Lund will have something, or ... I'll fuse some dynamite and throw it at 'em." A smile grew behind the hand he held to his face.

"Hey. Dynamite! That's not the worst idea I've heard this morning ... or afternoon, I guess," Mary retorted. "Or how 'bout we make molotov cocktails with the wine bottles in the trash, Mr. Tanner?"

Tanner sighed again, but he was smiling and Mary was on the verge of laughing out loud at the ridiculous turn of their conversation. Since they had risen so late, the sun was almost down behind the mountain when they finally agreed that for the moment they had only one reasonable course of action. They would continue to watch Goldenrod, shadowing her movements should she shift her anchorage.

Rain drummed on the cabin roof and the night turned bitterly cold

29

The next day started heavily overcast and there was a dark mournful light over everything. Rain squalls came and went, drifting and swirling about the mountains, drumming on the sea and drenching everything. Sharp wind gusts shook the trees and thrummed in the rigging, adding to the miserable conditions. The bone-chilling cold remained. Except for keeping watch on the inlet, Tanner and Mary stayed aboard, out of the weather.

Around eleven in the morning, the sound of the rain on the cabin roof seemed to grow louder. Gradually it took on the mechanical sound of an engine. Tanner leaped to his feet and scrambled up the ladder to the cockpit. When he jammed his head above deck, he found himself practically face to face with the pilot of a single-engined Cessna float plane. It was flying past them just a few feet above the water. Tanner was sure it was the same plane he'd seen resting beside Goldenrod two days earlier. Had the pilot seen them?

It was no a time to take chances. "C'mon, Mary, we've got to get out of here!" He yanked the tarp off Sea Queen's stern and dumped it in the cockpit. Then he ran forward to the bow. Now Mary's foresight in rigging the mooring lines to lead back to deck cleats was fully appreciated. It was the work of only moments to cast off the bow line and haul it, wet and dripping, to an untidy pile on the foredeck. Tanner felt Sea Queen's engine come to life while he worked.

Already a gap was widening between Sea Queen's bow and the bluff as Mary skillfully backed the boat, pushing the stern against the restraint of the stern lines, forcing the bow toward open water. Tanner jogged down the deck and uncleated the midships spring line. The stern lines were bar taut. He dragged the spring line down the deck as he trotted back to the cockpit.

There was a sharp twang in the trees above them when the mast freed itself from overhead branches. Mary shifted to forward and increased the engine speed. For a moment the yacht rested in place, then the big propeller thrashed under her hull, took hold and they began to turn out into the inlet. As soon as she had room at the stern, Mary pushed the throttle lever fully against the stop and swung the wheel hard to the right. At the same time Tanner loosed the slackened stern line and hauled it in as they came free of the tree on the bluff. Sea Queen lunged forward in a short sharp arc and pointed into the channel. Tanner jumped into the cockpit and looked up the inlet.

"Turn the radio on," Mary said. "We better monitor channel 16."

Half a mile farther up Butte Inlet, Goldenrod's crew watched the approaching plane from the shelter of the bridge. Rain streamed down the windshield and dimpled the sea as the little floatplane made a gentle turn and eased down onto the surface, two hundred yards away. The pilot kept the power on and steered toward the yacht. He repeatedly triggered a powerful flashlight that he aimed at the yacht. On the bridge, a man at the helm recognized with a jolt that the pilot was sending an SOS over and over. He couldn't figure why the pilot didn't use his radio. The captain swore at the pilot and sent a man into one of the launches hanging in the davits. By the time the plane closed to within twenty yards and stopped, the launch was already crossing the rain-lashed strip of water.

The pilot cut his engine and threw open the cabin door, ignoring the rain that now poured down on him.

"You okay?" called the boat driver. "Whatsa matter?"

"I'm okay, but your captain won't like this. I saw a sailboat just down the channel around that next bend. It's moored against the cliff."

"What? Another boat?"

"Yeah," shouted the pilot. I didn't want to use the radio. I couldn't see her name, but it sure looked like that boat you told me about. They scattered some brush on it to hide it. Christ, if it's that guy Tanner and he's been watching the transfer, we're in deep shit! I'm splitting without loading the rest of the shipment. Besides, there's a front moving in. Go back and tell the captain. I don't care what he does with the rest of the stuff."

Without waiting for a reply the pilot slammed the cockpit door and started his engine.

On Goldenrod, the crew watched, cursing, as the little plane turned away. By the time the man in the launch returned to Goldenrod's boarding ladder, the plane was making its takeoff run up the bay.

"Goddamn!" bellowed the captain when the man reported. "Get the anchor up! Start the engine. I knew Tanner was some kind of agent. We're gonna finish him right now."

"What about the launch?" asked the mate.

"Sink it," snapped the captain. The mate switched on the power to the electric windlass and started bringing up the anchor. "We don't wanna lose that boat and we've got to nail him before he can talk to anybody." Goldenrod was already answering to her helm, swinging around to point down the channel. They waited, poised impatiently, for the anchor to rise to the surface.

The mate left the bridge and moments later the heavy boom of a shotgun could be heard as he blew away the bottom of the launch and it disappeared under the water without a trace.

The rain beat down harder. It stung Tanner's face when he looked up to the top of the mast and beyond to the gray sky. Fat drops bounced off the sea around them. As the rain closed in, he looked aft up the inlet toward Goldenrod's anchorage. Only the sodden trees, clinging to the streaming shoulders of the mountain and a few glistening rocks and boulders were visible. The deck vibrated under his feet.

We're going too fast, he thought. His vision was sharply limited by the rain. The shore line twisted and turned then faded away as Mary pointed Sea Queen more into the middle of the inlet.

They were really moving now in a gray circle of dappled

sea water the color of old unburnished steel. They faced high risk of hitting the shore, or holing Sea Queen below the waterline before they could stop her headlong rush. But they had to put distance between themselves and their enemy. They stood together in the cockpit, water streaming down their faces. They were soaked and shivering miserably.

"Slow down," said Tanner. "We've gotta get dry or nothing else will matter."

"Go," Mary said. "I'll be okay while you change."

He ran below, shedding his clothes as he went, leaving a trail of dripping, sodden, tangled clothing on the floor of the cabin. Static from the radio assaulted his ears as he went by.

From his duffel, he grabbed a big towel, dried off and threw on fresh underwear, a wool sweater and flannel-lined jeans. Heavy socks. Over it all went his hooded foul weather suit and sea boots out of the wet locker.

When he returned to the cockpit, he found Mary stripped to bra and panties, her soaked outer clothes piled neatly in a corner of the cockpit to keep them out of the cabin. She flashed him a sour grin and disappeared down the companionway while he took the wheel. He looked after her disappearing form, fleeting, confused thoughts of the night on the cabin floor in her sleeping bag, rising briefly in his consciousness.

Looking ahead, Tanner found he could see the bow thirty-plus feet ahead, but only vague, gray textures to either side. He assumed that the unrelieved grayness was also about thirty feet of sea and rain-filled mist, but since everything was the same color it was difficult to be certain. Dry and warmer, he began to calculate possible actions they could take. What would Goldenrod do when the pilot reported seeing Sea Queen? Would they ignore it or had the pilot recognized Tanner as well?

When Mary reappeared, she was dry and clad in her own bright red foul weather suit. She'd stopped in the galley and got the stove going for hot tea and soup. Suddenly uneasy about their position, Tanner throttled back.

"What is it?" Mary asked.

"Don't know, just a feeling." He tried to listen beyond the

echoes of their own engine off the mountains on either side. He heard only the hissing rain on the sea. He wished for wind so they could sail silently down the inlet.

"Michael! Dead ahead!" Mary suddenly cried out.

He looked up in alarm. There, appearing out of the mists, were branches and boulders. They were headed straight for the shore of the inlet! Tanner threw the engine into reverse gear and twisted the wheel over.

"Hang on," he called, bracing his feet. Mary grabbed the backstay and stared ahead.

Sea Queen hesitated, then with agonizing deliberateness, began to swing her bow to the left more and more rapidly. Rocks and trees continued to appear closer and closer. Tanner held his breath. Were they in time? He glanced at the depthfinder. Twenty feet of water. No danger of hitting submerged rocks, only of ramming the shore.

When he looked ahead once more, there was only grayness. He glanced over the stern and shifted to neutral, dropped the engine to a fast idle. He was sweating.

There were no recognizable landmarks to be seen. Tanner looked at the compass. Then he shifted to forward and they again began to slide, now more cautiously, through the dripping universe. Tanner guided the yacht around in a big circle so they were once again headed toward the Georgia Strait. Mary went below to get the navigation chart.

"I think we must be right about here," she called. She came part-way up the companionway ladder and held up the chart, pointing. "But it's hard to be sure. I lost my sense of place during that little panic maneuver back there." Her tense smile flickered at him.

She reached over and turned up the volume on the radio. She picked up the microphone. Static crackled through the cabin. She frowned and keyed the transmitter.

"Hello world," she said, trying to sound bright and cheerful.

There was no response. She tried again. Still nothing but static and occasional electronic whistles.

Tanner called down the companionway, "We must have damaged the antenna. I heard something twang in the branches overhead when we left."

Mary groaned aloud and returned to the cockpit. Loss of the radio was a serious blow. If they sent out a distress call, they wouldn't know if anyone heard them unless they could receive, and there was no way to tell if they were sending. They were both jittery and tense. The smiles came hard.

"Look," Tanner nodded at her. "If you take the wheel and I go to the bow, I'll be able to see farther ahead and I can warn you if there's a problem. Even with radar, I don't think Goldenrod can catch us in this soup before we reach the mouth of the inlet. After that we'll have more options. Plus, it'll be night soon."

"Okay. You go sit at the bow. Take a harness, though. This boat is very responsive to the rudder and I don't wanna have to stop to fish you out of the drink." Mary's smile flickered again.

"Give me directions by pointing with your arms," she said. "If you want a sharp turn, wave your arm up and down. The faster the wave, the faster I'll turn. Point the direction you want me to turn. For stop, wave both arms fast, like you're trying to fly away, which you may want to do, since you'll get wherever we're going first. I'll watch you and keep one eye on the depthfinder." She pointed at the bulkhead-mounted instrument. They were in over 80 feet of water. While she gave him instructions, Mary re-engaged the engine and they began to move forward at a sedate pace.

Tanner ran forward and secured himself in the safety harness, then hooked the tether to a lifeline. Peering ahead through the rain, he felt the deck begin to vibrate more strongly as Mary increased their speed. Looking down, Tanner saw rising waves creaming off either side of the bow. She was already driving the boat faster than he would have dared, confident of her lookout and her ability to handle her boat. For two hours they raced down the inlet through the gray murk. Night came. The rain slowed to a drizzle and finally stopped altogether.

"I don't see how they can find us now. Let's anchor for the night."

Tanner recalled Goldenrod's radar. He wasn't so sure they were safe. He remembered that radar had helped Goldenrod find and smash down another boat not very far from where they were.

"Okay. I guess it'll be safer than charging around out here blind. If we put Sea Queen close to shore, I think it'll be harder for them to find us on the radar. Too much clutter. But we won't have a sheltered bay."

"I know, but I won't sleep much anyway."

Motoring as close to the eastern shore of the inlet as they dared, they located a shallow indentation. In no way was it a cove or bay, but it did give limited protection from the broad sweep of the inlet. Tanner lowered the bow anchor. Thinking ahead to the probable need to raise it again in a hurry, he put out just enough line to secure Sea Queen to the bottom. "What's the state of the tide?"

"Almost high tide. Mary's calm-sounding voice floated down the deck.

Back in the cockpit he said, "I put out very little line. We'll have to stand watches." She nodded. It was an uneasy anchorage in which they rested.

30

Tanner was dozing fitfully on the settee in the main cabin when Mary roused him two hours later. It was full dark and bitterly cold. The damp penetrated his clothes, even under the foul weather suit. There were no lights. Tanner thought he'd left a single red light burning over the chart table. The ship felt lifeless.

"Shhhh, there's a boat nearby," Mary whispered shaking his shoulder, her lips close to his ear.

Tanner's stomach turned over. "Small or large?" He felt her shrug.

Hand in hand they stole soundlessly to the cockpit. Standing by the wheel, staring into the blackness, they listened. It was very still. Damp fog brushed across their faces like invisible feathers. Then Tanner heard it, the rumble of twin, deep-throated, diesels drawing closer, terrible, menacing. Just as he imagined the doomsday boat might sound. Were he and Mary now the doomed?

And he remembered. With awful clarity he remembered that sound from another day two years earlier.

Tanner shuddered deep in his gut. He felt a light pressure from Mary Whitney's arm around his waist as she reached out for support and in the same motion offered comfort.

The sound grew louder, but still they saw nothing.

Goldenrod's passing seemed to take forever. The white yacht may have been some distance away or very close, sailing without lights. There was only sound, the steady rumble of her engines, the faint thrashing of her propellers. When the sounds finally faded, Tanner took a deep breath, his first conscious breath in many minutes. He'd been standing with his joints locked, muscles rigid. Feeling the ridges of muscle through his clothes, Mary Whitney had an even greater understanding of the depth of his anger. They waited for their racing hearts to slow as Goldenrod sailed away down the channel.

Morning brought more light and some relief from the fog which now hung over the water in patches. Minutes after raising anchor, they discovered they'd reached the mouth of Butte Inlet. They turned Sea Queen south, still cautious, feeling their way down Calm Channel toward the Redonda Islands. Without knowing it, they passed within 150 yards of Goldenrod, which was anchored on the north side of the entrance to Butte inlet.

The game of hide and seek played on. Goldenrod, larger, with more powerful engines was faster. With her radar to guide her, she moved through the fog with greater surety. Sea Queen, shallower of draft and more maneuverable, could run closer to the shore, reverse direction in her own length, dodge among concealing headlands. Tanner and Mary took advantage of small islets and shoals where they could go and Goldenrod could not follow. They stuffed towels and clothing in the rigging and along the boom to muffle creaking and banging sounds when they shut off the engine and drifted. With the engine off they listened, trying to pinpoint and out-think their adversary. Had there been wind, they could have sailed silently away. But there was no wind and again the fog closed in around them.

"Mary, you know boats. What kind of speed can Goldenrod make?"

"Twelve, maybe fifteen knots."

"Better than twice what we can do."

"Sure, unless we're sailing in a gale."

"But we've got maneuverability and a much shallower draft."

"She must draw ten or twelve feet of water."

"We'll try to take advantage of that."

Once the game was nearly ended. Through the muffling atmosphere, Tanner heard a strange whump. It came again and with a spang, a heavy slug whined off the upper side of the boom, leaving a bright gash.

"Get down!" he hissed, dropping flat on the cabin roof. "They're shooting at us!"

Mary dropped to the cockpit floor, holding the wheel at the bottom and craned her neck in a vain attempt to watch her compass heading.

"How did they spot us?" she whispered when Tanner crawled back into the cockpit beside her.

Tension deepened the lines in his face to craters. "I don't think they did," he muttered in a low voice. "Probably just a random shot. They must be getting frustrated."

"They seem to have stopped shooting."

"Yeah." Tanner grimaced sourly and peered over the side. "Dumb idea, shooting at us. It'll be pure luck if they do any real damage, and they'll be in serious trouble if they hit someone else out here. What if there's another boat around? Gunshot wounds are hard to explain."

"What now?" she whispered. Ten silent minutes passed. They sat in the cockpit and stared around them into the thick fog. Mary had killed the engine after the first shot and Sea Queen drifted in the peaceful grip of the outgoing tide.

"It must be close to slack tide," she murmured.

Tanner bent his damp curls closer. "Let's just drift a while longer." His finger on the chart he'd retrieved from the deck, Tanner traced the western edge of Calm Channel from their approximate location to the lower end of west Redonda Island.

"There are several small islands along here. We can try to confuse their radar by dodging in and out among them. And these narrow little channels off this main one look shallow enough on the chart so they won't be able to follow. I wish I knew exactly where we are."

"Why don't they use their launches to find us?" Mary asked. "They have two, I think,"

"They don't know much about us. Probably assume we're

armed. I wish we were. Unless the fog goes away completely, it'd be tough for them to get back together with the launches. And they'd have to split their forces. We don't know how many are on board Goldenrod and they don't know how many we are. For all they know, we have a heavily armed assault force hidden in the hold."

Mary snorted. "I saw eight or nine people on board Goldenrod my last trip. People who weren't guests," she said.

Tanner glanced at her wan face. She looked exhausted. The rollercoaster of fright, anger and calm, was taking its toll.

"Be right back." He dropped down the companionway. Alone in the cockpit, Mary checked the compass and peered around, rocking the wheel nervously from side to side. Would they survive? Sailing rings around her opponent was one thing; fighting weather, tides, that she could do. Evil men with guns, that was a dimension beyond her capability. Tired, frightened, she turned to comforting routine. She checked once more to make sure the engine controls were positioned so they could start it quickly if necessary. Careful attention to such details might yet save their lives.

31

The smell of hot coffee drifted up through the open hatch. Thank God, Mary thought. Tanner was also fixing hot food. He was famished. He assumed Mary was too. They needed food to replenish their strength and help their morale. Moments later he appeared holding a tray with two steaming bowls of porridge and two small apples sliced into sections. Setting the tray on the cockpit bench, he smiled at her.

"Here. I'll take a turn at the wheel. You eat this mush. My culinary talents are limited, but we have to stay healthy."

"True. My grandfather always said eat to keep your strength up and your senses alert." She gratefully slipped aside and they changed places.

"I checked the water supply," said Tanner around a mouthful of apple. "We better not take any showers until we can fill the tanks."

Mary grimaced and scratched her head. "To tell the truth, it wasn't something I've been thinking about a great deal the last few hours."

In spite of their situation, as perilous as he knew it to be, Tanner was now beginning to believe that they could continue to avoid Goldenrod through superior seamanship and the greater maneuverability of Sea Queen.

"Listen," said Mary. "What if we just abandon Sea Queen and go ashore? Or we could try to get away in the dinghy."

"I dunno," he said. "You know how dense the underbrush on these mountains is. If we get off Sea Queen and if we got lucky, we might find a logging camp or a backpacker with a radio in the first day or so. If it took longer, we could get real lost and die of exposure. We don't know exactly where we are, remember."

"There's a town on Redonda," she persisted, waving generally over the starboard side with her free hand while she continued to shovel in the hot porridge with her other. "Guess I was hungrier than I realized," she told him between mouthfuls. "Anyway, what about going to the town?"

He glanced at the compass and then said quietly, "I think Redonda is in that direction," pointing the opposite way.

She glared at him for a moment, then chuckled softly.

"Jerk. Of course we'd take the small compass." She looked at him silently. "You're still trying to figure out a way to nail them, aren't you?"

Tanner shrugged an affirmative. "I don't want to run away now just because we've got their attention. I still need something to take to the authorities. I'm sorry I got you into it. You and Sea Queen. I guess I've become as obsessed with getting my pound of flesh as my partners back in Seattle told me I was." His shoulders slumped. God, he thought. An image of a crushed Queen Anne rose in his mind. It's happening again. I've managed to put someone else in danger.

Mary watched him closely, suspecting what he was thinking. "If I remember my Shakespeare, or the Bible, there's a reference to an eye for an eye. Since you chartered Sea Queen, your insurance will cover any damage. As for me, I stowed away, you didn't shanghai me." she smiled tiredly and then sat up straight. Now she made one of her periodic visual sweeps around them and at the gray ceiling above. "Between you and me, sailor, we are going to figure something out." She stiffened. "Michael look!" She pointed urgently at a patch of blue overhead. The fog, more friend than foe, was receding. If it disappeared completely, Goldenrod would see them from a distance and in the narrow confines of Calm Channel, they'd have little chance to survive.

Mary threw the rest of her apple over the side and stepped to the wheel. Automatically she checked the instruments and the engine controls.

"Oh hell. What's happened to the depthfinder?"

"What?" Tanner was in the cabin, writing a quick entry in the log book. Without saying so, both Tanner and Mary were keeping the log current with frequent entries because they hoped that if disaster caught up with them, there was the chance the log would survive and be turned over to the authorities.

"Depth?" he called.

"Dunno. It's dead."

"Great. Just what we need. I better--"

"No time. Look," she told him. The circle of blue sky was growing larger by the moment. "Michael, I can see treetops over there. The fog's really going this time."

Tanner dropped the log and climbed into the cockpit. "Those trees must be on the mountains," Tanner said.

Mary switched on the blower. After a few moments, she started the engine, engaging forward gear in almost the same motion, so even as the fog began to draw away, Sea Queen actually drove through the remaining curtain into open water. The sea around them for a hundred yards in any direction was pale blue like the sky overhead. Off the port side, she could see a long way down the channel. Tanner glanced back at the chart and then at the shore line--trying to precisely pinpoint their location. He knew an exact location would be vital if the fog closed in again.

Mary looked over the left side and there was Goldenrod. She was riding at anchor three quarters of a mile away near the eastern side of the channel. The sun glinted off her creamy white hull and gleaming superstructure. Beautiful vessel, she thought sadly, beautiful and deadly.

"Michael! It's them!" Mary pointed toward Goldenrod. Tanner turned at her cry and then was flung back against the lifelines as Mary throttled up to full speed, turning toward the fog bank. It lifted and drew away before they reached it, revealing jagged rocks and boulders that rose sharply out of the water at the edge of a point of land. Mary whipped the wheel over and as they swung abruptly left, the piercing beep of the shallow water alarm on the depthfinder sounded its sharp warning.

Tanner glanced at the dial, but there was still no reading. "What's the shallow alarm set for?

"Don't remember."

Mary spun the wheel again and the alarm stopped. She drove Sea Queen parallel to the shore, chasing desperately after fog that seemed to retreat at almost the same speed they were moving.

"I'm catching it," she said, breathlessly, as if she herself were running the race. "And I take back all my earlier complaints about how miserably damp it's been."

Tanner compared the shoreline to the chart, figured out their location and made a quick note. He dropped chart and pencil, grabbed the binoculars and trained them on Goldenrod. There was no human movement aboard her that he could see, but the anchor chain was being raised and there was turbulence at Goldenrod's stern. Her engines were running.

"They've seen us!" The high knife-like bow began swinging toward them even before the anchor was clear of the water. Tanner saw from the angle of the chain that Goldenrod was already moving forward. A dangerous maneuver because the rising anchor could damage her hull. Tanner watched through the glasses and saw the beginnings of a frothy bow wave start to climb the sides of her hull. It all seemed to be happening silently at this distance, in slow motion, and at the same time, entirely too fast for his peace of mind.

Tanner lowered the binoculars and glanced at Mary standing tensely at the wheel, alert for any indication of trouble ahead. "I'm ..."

"Sorry? Don't be. Unless we lose the game." She spared a quick glance over her shoulder at Goldenrod and then back to her course.

"There are several small islands out here," Tanner reminded her quietly. He pointed ahead and a little to the right. "We can try to hide among them. With a little luck and more fog. But without the depthfinder, it's risky."

"Luck coming," she told him. They were approaching maximum speed, faster than Tanner had ever gone on Sea Queen.

The fog was no longer receding, they were rapidly gaining on it.

"Slow down a bit."

Mary raised her eyebrows but complied. An island appeared as the fog continued to recede down the main channel. Mary changed course again to skirt the land without losing more ground to Goldenrod.

"How do you feel?" asked Mary, glancing back and forth between the fog bank and Goldenrod, now fully under way and rapidly narrowing the gap of water between them.

"Excited, scared. I don't know. Frustrated too, I guess. Tired of running away. Damn them."

Mary changed course once again. The deck vibrated beneath their feet and the roar of their engine was all around them. She turned back toward the center of the channel to give them a little greater safety margin on the right side. The depthfinder suddenly beeped, causing both of them to flinch. The readout was still blank.

"Must have been a fish, or just cavitation from the keel. If we had a known depth, we could probably adjust the shallow alarm to give us some warning," Mary said. "But we're probably going too fast for it to help much."

Tanner's head was bent over the chart again. He used the hand-held compass, taking bearings from the few recognizable landmarks.

"Speed?" he asked quietly and made a note. "How 'bout heading?" Mary answered and watched from the corner of her eye while Tanner made another note and consulted the stopwatch built into his wristwatch. He certainly seems calm, she thought. Then she looked over her shoulder at Goldenrod less than half a mile away, charging across the open water toward them. While she watched, the other yacht disappeared as fog enveloped Sea Queen once more. It grew colder. Moments after entering the fog bank, Mary made a sharp turn to the left and dropped their speed to a fast idle.

"Good," Tanner said. "Run this direction for five minutes and then go to this heading." He scribbled on the edge of the chart and showed it to her. "Maybe if we zig and they zag, they'll make a mistake and go aground or something. The closer we stay to the shore, the harder it will be for their radar guy to pick us out on his screen." Tensely, Tanner continued to navigate Sea Queen down the channel.

"My stomach hurts," complained Mary a few minutes later after they made their second turn.

"Tension," Tanner grimaced. He felt it too. He was concentrating on the chart and the stopwatch again. "I felt like that after the night in the dinghy, eavesdropping on Goldenrod. It was like somebody'd been pounding me in the belly or after a really heavy workout in the gym. That wet mist didn't help, either."

"Did you do that a lot? Before?"

"Work out? Oh, some. Elizabeth got us a family membership at a health club once. I overdid it, early on." His voice faltered and he stared out away from the chart in his lap to the fog that again surrounded them. For a long moment there was only the sound of their engine.

"Michael, I'm sorry." Mary reached out a hand and laid it on his shoulder.

He was still for another moment. Then his hand came up and touched hers, squeezed it. He turned his head and smiled, one of his bright, wide, smiles that he used to smile so often. He rose and wrapped an arm about Mary's shoulders.

"Hey. It's okay." He leaned down and kissed her cheek, still smiling slightly. "I'll never forget her, but I have to let her go and I have. Now, however," his voice hardened, "we have to keep playing this game of hide and seek until we figure out a way to extract retribution."

"Extract retribution?" Mary's eyebrows rose. "You P.R. types certainly have a way with words." Even as she spoke, her mind continued to sift conditions and options.

"In about two minutes, we should clear that island and we can turn into this little channel here." His finger traced their proposed course on the chart he held for her to see. "If my calculations are on the money, we can stay at this speed and heading until we reach this shoal area, just north of the island.

Then we'll ease in here and tie up for the night. It's shallow enough so that even if they get lucky and figure out where we've gone, they'll have a very dicey time trying to reach us. We're going to need some rest. I don't know about you, but I can feel it. I'm starting to get punchy. Trouble concentrating."

"Without a depthfinder, we could be in big trouble."

He tapped the chart, betraying his nervousness. He knew Goldenrod might decide to send a small boat of armed men after them, particularly if they discovered Sea Queen had stopped for the night.

He also fervently hoped his navigation was on the mark, otherwise they'd have lost again, in constant danger of running into the shore.

"Michael, I just remembered something."

"Good, I hope."

"My uncles taught me not to rely too heavily on electronic stuff on the ships. So we've got a lead line."

"A what?"

"A lead line. A long light line with a heavy piece of lead tied to one end. Its length is marked. Somebody stands at the bow and throws it forward. You can read the water depth with it."

"I get it. Good. We can use it when we get into the side channel."

While they made their cautious way through the fog, other questions nagged him. Where was Goldenrod? Had they broken off the chase? He had fully expected to hear Goldenrod charging after them in the fog, but he couldn't detect her. After a moment of indecision, Tanner said, "Shut down the engine, will you? Let's just listen for a minute."

Sea Queen's engine died and the sound drifted away. They heard no other. The fog blanketed everything.

32

"I've lost 'em in the clutter, Captain."

"Damn it! What's the problem?"

"It's this new radar, sir. I don't think it's set up right. I seem to be getting a lot of false echoes. Plus they don't have a lot of superstructure to give us a good reflection. They could've slipped behind an island." The sweating crewman was bent over the radar manual, not daring to look the captain in the eye.

"All right," he snarled, slamming his big hand on the steering console. "Reduce speed to just over three knots and move into the middle of the channel. You can find that, I suppose?"

Crew members posted on both sides of the bridge and at the bow peered tensely into the fog. They were armed with shotguns loaded with heavy double-O buckshot ammunition and slugs. Double-O buckshot will shred an automobile body at 100 feet. On the bridge the captain cursed steadily. Tanner and Mary Whitney would not have been pleased to hear his threats.

"There's still nothing on the radio. He's not sending unless he's got a special transmitter." Goldenrod's radio operator was using all the available communications equipment carried aboard the yacht to listen for a transmission from Sea Queen.

"I don't get it," grunted the captain. "Maybe their radio's on the fritz. I was them, I'd be screamin' for the Coast Guard."

Aboard Sea Queen, Tanner and Mary Whitney proceeded as planned.

"Look Michael!" Mary's whisper was urgent. For twenty

minutes they'd been ghosting through the fog at the slowest speed possible and still maintain steerage. The tactic reduced their noise as well as the danger of going aground.

Tanner looked up to see branches and leaves projecting out of the fog. Mary shoved the gearshift lever into neutral and rotated the steering wheel to the right. Now they were ghosting along parallel to the island shoreline, angling away from the main channel. By comparing their compass course to the chart, Tanner verified their location for only the second time that day. He dropped the chart.

"I'll go forward with the lead line and measure the depth now."

"Good."

Tanner went forward, stumbling against a cleat. He grabbed the forestay to keep from falling. Sheesh, he thought, I'm gonna fall asleep standing up pretty soon.

In a few moments they both felt them, even before seeing the fuzzy, indistinct, images of trees closing in on one side. Mary changed course again, this time slightly to the left.

They had found their target and slipped into a narrow, shallow channel, no wider than two boat lengths. Again and again Tanner swung the lead line overhead and cast it forward into the water. He called out the depth in weary monosyllables. The line indicated less than ten feet of water when Mary brought Sea Queen to a halt. They had made it to temporary shelter. While Tanner eased the anchor over the bow chock as silently as he could manage, and then into the water, Mary shut down the engine. She looked at the hazily-seen shoreline, a mere ten feet off their port side. The western shore was totally obscured in the fog, but she could sense its presence.

"Okay," said Tanner when he rejoined Mary in the cockpit. "The only way Goldenrod can reach us in here is by small boat."

"If they try that, we'll beat 'em off with the boat hooks," Mary said.

She felt the knot of tension in her stomach begin to loosen and her shoulders relaxed their stiffness. Sea Queen drifted backward. A silent moment passed, then they both felt the tiny jar as the anchor took hold. Mary watched the shore as the boat began gently to shift in the slight current. Satisfied that they were all right for the moment, she considered her next move.

Food, her empty stomach growled. She went down to the galley and looked over the possibilities. I better not cook, she mused. There's no telling how far cooking odors might travel and give us away. The result of her survey was two thick tuna fish, lettuce and mayo sandwiches. The bread was getting stale, but as they quickly discovered, they were so ravenous after their most recent encounters with Goldenrod that a little stale bread was inconsequential.

"Michael, what about the radio?"

"I think the antenna has come adrift," he mumbled. They were in the main cabin, sitting across from each other at the table in the dim glow of a single red night light. He rummaged under one of the benches and came up with two cold beers.

"I could go up the mast in the bosun's chair and take a look at it. But I don't know if I can fix it, even if I find the break. And I don't like the idea of being up there if those lowlifes suddenly show up. Good sandwich," he said around another big bite. "Really hits the spot."

For a time they watched and rested, struggled to stay awake while the fog hung on and night came. It was difficult to tell when the sun set, the day had become so murky. They dozed fully clothed, half sitting, half lying on the cushions in the cabin. Sleep deprivation and tension combined to take them both deeper into sleep than they had intended.

At seven, Mary rolled to her left and almost fell off the bench. She flung one arm out and cracked her elbow on the table. "Ow!" The pain was brief, white-hot, lancing down her forearm to her fingers. She pulled her elbow in close to her side, slid down prone on the seat and went back to sleep.

At eight-thirty, Tanner sat bolt upright, hearing a strange gurgling sound. He'd never heard it before, but his instinct told him it shouldn't be. It came again and now he felt the motion of the yacht. No longer did it have that soft cushiony feel. It felt solid and the deck was slightly canted.

"Mary! Quick! We've gone aground!" Tanner stumbled to his feet and leaped for the hatch. Mary was right on his heels. In the dripping darkness, Tanner leaned for the engine controls, but Mary's warning stopped him.

"Michael! Stop!" she hissed. "It's too late. We're already hard aground. The engine alone won't get us free."

"Shit." Tanner straightened up. "What do we do now?" The gurgling came again, longer this time. "What the hell is that noise?"

"Water draining from a through-hull, one of the outlets for the galley sink or the toilet. Is that what woke you?"

"I guess so. Never heard it before. Now what?"

"We have one immediate problem. We have to secure Sea Queen so there isn't any damage and so she doesn't turn turtle when the tide goes all the way out. After that, all we can do is wait."

"Wait? For what?"

"For the tide to come in and refloat us."

"How long?"

"Four, five hours. Check the tide tables."

"Jesus!" Tanner exclaimed.

They stopped and peered at each other. Four or five hours aground, unable to maneuver. Sitting ducks for the killers aboard Goldenrod.

Tanner blew out his breath between pursed lips. "Okay. Tell me what to do to secure this boat." He turned and started back down the ladder.

"Wait. Michael, maybe we should get off. Abandon Sea Queen."

Tanner shook his head. "I still don't think so. If Goldenrod does find us, I think our chances are better on the boat. We'll sleep better here and I can rig some kind of alarm. This is pretty wild country. And we aren't exactly equipped for overland trekking. If we get off Sea Queen and they find her empty, they'll probably destroy her."

"I guess I agree. My instincts say to stay with Sea Queen

too, even if logic isn't so sure." She stopped and swallowed. Mary felt her stomach knot and her throat closing. A spasm of trembling passed over her, unnoticed in the dark. She swallowed carefully, forced her mind away from Goldenrod to more immediate issues. "We don't know how shallow it'll get, but look here." They were in the cabin looking at the chart under a carefully shielded flashlight, leaning against the table as the deck beneath them slowly increased its slant.

"Worst case, we'll fall over on our side, but only partway. The wide part of the hull will keep us from going completely over. If the mast doesn't hit any trees and break something or get tangled, there's no problem there. But we have to be sure we don't lean toward deep water, otherwise the cabin could flood from the incoming tide before we float again."

"Your voice sounds a little weird."

She glanced at Tanner, swallowing rapidly. "Yeah, I know. I have a little problem in my throat. It only happens when I'm under a lot of stress or tension."

"Uh huh."

"The first thing is to be sure we're leaning the right direction."

Tanner popped his head out of the hatch and listened hard. "Damned if I can see anything, but we're certainly leaning toward the island."

"Good. We won't flood then. Now we have to put everything that's heavy and loose on the floor and be sure the cabinet doors are tied shut. The boat will lean way over and we don't want to get conked or break something."

With Mary giving terse directions they went swiftly through Sea Queen, moving a few things to the cabin floor and tying shut cabinet doors and drawers. After they finished, Tanner strung some tools and empty pots and pans along the deck where intruders might try to come aboard. The noise would give them some warning while they dozed in the cabin. After that there was nothing to do but wait. And hope.

Their concentration on securing Sea Queen had pushed their peril away for a time, but now Goldenrod intruded more and more. They heard a quiet metallic pong when the gimbaled stove fell against its stops. Sea Queen continued its slow, inexorable lean, canting more and more at a crazy angle. Every so often there were other sounds as gear in the cabinets and lockers shifted to the call of gravity. It became impossible to stand on the cabin deck. Tanner half lay against the back of a bench seat in the main cabin.

"Michael?" Mary's voice was small in the darkness from the floor at the forward end of the saloon where she'd stopped earlier in her final crawl to check the forward cabin.

"Listen. I ..." For a moment his self-assurance and glib tongue deserted him. "Can you make it over here? Everything considered, I'd rather be a lot closer to you if this is our last night together."

"My very thought. Great minds and all that." Her voice became warm breath on his face when she crawled onto the cushions and up along his body. "And I have here ye olde sleeping bag."

"But how do we stay awake?"

"I'm not sure I much care, right now."

Tanner smiled in the dark, wrapped his arms about her while Mary adroitly pulled the sleeping bag over them. His foul weather jacket crackled in the dark. She pulled the zipper on Tanner's jacket down a little and peeled the collar away from his throat. She burrowed her face into the warm curve of his jaw and neck.

"You could use a shower, my man." Her voice was a hazy murmur. Her breathing changed, deepened and she drifted into an exhausted doze.

This would be incredibly sexy, thought Tanner, under other circumstances.

The mud gave a sucking groan and Sea Queen rolled still more onto her beam ends, coming to a stop with a soft bump. Unable to run, stranded until the sea returned, Tanner too fell asleep wondering if the next thing he saw would be the muzzle of a gun in the hands of a crew member from Goldenrod.

Tanner stared wide-eyed into the darkness. What had awakened him? Had he heard someone approaching? Then he realized what it was. Sea Queen had shifted into a more upright position. A pan outside scraped slowly across the boarding ladder. He eased Mary's weight to one side. The bench back was now almost vertical and Sea Queen trembled as if she was about to float free. He crawled up the ladder to the deck and looked around. He didn't feel the presence of an intruder. A pan clanked softly. Moving with slow care he slid across the canted deck and retrieved the pans hung around the cockpit. Then he went below.

"Well, I feel a lot better." Mary was sitting up on the bench. She rubbed her eyes. "I take it we're still alone?"

"We are and now I want to move. It's just after one in the morning. We'll be free in a second. It may not be the wisest thing to do but I can't just sit here any longer. Maybe we can provoke them somehow. If you see it happen, I'll have another witness. Then we can hightail it for safety and call the cops."

Mary only smiled to show her agreement, then turned and led him up the ladder to the cockpit. She rolled her shoulders under her jacket. They'd both been in the same clothes for nearly two days and she felt sticky and uncomfortable.

"There's probably enough water to wash your face and brush your teeth. That'll help a little," Tanner suggested.

"You go while I check things topside." Tanner turned and went down the ladder.

A few minutes later, they changed places and then Mary joined Tanner in the cockpit.

Everything was quiet. Sea Queen, with dampness collecting on all her exposed parts, still enshrouded in fog, waited quietly for new commands. Mary started forward to the anchor.

"Mary," said Tanner quietly, "I'd appreciate it if you'd take the wheel. I'll raise the anchor and take lookout again. You're better at running Sea Queen than I am, especially if we get into another tight situation."

Recognizing the logic of his statement, Mary stepped back to the wheel and switched on the bilge blower. A low hum started, then they detected the smell of engine oil.

"You know," said Tanner. "Goldenrod could be waiting in the main channel right off the entrance."

"Well, let's go find out." She leaned to the starter and said, "let me check out the engine. Being on its side like that might have clogged some lines." She pressed the starter switch. The engine started, coughed and settled into its normal rhythm. Tanner checked over the side with a flashlight to see that cooling exhaust water was being pumped out of the hull. The dimly lit gauges registered normally.

"Okay, I guess," Mary said after a moment, thankful once again for the extra insulation the previous owner had installed in the engine compartment. "I'll keep an eye on the temperature."

Tanner went forward in the chill night air and hauled the anchor out of the water. When he signaled it was clear, Mary shifted to forward. Slowly they motored through the narrow waterway and emerged into the main channel. They passed the entrance to Teakerney Arm, unseen in the dark. Gradually the land fell away and they motored into the seaway. In the distance they heard the faint mournful sounds of fog horns from traffic in Georgia Strait. Now only the broad sweep of the Inside Passage separated them from Campbell River and safety. Under their feet, Sea Queen began to rise and fall to the long swells rolling up the strait.

"How far are we from Campbell River?" asked Tanner.

"Four hours sailing, I'd say."

For a long time there'd been no sight or sound of Goldenrod. Mary and Tanner knew that every hour, every mile that separated them, offered both more safety and a greater possibility they would leave Tanner's mission unfinished. He stood at the shrouds amidships and mulled over the situation. He couldn't decide what their next move should be. In a part of his mind he thought about Goldenrod and Sea Queen, and about the wind and the night and the fog. Could he use this natural environment to somehow bring down his enemy?

"Michael," said Mary, "we're entering that stretch beyond Refuge Cove. There are some islands up ahead to think about."

"I remember. It'll be easier for their radar to pick us up

now, in all this open water. At least until we get a lot closer to those islands."

"If they haven't just gone."

Tanner didn't believe it. Somehow, he still hoped to confront Goldenrod in a way that would give him the upper hand. It was a forlorn hope, and it became less likely with the passing minutes.

A sound came to them then, rising over their own engine noise. It was the sound they had both learned to recognize, the deep-throated rumble of Goldenrod's powerful diesel engines. She was behind them and closing fast.

"Michael!" Mary cried in an alarmed voice.

Tanner looked astern, trying to estimate the distance between the two vessels. How had they gotten so close? He went back along the deck to stand beside Mary.

"Don't change course!" His voice was harsh. Tanner reached for the throttle lever, giving himself a sense of how much reserve power they had.

His turbulent emotions stilled suddenly. He stood like stone, muscles tight, staring over the stern. Without warning a bright blooming glow arose behind them. Goldenrod had switched on a powerful light.

"Searchlight!" cried Tanner. "They must have us identified on their radar."

"What'll we do?" shouted Mary.

Tanner leaned forward and fumbled in the dark with her safety harness. It took a moment, then he had the tether and hooked it to the life line. He did the same with his own harness.

"You can out-maneuver them," he said. "Sea Queen is pretty agile. Okay," he gritted, anger rising like bile in his throat. "I'll watch 'em. You run the boat. When I yell, you give 'er full throttle and turn hard right. I mean, tight and fast as we can go." Side by side in the cockpit they waited tensely. Suddenly, almost like a physical blow, Tanner flashed back to that horrific day when he stood with another woman he cared about and endured a death-dealing collision. Was history about to repeat itself?

The misty glow from the searchlight, sweeping back and

forth, grew and grew until, coupled with the roar of her engines, Goldenrod presented a fair imitation of the apocalypse swooping down to claim Mary, Tanner and Sea Queen. The high sharp prow of the white yacht gleamed in the reflected beam of the searchlight. When it seemed that Goldenrod would smash them into shards of bone and fiberglass, Tanner shouted.

"Now!"

Mary threw the wheel full against its stop, all the way to starboard and at the same instant slammed the throttle full open. Sea Queen heeled heavily on her side as the engine roared its own challenge to Goldenrod. The sailboat slewed around in the water, gaining speed more rapidly than Tanner had believed possible. A wave crashed over the prow, sending green sea water sluicing down Sea Queen's deck. Goldenrod stormed by in a great wave of sea foam scant feet from their stern. In seconds the two boats parted and were lost in the fog. Goldenrod's searchlight died.

"Throttle back and head for King Horn," Tanner waved in the general direction of the island. Mary, more familiar with the area, recalled the approximate heading and changed course. They were now running almost parallel to their earlier path and to Goldenrod.

"Why go slower than we can?" Mary questioned.

"The longer we can avoid showing our true top speed, the longer we have something else to play with. It's an edge."

"Things have changed now, Michael," she said. Tanner looked at her. "Now you have a witness. I've seen them in action. They deliberately tried to run us down just now. I can testify to that in court. Now they have to kill us."

33

Twice more, Goldenrod rushed at them out of the dark. Twice more Mary and Tanner managed to avoid being run down. Once the space between them was so narrow that Goldenrod's bow wave severely rocked Sea Queen, shoving her contemptuously aside and they were glad for the extra security of their safety harnesses. On the last pass a man on Goldenrod got off a blast from his shotgun. The heavy shot tore a ragged corner off the cabin roof and scarred the deck.

In the next hour they reached the temporary shelter of King Horn Island. When they slipped behind it they were again lost to Goldenrod's radar. Swinging around the island, they found wind and rain added to the fog for a thoroughly uncomfortable mix of weather. A strong sea was running against the westerly wind, and Tanner estimated there was an eighteen-inch chop on top of the swells. The going was bumpier than anything they'd experienced before. But they had played the mouse to Goldenrod's cat and were still afloat, exhilarated on one hand, tense and afraid on the other.

"Look," said Mary as Tanner peered through binoculars at the island off their port side. "I think we ought to make a run for Campbell River. As you said, those guys still don't know how fast we can really go. We've always slowed down immediately after they've rushed us, so I bet they're still fooled. At least they don't learn too fast. Look how many times they've tried the same tactic."

Tanner looked at her across the soft glow from the

binnacle compass.

"Yeah." He stared at her, absurdly thinking how romantic the lighting was, how attractive she looked. He saw her in full dimension, tough, competent, able to hold her own at the wheel of a sailing ship at sea or in well-appointed corporate board rooms. His heart reached out to her.

"You're right. Thing is, they must be twice as fast or better in a straight line. So we'll have to be sharp."

"Random course changes will help. I think we'll probably have to tack anyway to reach the harbor."

"I've been keeping track," Tanner said thoughtfully, "and we've turned right every time they've come at us. Next time they find us, we'll turn left, in case they anticipate our maneuver."

Mary nodded and spun the wheel. Obedient as always, Sea Queen changed course and headed west across the lumpy waters of the Georgia Strait.

"I'm gonna see about that damned radio. Get the Coast Guard out here." Tanner climbed down the ladder. "I had an idea a while ago."

He stood in the cabin, swaying easily to the rhythm of the Tartan as she battered her way across the water. He felt behind the radio chassis and unscrewed the antenna connector. He then fished the antenna cable out of the channel behind the hanging cabinets until he had it loose all the way to the place where it entered the mast.

"Mary, where's the tool chest?" He called up the hatchway.

"Look under the oven. There's a recess that just takes it," she called back.

There it was. He picked out a screwdriver and removed an access panel on the mast. Then he took a large pair of pliers and reached up into the mast, grabbing the antenna cable. He swung all his weight on the wire which suddenly parted somewhere up the mast, dumping him on the deck with a loud thump.

"Michael? Are you all right?"

"Yep, just lost my footing."

Now he needed an antenna. His eyes lit on the Loran receiver over the chart table. Where was it's antenna?

"Mary, is the Loran antenna on one of the rails topside?"

"Yes, it's bolted to the rail behind me."

Tanner reached under the instrument case and felt for the connector. It wasn't the same as the radio antenna connector and wouldn't fit. "Naturally," he muttered, "it couldn't be simple." Tanner cut the cable to the Loran and spliced the radio cable to the end of the other cable. Then he wrapped the connection with electrician's tape to hold the crude splice together.

"Well, here goes," he announced, flipping on the power switch. The LED channel indicator glowed 16, the universal emergency and hailing channel. He adjusted the squelch and heard only silence. Then, faintly, slightly distorted, he made out voices. There was a lot of static, but the reception was intelligible. For a moment he stared at the radio. Then he picked up the small microphone and pressed the transmit key. A tiny red light glowed.

Tanner hesitated, clicked the button a few more times and then said softly, holding the microphone close to his lips, "Mayday, Mayday."

For a moment there was no response and then a strong military-sounding voice burst from the speaker requesting that the Mayday caller identify himself and give his position. Tanner grinned, hung up the mike and flipped off the radio. Giving false emergency calls was a serious offense, but it had insured an immediate response without his having to give his name. Now he knew they could transmit and receive. Still grinning, he bounded up the ladder to give Mary the news and a quick hug.

"Now we can call the Coast Guard to come get us. They'll protect us until we get to Campbell River." I'll switch on the running lights too." He turned to go back to the cabin.

"Wait a minute," said Mary.

Tanner frowned and turned back.

"We have no way of knowing how far away a Coast Guard cutter is. To get them out here, you'll have to identify us and give our exact location. Goldenrod will hear it and find us first. In fact, they might even call the Coast Guard and offer to respond."

"God, I never would have thought of that."

"I think we better just keep on running and call when we get closer to Campbell River. In fact, let's put the main up. It'll give us more speed now we've got some wind. Even if we have to maneuver, the sail won't slow us down unless we get backwinded."

Tanner hesitated, and then shrugged. He knew the big white mainsail would make them easier to spot. But they'd managed to survive thus far. Fumbling in the dark for the main halyard and winding it around the big winch he said, "I'm angry enough to want some kind of personal revenge, but if we don't get outa this alive, we sure won't get back into court."

He soon had the big sail up and drawing, and it added noticeably to their speed. Tanner went below and switched on the running lights. He returned to the cockpit just as a squall swept across their path, drenching both of them in icy rain. Water ran in rivulets down the sail and dripped off the boom. Still dry in their red and yellow foul weather suits, Tanner and Mary Whitney kept a sharp watch as they raced through a night only a dedicated sailor could love. They left Kinghorn and its group of smaller islands behind and entered Georgia Strait itself. Now they had be alert for other traffic as well as for Goldenrod.

Wind and fog patches continued. Another nasty, hissing squall pelted down and the sound of the stinging rain masked other sounds. Mary and Tanner had to shout to be heard. The wind rose and gave voice to itself in the rigging. Even though only the main was up, Sea Queen heeled more and more under the pressure of the wind. The yacht charged across the sea and Tanner began to think about reefing the sail.

Concealed by the weather, Goldenrod pounced on them once more. This time, on the edge of exhaustion, worn down by the pressure and the long hours, this time they weren't quite fast enough. With a speed that shocked them into startled immobility for a fatal instant, Goldenrod roared viciously out of the night.

Tanner snapped his head around and stared at the

onrushing bow. It looked as if it had grown teeth. At the last possible moment, screaming with anger and fear, Mary shoved the throttle lever so hard against its stop, she bent the rod. At the same instant she whipped the wheel to the left. Off balance, Tanner lost his footing and was flung back to bounce off the lifelines. His head cracked against the edge of the cockpit coaming, momentarily stunning him. Goldenrod's bow seemed to rise up out of the water and smash down on them. It struck Sea Queen a glancing blow at the stern and carried away the dinghy, its outboard motor, the rear pulpit and the boarding ladder in a shrieking, grinding, explosion of sound. Gone too was Tanner's jury-rigged radio antenna.

Mary held on, hunched over the wheel, sobbing in terror and anger. Their engine raced at full speed, driving a damaged Sea Queen furiously away. The sail cracked and filled. Goldenrod tried desperately to circle back for a final killing blow, but Sea Queen disappeared in the rain and fog. Mary turned sharply to port, pointing higher into the wind. It took them away from their course and the mainsail began to flap loudly. Tanner saw that she was unharmed and had already struggled back from the shock of the collision. His own emotional state was more uncertain. His head throbbed from the blow he'd received.

He looked down at his feet. A raw stub of black antenna cable lay on the deck. "Damn it, what a mess. I'm gonna kill the lights." He stumbled below and flipped off the switch. He looked at the radio which was awry in its bracket. Electrical and other wires had been torn loose from the radio chassis when the antenna cable was dragged over the side. When he returned to the deck to report, he saw that Mary had loosed the main halyard and dropped the sail. It lay, flapping listlessly, in an untidy bundle of sodden cloth on the cabin roof. The terror of the moment behind them, Mary once again functioned with precision and competence. But in her throat she felt the familiar pressure building.

"Michael," she called urgently, "we've got to check for damage to the hull. I'll run into the wind while you look things over."

Grimly, still watching for Goldenrod, she began a methodical check of the steering and other systems. Her eyes scanned the hooded, glowing navigation instruments and engine gauges mounted on the cabin bulkhead in front of her.

"Depthfinder, log and windspeed all look okay. Hey, the collision jarred the depthfinder back on. The engine seems okay too. We aren't losing oil pressure and the temperature's right where it should be," she reported tensely. "The binnacle compass is still working. We can check it later with the hand compass."

"The gauges in the nav station tell the same story," Tanner called from the cabin.

Mary looked all around at the black empty sea, searching for Goldenrod. The wind continued to moan through the rigging. The wet sail flapped soggily, and the boom swayed overhead. "The rudder works, but the wheel doesn't feel right." She changed course, continuing their pattern of zigzagging in a westerly direction.

"Damn! The antenna is gone and pulled the radio apart. This thing is a piece of junk. Whaddayou mean about the wheel?" The pale oval of Tanner's face appeared in the open hatch.

"Well," she responded, "the wheel just doesn't feel the same. A little stiff. Maybe the rudder shaft is bent."

"I'll take a look," called Tanner, disappearing again. Moments later Mary saw a flickering glow as he waved a flashlight about in the main cabin. He opened an access port behind the refrigerator to peer at the engine and the end of the mechanism that linked the wheel with the rudder.

"I can't see anything wrong down here," he called again. After another long look around, he replaced the cover and climbed back up the companionway ladder to the cockpit. "Anything else?"

Mary shrugged. "I dunno. Are we holed? The rear pulpit is gone or hanging over the side, I guess."

"God," Tanner husked, "I think I wet myself when they hit us."

Mary giggled, the small attempt at humor helping to settle

their jangled nerves a little. Tanner glanced around in the dark night. There was still no sign of Goldenrod, but they had no doubt she wasn't far away. He covered part of the flashlight lens with his fingers and leaned out over the stern on his knees. The rear pulpit had been torn loose and was gone in the sea, as was the swim ladder that had been attached to the stern. There was a gaping hole in the hull where the ladder had been. The hole ended just above the waterline. The teak trim on the decking edge around the stern was also gone. Ragged holes showed where bolts had been ripped from the fiberglass. Tanner lay flat on the deck at the edge of the cockpit and leaned out over the stern as far as he dared. He aimed the flashlight toward the rear portion of the keel where the rudder was attached. Only blackness and bright reflections from the water could be seen.

"I can't see the rudder. There's a big jagged hole in the stern here."

He also saw several long jagged gouges in the above-water portions of the hull where Goldenrod's bow or the ladder or the pulpit had scraped.

As Tanner rose to his knees, he put his left hand on the backstay and the hair rose on his neck. "Oh my God," he mumbled. He shone the flashlight on the plates at the stern where the backstay attached to the hull.

In the flickering light of the flashlight, Tanner saw just how close to losing their mast they had come in the collision. On both sides of the boat at the stern, the plates which had so recently held the stern pulpit were bent and damaged, but the bolts holding them to the deck were still in place and still felt secure. If the cracks in the decking had reached the plates where the backstay was secured, the stay itself could have torn loose, transforming the stay into a lethal snake of cable, able to inflict great damage and even death. And the mainmast would have collapsed around them.

Tanner wondered if he ought to rig some temporary strain relief in case there was other damage that could rupture the decking later on. It was too big a job for right now, he decided and his questing fingers found no cracks or distortions in the area around the deck plates for the backstay.

"Well?" asked an anxious Mary.

"Lots of superficial damage and a few holes in the upper part of the hull where the ladder was attached. I checked the bilge while I was below and we don't seem to be taking on any water."

"That's a relief. Maybe something's tangled in the rudder. That could be what's causing the drag on the wheel."

"Here," said Tanner. "I'll relieve you for a while. Their cold hands touched briefly as Mary slid sideways and picked up the flashlight.

"I'll just check the bilge once more and see if there's been any change." She disappeared below and Tanner, looking up at the dark masthead, realized that beyond the top of the mast he could see stars. A slow scan around their perimeter revealed that the fog was dissipating. Now he could see lights lower down, flickering red and green lights from ship traffic on the water.

"Well," Mary reported from the hatch, "I don't see any more water in the bilge than usual. Looks like we were lucky again."

"Fog is pretty much gone," responded Tanner. "Don't show any lights now."

Before long, they discovered that the fog had only retired for a time. As they headed now in a northwesterly direction, they continued to encounter dense patches of fog. Mary and Tanner raced on with no lights, constantly on the alert, not only for Goldenrod, but for other traffic in the strait.

34

The cold black hours before dawn seemed endless. They raised the mainsail, then the big jib and carried on. Tanner, at the wheel, looked at the sky for the sixth or seventh time and realized it had changed again.

He called down the companionway to Mary, "The stars are gone again. More fog or clouds."

Mary, hearing his voice, came on deck from the cabin where she'd been resting.

"It'll be light before too long," she murmured, fatigue in her voice. She raised her head and brushed the tangled hair back from her forehead. She looked again over the stern into the stygian darkness.

"Take the wheel a moment," he said. "We took a couple of major waves a little while back. I think I ought to check the bilge again."

It was then, as if in answer to their unspoken question, running lights that could only be Goldenrod's appeared just behind them. The wind chose that moment to die and Sea Queen slowed as her sails went slack. Goldenrod came on, her searchlight sweeping the water and blooming off the mist.

A clot of fog swirled around them. The temperature dropped. Tanner shivered in his jacket. He threw his head back and tugged off the hood. They listened, straining.

"They're north and a bit east of us," said Mary.

"Yeah, if we come about now and head directly toward

Campbell River, they'll easily cut us off."

"Assuming they know where we are. There's other traffic out here too, hear it?"

Tanner's nerves twanged. There was something not very far ahead and a little north of their position. A foghorn sounded. He changed course to a more southerly one, still closing on the vessel off their starboard side, the one coming south down the strait.

"Michael!" Mary stared at Tanner through the gloom. "We can't let Goldenrod trap us against that traffic."

He glanced at her and then back over their stern.

"We'll go behind, around that ship ahead," he said, throttling up. "I hope our fuel lasts."

Goldenrod continued to draw nearer. The fog went away, leaving behind heavy mists that swirled about the cockpit. Again they heard a foghorn, now much closer and soon, heavy thrashing propellers.

"It must be a tug," said Mary peering ahead for some sign.

Glowing lights appeared, hazy through the mist, and they made out more distinctive sounds of machinery, the engines, and the sound of the bow wave.

"Mary, I'm changing course." While she adjusted the mainsheet and winched in the boom, Tanner changed course to run nearly parallel to the boat ahead, but in the opposite direction. He brought Sea Queen even closer, staring across the water as the big tugboat came into view. It dwarfed Sea Queen's sleek profile with its bluff bulk. The tall black stack angled slightly to the rear added a rakish profile. As it passed and he looked into the long patch of empty water off her stern, he saw a glint of steel stretching behind. Tanner recognized what it was.

"It's a log boom, they're towing a log boom!" he said hoarsely, pointing into the mist. "It's being towed down the strait to the lumber mills."

"Michael! We're trapped between the boom and Goldenrod!" She yelled at him, trying to shake him out of his trance-like state. Tanner turned his head and stared at her, his mind racing.

"Maybe not. I just got an idea that might finish things once and for all. Coming about."

He brought Sea Queen around once more now to head south beside the big tug. Tanner reached for the throttle and increased their engine speed to near maximum. Then he turned the wheel gently to the right bringing Sea Queen to a converging course with the tugboat. Slowly they overtook the other vessel, moving ever closer until they were inside the broad width of the log boom itself.

Tanner eased Sea Queen closer until they were next to the towboat, separated by only a few yards of thrashing, turbulent water. A wave crashed over Sea Queen, then another, sending spray high into the air. For a few minutes Sea Queen ran beside the larger vessel, matching the tugboat's speed. Tanner checked the throttle. He hoped the proximity of the two ships would confuse those watching Goldenrod's radar screen. He hoped Goldenrod would also turn south, to follow Sea Queen rather than try to go farther west into the strait.

"I'm going to cross that tug's bow in a few minutes, staying as close as I dare." Tanner had to raise his voice to be heard over the combined engine sounds. "It's dangerous," he said unnecessarily. That baby isn't very maneuverable and you know it would take her a long time to stop at this speed." Tanner looked at Mary.

She looked back, nodded, understanding the risk. "Okay. I'll watch the towboat.

"They're probably screaming at us on the radio already." Tanner stretched his mouth in a stiff grin and nudged the throttle lever forward. The sail cracked in the wind.

"With the wind from the west, we'll be headed at one point. Let me harden up the main so the boom doesn't crash about."

Sea Queen began to draw ahead, moving still closer to the towboat. They continued in that way, Sea Queen gradually moving out until the cockpit of the yacht appeared to be next to the bow of the tug, until Tanner judged they could just make it across the other's course. The noise of the towboat and their own

engine was very loud now, and they had to shout to be heard.
Mary looked at the bridge of the towboat and thought she saw a
man waving Sea Queen away with frantic motions from inside the
wheelhouse. Tanner was certain Goldenrod must be close now.
If his plan was to succeed, they had to get across the path of the
tug before Goldenrod closed to visual range through the mist.
Tanner's stomach jumped. He changed course again, angling
across the path of the towboat. He held his breath.

"Fifty yards," Mary shouted the distance as Tanner
changed the angle again. God, it was taking forever.

"Forty yards."

Tanner shoved the throttle all the way open, increased Sea
Queen's speed to its maximum. The wind held. He glanced at the
blunt, rope-festooned bow of the towboat. In the night and mist
it loomed over them, coming inexorably closer. They were on a
collision course.

"Thirty yards."

Now they were committed. Tanner spared a glance for
Mary, for Sea Queen, for the compass. A patch of thick fog
swept over them The sound of the towboat's horn pierced the
night in a quick series of warning blasts. The blinding glare of
the towboat's spotlight swept over them and Tanner shielded his
eyes.

"Twenty yards!"

The fog went beyond them leaving the towboat and Sea
Queen in a light mist with a thick fog bank between Sea Queen
and Goldenrod. The towboat appeared to increase its speed and,
to Tanner, Sea Queen seemed to slow to a standstill. A wave
crashed over her bow and flung stinging spray through the
cockpit.

"Fifteen yards!"

It was taking forever. It was taking too long.

I've misjudged it, he thought despairingly. After eluding
Goldenrod for so long, now it appeared they were going to be
crushed under that onrushing tugboat. Rain stung Tanner's face
but he hardly noticed. Beside him, Mary clung to the lifeline,
staring at the tug.

"I can see the other rail!" Her voice was an excited shout. She turned and clutched Tanner's arm, fingers biting into his muscle. "We're across! We've made it!"

Tanner grinned at her, relief washing over him like a warm shower. A minute more and he turned the wheel to the right. Now they were angling northwest of the tug's course less than fifteen yards away. Mary saw a crew member on the near side deck about to enter the cabin, stop and look up in astonishment as the Tartan, still without lights, finished her turn and raced north. Heavy wake from the tugboat smashed into Sea Queen's bow and forced her to port. Tanner throttled back.

"Keep watching up ahead for some kind of light low to the water. They'll have something to mark the outer corner of the tow. Probably a red lantern. We don't want to hit those logs."

A moment later Mary saw the lantern and pointed. Tanner checked his watch, turned sharply left and they began to motor at right angles away from the log boom. The sail cracked and flapped uselessly.

"Listen," Tanner said tensely. "If we get lucky, Goldenrod will turn west again to intercept us. I hope they haven't seen the towboat yet, except on their radar. The log boom is so low they may miss it altogether on the screen. If they try to cut some distance by crossing as close behind the tow boat as they can, they might run into the log boom." He stared into Mary's eyes. "If they hit the boom at high speed, that'll end it right there. Some of the people on Goldenrod might drown if she sinks."

There was no hesitation in her response as Mary looked back at him. "I think it could be called retribution."

Tanner nodded, sighed, and looked to the right across the dark water where he knew the log boom was sliding south between Sea Queen and her pursuer. Higher up off the water, he noticed the faint outlines of distant mountains and knew that dawn would soon arrive.

Out of the fog and into clear air charged Goldenrod, only half a mile away. Mary and Tanner stood in Sea Queen's cockpit watching their enemy race toward them. At full throttle,

Goldenrod smashed into the log boom, and her bow lifted high out of the water. Suddenly a huge fireball enveloped the yacht, followed instantly by the concussive sound of a massive explosion.

"Michael, it blew up!" Mary's awestruck voice echoed in Tanner's ears. What had happened? He opened his mouth to speak when a second explosion sent another thunderous wave of sound rolling over the strait. A ball of yellowish orange light flickered in a bright fireball that mushroomed swiftly upward and then died. Tanner reached down and throttled the engine down to an idle.

"My God, that was enormous! What could have caused it?"

Tanner thought a moment. "I guess we interrupted the transfer of explosives to that floatplane up in Butte Inlet. They must not have unloaded everything in the keel pods and the shock from ramming the logs set it off. Remember, I heard one of the crew mention how unstable some of that stuff was? "When those logs tore into Goldenrod's bow there must have been a tremendous shock wave. Wow."

"Michael?" Mary's voice quavered. "That could have happened when they hit us."

He shivered. "We could have been blown to smithereens." They looked at each other, remembering.

Mary and Tanner dropped their sails and turned Sea Queen back to stand off the log boom and wait for daylight. They were certain it was Goldenrod that had exploded, but they wanted to see the wreckage. When the new day came, the sun rose on a clear, breezy morning and blew away the remnants of the fog.

Debris was everywhere, strewn about the log boom and in the water. Logs separated from their tether by the blast bobbed in the sea. Several other vessels had by now arrived and were tied to the boom or were slowly circling the scene.

"Michael, look," called Mary from her position at the rail, forward of the mast.

He turned to see what she was pointing at. Lying amid a loose pile of oil-streaked shards of aluminum and fiberglass was a fractured wooden piece carved in an intricate design. It was an artist's rendering of the symbol of the California communications company that owned Goldenrod. Tanner remembered seeing it on cabin doors during his midnight prowl.

Mary scrambled back to the cockpit. She stood in front of Tanner, gripping his arms. "It was them, Michael. It was Goldenrod. Its over. It's really over."

Tanner looked at her and there were tears in his eyes.

"Yes," he said. "I knew it was, when the ship exploded. I felt it the way you feel a sea change, or when you pass through a pressure cell." He sighed. Then he smiled and wrapped his arms around her.

A Coast Guard loud hailer interrupted their euphoria. Politely but firmly, they were ordered away. The authorities had taken control of the scene and the growing gaggle of boats was becoming a danger to navigation and an impediment to the accident investigation. Mary and Tanner were not reluctant to go. He checked the mountings of the backstay and hoisted sail, bearing off and headed south in the sparkling sun toward the San Juan Islands. Sea Queen seemed glad to go. Her wake stretched out in a clean, widening, vee behind her stern.

35

There was only a dim glow from Seattle's night in the window when she was awakened by a weight easing down onto the bed beside her. She sighed. A warm hand snaked cautiously over her hip and up her chest between her naked breasts.

"Hey, Mr. Tanner," she murmured sleepily.

"Hey, yourself, Mrs. Tanner. Sorry I woke you."

"Is it late?"

"Very. Or early."

"How's our lady?"

"Looking better than ever. Boatyard guys are doing a really nice job. "Repairs on the hull are finished and most of the new standing rigging is in place."

"Good. Martin was right. That Vancouver shipyard knows its stuff. Still. Really late, my man."

"Had a visitor and a long talk. Interesting information."

Sensing Tanner wanted to talk, Mary rolled onto her back, holding Tanner's hand in place. "So tell me."

"Remember that Coast Guard lieutenant? The one who rescued me? Stark?"

"Of course. Twice."

"Remember how his boat showed up at Campbell River that night?'

"Sure."

"Not an accident. They were following us."

"Ah. I wondered why they'd posted a watch."

"He told me they'd been detailed to watch for Goldenrod the year before. It seems our government, ATF or somebody like that, and the Canadians were pretty sure for a long time that the

Goldenrod crew was hauling illegal cargo. Knew they were smuggling guns and explosives from Mexico. Last year they started carrying drugs as well. Anyway, Lieutenant Stark was supposed to be monitoring our activity and looking for Goldenrod. But he decided on his own we might be in more danger than we knew."

"Are you telling me they knew all about Goldenrod before she rammed your boat?"

Tanner sighed and nodded in the dark. "Apparently so. In fact, they had a small power boat in the area shadowing Goldenrod that very day. I faintly recall hearing another boat around that time."

"Why didn't they arrest the bastards?"

"Not enough proof, I guess. Afterward, some ATF guy named Jenkens had the thought that I might be their local drug connection."

"Those people seem to see conspiracies everywhere."

"Anyway, they were watching me for a while. Followed me to San Diego and Long Beach. It was probably their guys who saved me from a crack on the head in that bar brawl. Stark said that Jenkens was on his cutter that morning after Goldenrod blew up. Said he admitted searching my room at the marina and even talked to me early on. Jenkens told Stark they were disappointed not to get to talk with Goldenrod's crew. He wanted the pilot and the people ashore. I guess we spoiled their little game." Tanner sighed again and pulled Mary closer.

"Jenkens even admitted he still wasn't sure whether to believe my story about the ramming.

"I wonder what would have happened if we'd made it to Campbell River and gone to the authorities."

"Stark said he asked Jenkens about that. Jenkens told him they'd probably have cut a deal in return for testimony."

"Sure," murmured Mary, "a few years in jail but nothing for the murder of Elizabeth and Alice. And what about the people behind Goldenrod? There must be somebody out there."

"S'pose so. Now they'll probably never know. Thought any more about what you want to do when we put Sea Queen back in the water?"

"Sure have. There are several things I haven't had a chance to try on that boat." She rolled toward Tanner, pressing closer. "Most of them don't have anything to do with sailing."